The Trouble with Telling

The Trouble with Telling

Bickford "Bick" Penn

St. Petersburg Press

Published by St. Petersburg Press

St. Petersburg, FL

www.stpetersburgpress.com

Design and composition by St. Petersburg Press and Isa Crosta

Cover design by St. Petersburg Press and Amy J. Cianci

Paperback ISBN: 978-1-964239-10-1

eBook ISBN: 978-1-964239-11-8

First Edition

To Leah and A.G.M.

For their encouragement and unfailing support in my ongoing
journey to become a published author

CHAPTER 1
NOVEMBER 28, 2015

Thomas Johnson Telling III stood out from the crowd like Mister Rogers at a Def Leppard concert. His innocent trust in fallible humans often led to his downfall; his unwavering humility and obsessive-compulsive tendencies could be tiresome. Unencumbered by self-awareness, he navigated his adolescence by ignoring his detractors and doing what he was told. But this smooth flight into adulthood developed unexpected turbulence, and late in his 21st year, his seat belt came unfastened.

It began on a dreary day. A light mist engulfed the gridiron as State's coach paced up and down the sidelines. "Where the hell is Johnson?" he screamed. "Who does he think he is? I should bench his ass when he gets back from whatever he's doing. What could possibly be more important than a game against Tech?"

The team's execution thus far against its bitter rival had been lackluster. On offense, gems that had shined so brightly in practice disappointed like cubic zirconia, and the usually impervious defense was "profanely pervious," according to one colorful critic. Even the trash talk was weak. The vulgarity had little edge and the maternal aspersions were trite and uninspired. Everyone knew exactly how fat their mama was. Only the marching band's renditions rose above the level of embarrassment.

Given his exceptional performance thus far, Johnson's disappearance was baffling. Throughout the season, his drive and work ethic had been unmatched. He was fanatically devoted to the team, arriving early for practice and staying late, studying videos of the opposing teams for hours. And he was a maniac in the weight room. It was impossible not to root for him.

At an early age, Johnson had learned the value of discipline from grandparents who'd raised him in a strict environment. He'd been a good student, but his size, shyness, and clumsiness had made him an easy target of ridicule. Over time, his coordination had improved, but his lack of social skills had led to the dork label that stuck with him.

Football offered an escape. Coaches had little interest in his persona out of pads. They marveled at his stamina and innate ability to steamroll competitors. As word of his unique attributes spread, his high school career became storied, earning him a full scholarship to State, where he'd dedicated himself to excellence both on and off the field.

Before the second half started, players huddled to speculate on Johnson's whereabouts. To many, the possibility of a tryst was laughable. No one could document a single instance of the burly co-captain conversing with a female for more than a few tongue-tied seconds. He was in love with football and equally enamored with computer science, more apt to be intimate with a complex programming algorithm than a fawning first-year student. Still, the possibility of a quickie couldn't be ruled out. Even a life-long celibate like Johnson might succumb to temptation at least once.

Naysayers maintained that his penchant for thoroughness and attention to detail precluded a rushed rendezvous. Devon Clark, a frequent mimic, illustrated the point by taking his teammates through one likely scenario in Johnson's stilted language and mannerisms.

"'Now Hyacinth, before we begin our session, let's review the specifics one more time. I'll start with the standard four minutes and thirty-three seconds of kissing, mostly on the lips, with some focus on your ear lobes and neck. After that, I'll remove your brassiere and begin touching your breasts, which will require your *a priori* permission.'"

"At this point, Johnson is facing a conundrum. What does he have to do? Anybody have a clue?"

The players shouted their guesses.

"Remove her top?"

"Unhook the bra?"

"Name them?"

"Wait—explain *a priori*. Is that a lesbian thing?"

"No, you idiots," Clark chided. "He has to decide which breast to start with. Now let me continue with Johnson's monologue. 'Unless you have a preference, Hyacinth, we'll conduct a Bernoulli trial to determine the starting side. Thereafter, I'll alternate between the two. As you know, tactile stimulation of the nipples has been proven effective. I'll modify the pressure and technique based on your non-verbal cues. I hope that's okay.'"

"What's a Bernoulli trial?" cried a linebacker.

"I think it's something they did to the Nazis," replied a tackle.

"No," Clark said. "You guys are so pathetic. A Bernoulli trial is just a coin flip. At this point Johnson would hand her a document displaying her arousal level as measured by his smart watch, the tensile strength and reliability of the condom, recommended positions, and the required disclaimer for latex allergies."

They laughed, then considered other possibilities for his absence. Johnson had a falling out with Kupert, Tech's linebacker, but it wasn't in his character to mastermind a system of armed drones to attack him. Such was the act of a devious mind, not the awkward, lovable nerd they had grown to admire and respect. His motives were always pure.

The reason for the rift had never been fully explained. When the press caught wind of it, the resulting firestorm of attention nearly overshadowed the game itself. Johnson ignored the hype, preferring to make his statements on the field. But Kupert relished the opportunity to lampoon his enemy on social media, boosting his ego in the process. His memes were rude and demeaning, often depicting Johnson as awkward and clueless, with an affinity for certain barnyard animals.

* * *

Almost five minutes had elapsed when Johnson reappeared, looking more contrite than usual. The coaches lit into him immediately and subjected him to an inquisition so brutal some claimed only the famous Spanish tribunal matched its intensity. He survived with his reputation intact by pairing a vague excuse with a healthy dose of humility. Tyrell Cornelius Brown was among the interested bystanders.

Like Johnson, the lanky quarterback had been an Army brat who had lived all over the country and knew what it was like to be an outsider. Soon after he joined the team as a junior, the two developed a kinship, sharing a dorm room and a passion for football. But the two men were vastly different in terms of personality and lifestyle.

Johnson avoided the limelight whenever possible, preferring to spend his time practicing, studying, or writing code. On rare occasions, friends managed to drag him to a social event, only to regret the gesture when he flooded their inboxes with endless questions about the minutiae of the evening. He was physically appealing and easy-going, but to the opposite sex, he was an enigma.

Tyrell, on the other hand, was an extrovert, oozing with confidence, attractive in a Hollywood way. He spent his abundant free time at parties surrounded by throngs of swooning women who hung on his every move, each of them hoping for the slightest indication that this Adonis might become more than a casual acquaintance. As his campus exploits increased, dreams were shattered and broken hearts were scattered like wrapping paper on Christmas morning. Nevertheless, he remained grounded and loyal to a close circle of friends who suffered with him as he struggled to prepare his tedious roommate for mainstream society.

"Where the hell have you been?" Tyrell barked when he saw Johnson back on the field. "Coach was about to have a coronary."

Johnson stared at the ground. "Well, I lost track of time."

"Doing what? Please don't tell me you went back to the computer lab in the middle of a game. Are you still working on that infinite loop problem?"

"No. Not this time. I solved that. Now that you mention it, I developed some cool syntax last night. You just take an array—"

"Not now! I love you, man, but you need to drop it. Kupert is a bigger prick than usual. Now he thinks you're a wuss."

"A wuss?"

"Do you need a translation?"

"Being a wuss is insulting, right?"

"Yes, it is."

"So what? I'll flatten him again if I have to. Within the rules, of course. I would never let an angry opponent stand in our way. We're seniors now, playing what may be our last game. Let's go out in style with a win... Are you touching me?"

"Am I what?"

"Bro, I asked if you were touching me."

Tyrell looked at him, aghast. "I may be your bro' but I am definitely not touching you."

"Sorry. I guess that's not how it goes. I mean are you *feelin'* me?" With a freakish grin, Johnson tried to approximate the swaggering moves and hand gestures of a popular rapper, but instead resembled Charles Manson on quaaludes.

"Oh my god, dude," said Tyrell. "That's about the most terrifying thing I've ever seen. Don't ever do that again in public. On second thought, don't ever do that again anywhere."

* * *

The punt sailed out of the end zone and State started from its own twenty-yard line. On the next play, Johnson took the ball on a handoff, grinding his way into Tech's secondary. Forced out of bounds on a four-yard gain, he wheeled around in response to a groan.

Richard Kupert, his large, tilted nose visible through the face mask, was standing behind him. "I thought something stunk around here," he said.

Johnson took a step closer. "I see. Do you think your prominent proboscis enhances your sense of smell? If so, you should know that's a fallacy."

"My prominent what?"

"I think it means nose—like an elephant's."

"That's rude, don't you think?"

"Huh? In one of my courses there was a statistical analysis that showed there's only a weak, non-significant correlation between olfactory sensitivity and nostril size. Counterintuitive, isn't it? Anyway, what exactly did you smell?"

"I smelled you, you ass wipe."

"Sorry, you'll have to be more specific. Ass is ambiguous. Are you referring to a male donkey or a human's anatomy?"

"Yours, you jerk wad. You're an ass wipe."

"Now I'm really confused. Am I a jerk wad or an ass wipe? And what exactly *is* a jerk wad?"

"Oh—I forgot to mention you're a dick, too."

"No, my name is Thomas, not Richard. But let's get back to the jerk wad and the ass wipe. They're not mutually exclusive? How much overlap would you estimate? I'm trying to picture the—"

"So help me," Kupert wailed. "If you start talking all that math shit and Venn diagrams I'm kicking your ass right here, right now."

"I actually prefer the Euler diagram to the Venn."

"There it is. Holy shit. You're a giant douche."

Johnson grinned. "You're all over the place today. Let's begin with the term douche. I know that one. It refers to the rinsing of a body cavity, so it must be like an enema. I get it, you think—"

"That's it, you hopeless nut sack," Kupert screamed. "You're going down."

"Excuse me, guys," a referee growled. "I hate to break this up, but there's a game going on. You need to finish this love fest on your own time."

Heading back to the huddle, Johnson felt the icy stare from his nemesis. "You won't be so lucky next time," said Kupert.

* * *

When play resumed, each team scored and drew penalties for showboating. Kupert bestowed insults on any opponent within earshot. The rabid taunts were lost on Johnson, but Tyrell declared war. Skirmishes continued until the fourth quarter when Tyrell reached his breaking point. A shoving match ended in a retaliation punch, and he was ejected from the game.

With time running out, State had the ball in Tech territory, down by six. Then a sudden downpour turned the field into a patchwork of splattered sludge. The drenched players were unable to gain traction, and the offense stalled. On fourth down, Johnson recovered his own fumble. He tossed a wobbly pass to a wide-open receiver who scored a touchdown. As the last second ticked off the clock, the local townies and barely lucid students went berserk.

With the crowd still roaring, the kicking unit trudged out for the extra-point attempt. The execution was perfect, and the ball sailed through the uprights. Celebrations broke out everywhere, then ended abruptly at the sound of a whistle. An infraction against State nullified the result and moved the ball back five yards. Livid fans moaned and cursed in anguish as the rain slowed to a drizzle.

With Johnson back in the game for his exceptional blocking, State lined up again in the hushed stadium. The placeholder struggled with a high snap, and the mistimed kick was partially tipped. A Tech lineman snatched it from the air, but the slick pigskin squirted through his hands. Kupert came up with it deep in the end zone. The defense now became the offense and play continued.

Kupert dodged his pursuers as they slipped and skidded on the soggy turf like Keystone Kops. Then he found an opening, lowered his helmet, and churned straight ahead, hellbent on crushing anything in his path. Johnson, who was the only thing standing between him and yards of open field, charged forward with equal abandon.

Their impact sent shock waves throughout the stadium. And it was game over.

CHAPTER 2

Charlie awoke disoriented and woozy from her latest binge. The gray, graffiti-covered stairwell looked unfamiliar, and the granite floor beneath her felt cold and unforgiving. Above her, a fluorescent light hummed and flickered, throwing faint shadows on the wall like a projector from a bygone movie house. In a corner, a mousetrap lay unsprung.

A radiator banged and hissed in the chill of the raw evening. Thoughts swirled in her head. *Is this my dorm? How did I get here? How many did I have? Ugh, I'm never drinking again.* She grabbed the pitted metal railing for support. Rough and biting to the touch, it offered little comfort. Her stomach churned.

Since pledging Omega Chi, her life had become a non-stop Ferris Wheel of wild parties, humiliating duties, and unique challenges, each more bizarre than the last. Her first assignment had been tame. She'd been ordered to crash the president's annual faculty dinner. Then she appeared at her Psych 101 class dressed in a makeshift suit of armor, which garnered rave reviews from her peers. After that, commandeering a live chicken from the vet school seemed too easy. But today's task was far outside her comfort zone, even in her current chemically induced state. Maybe the campus Greek scene wasn't her thing.

Her throat was parched, and her head pounded as she attempted the stairs, pausing at times to steady herself, oddly comforted by the familiar musty odor of Anderson Hall. Outside, students celebrated State's remarkable win over Tech, gathering around the campus in throngs. When she approached her room on the first floor, the party noise grew louder and became unbearable as she flung open the door.

Inside, Amanda was flaunting braided hair and a gold bikini. The statuesque first-year student greeted Charlie with bloodshot eyes and an inebriated smile. "Hey, loser. What happened to your other shoe?"

Brie, in a loose-fitting football jersey hanging well below her knees, was gyrating to the music. "Come on, Charlie. Dance with me."

Wearing a T-shirt, faded jeans, and a silly grin, Crystal raised a glass. "Where the hell have you been all day? Want a drink?"

Charlie winced, shielding her eyes from the piercing bright ceiling lights. "Holy moly! My head is killing me. What's up with that outfit? Princess Leia, can you turn that down?"

"I can't hear you," Amanda said. "Let me turn this down for a second. What did you say?"

"Nothing you would want to know."

"Hey, what's with the attitude?"

"Sorry. You know when your mother tells you you'll have days like this? Well, I've had one of those days."

"So take off that bitchin' jacket, put up your feet, and hang out with us."

Charlie darted into the bathroom as the earsplitting hip-hop beat resumed. Amanda threw up her hands in frustration. "My nerdy roommate is on the rag again. What a surprise."

"Hey, mix me up another one," Brie said. "I am so stoked. I can't believe we beat Tech. That was some dramatic shit today."

Crystal tossed a handful of ice cubes into a blender. "Oh yeah, totally. And even without Tyrell playing at the end. Was anybody else turned on when he and that guy started going at it on the sideline?"

"Oh, I was," said Amanda. "Tyrell is frickin' awesome."

Brie took out her phone and scrolled through the photos. "Oh my god, I saw him before the game today. He looked amazing. I would *so* do him."

Amanda fanned herself. "Who wouldn't do him? They could make a bronze statue of his ass, and I'd buy one."

"Speaking of his ass, take a look at this shot," Brie said. "Damn, he is so hot. I hope he'll show up at the party tonight."

Crystal crossed her fingers. "Oh, I hope so. I think tonight may be my night."

Brie downed her drink, then poured another one from the blender. "Ooh, the big victory par-tay. I almost forgot. Don't forget to check your decency at the door. What are you bitches wearing, anyway? Wait, don't tell me. A pushup bra with a low-cut top, tight jeans, and no panties?"

The girls howled.

Crystal checked herself out in the mirror. "How did you guess? Are we slutty or what?"

"Not that slutty," said Brie in a professorial tone. "Now then, if we can measure degrees of sluttiness, and I think we can do that with some precision using today's technology, then some of those Omega Chi chicks are at the top of the scale, right, Crystal?"

"Absolutely."

"Yeah, and it's not fair," Amanda said. "They always get the hottest guys."

Charlie reappeared in a white cotton robe. Wisps of ash-blonde hair sprouted from a towel wrapped around her head. "That's because they're willing to do anything," she said. "It's sad but true. Going back to measuring degrees of sluttiness, would that have to be on a linear scale? I'm liking a construct with a non-integer base."

Amanda rolled her eyes. "Holy shit, Charlie. Did you really just say that? Who cares?"

Brie slapped down her glass, laughing. "Amanda, are you telling us you don't care about the metrics? I'm sure Charlie has given this a lot of critical thought. We should listen."

"Oh, shut up, Brie," Amanda said. "Nobody gives a shit. But, Charlie, what I *do* want to know is what was the task du jour? The way I see it, you're almost in."

Charlie groaned as she stumbled into bed. "Well, not *in* anymore. After what happened today, I'm done with the sorority thing. It's just ridiculous. I think it's time for me to grow up. At least a little."

Crystal shook her head. "No, girl, it is certainly not! Remember, you're only young once. Sow some wild oats. Howl at the moon. Raise hell. Celebrate life. This has been a public service announcement brought to you by all the chicks like you who are old now and regretted not having fun while they could. What happened?"

Charlie unwrapped the towel, revealing wet bangs and a thick bundle of straight, shoulder-length hair. "Let's just say I was pranked. And when I say pranked, I mean incredibly pranked. I can't believe how gullible I am."

"Oh, come on, you wuss," Crystal said. "Being pranked is part of the fun. It's a time-honored tradition. They just want to see how bad you want it."

"That's just it, Crys. I don't want it that badly. Ladies, I've seen the light. Just because my mom and her sister and half the town were Omega Chi's doesn't mean I have to be. Some things just aren't worth it."

Brie stared at Charlie. "Girlfriend, what's gotten into you? This could open a lot of doors for you. Not to mention all the guys."

"Exactly," Amanda added. "You can't quit now. Think of all the fun you'll be missing. Don't be such a geek. Let me fix you a drink."

Charlie pretended to gag herself with a finger. "No thanks. Look, guys. I get it. I'm throwing away an opportunity. I may regret this later, but right now I need to focus on my classes. I'm in danger of failing some. Believe it or not, I came here to get an education. There's so much I want to learn—science, technology, literature. I want to program computers, understand quantum physics, write a novel—even unravel the mysteries of the universe. I'm so far behind in everything. I've got a paper due on Monday I haven't started on, not to mention two big tests coming up on Tuesday and a project due on Friday. I'm not cut out for burning the candle at both ends. Okay, maybe I am a geek. I'm tired, I want a break and I desperately need to restore my dignity after all the crap I've been subjected to. So, if you'll excuse me, I'll go back to the bathroom and throw up!"

Crystal jumped aside as Charlie shot out of the room. "I never realized just how much of a nerd she is. I think she's serious. Should we try to talk her out of it?"

"I don't know," Brie said, ignoring the retching sounds coming from the bathroom. "She sounds like she's made up her mind. I wonder what weird thing they asked her to do this time."

"Who knows?" Amanda mused. "Maybe like steal Dr. Ganson's underwear?"

"Ew!" They squealed in unison.

Amanda doubled over. "Guys. That is so gross. What is he? Like fifty years old?"

"At least," Crystal said. "Brie, would you do him?"

They squealed again. "Ew!"

"Sluts, do you know it's after eight?" Crystal asked, then went to the bathroom door. "Hey, you in there. Coming with us?"

Sounds of violent retching continued.

"Yuck," Amanda said. "We'll take that as a big no. Brie, I'm coming with you. I need to borrow a top. Come on guys, let's go."

"Wait," Crystal said. "Shouldn't somebody stay here with Charlie, I mean, given her condition?"

Amanda patted her on the head. "That's a very noble gesture. Are you volunteering? You can help her clean up the bathroom, too."

Crystal pretended to ponder. "Let me think about it… Hell no! Anyone else want to volunteer?"

The room fell silent.

Brie headed for the door. "There's your answer, Charlie. We're off to get looser and do unspeakable things to those so inclined. Hope you feel better. If you change your mind, you know where we'll be."

* * *

Eventually, Charlie crept out of the bathroom, brewed herself some coffee, and crawled into bed. The room was in shambles. Plastic cups, paper plates, and empty liquor bottles had been abandoned in unreachable places. She was still under the influence, so her usual response to the disorder was subdued. Despite the repulsive smell of alcohol lingering in the air, hunger set in. She ripped open a nearby package of saltine crackers, opened her laptop and settled in for the evening.

She made good progress on her classwork but found it increasingly difficult to concentrate. *Come on, focus. Great Expectations. David Copperfield. Oliver Twist. Classics. Keep working*. On the last page of the essay, in a moment of weakness, she gave in. Dickens's literary brilliance was no match for the lure of cleaning. She ignored her buzzing phone as she re-organized, cleared trash, and scraped salsa off the floor. When the phone buzzed again, she snatched it up in anger.

"I don't care who you are or what you're selling. I'm not buying."

"Hello, is this Charlene Jankowski?"

"Yes, this is she. Who is this?"

"This is Dr. Nick Manolas at Parish General Hospital. I'm afraid your mother has been in an accident. She's in stable but critical condition. You should get here as soon as possible."

"Oh my god, what happened? Is she going to be all right?"

"It's too early to tell. She had to be pried out of her car and suffered significant trauma. I'll be able to tell you more when you get here."

"I'm on my way."

Charlie slipped into a T-shirt and worn jeans, grabbed her suitcase from the closet and filled it with whatever clothes she could find, then sprinted out of the room and kicked the door shut behind her. She fought back tears as frightening scenarios played out in her head. *No, this cannot happen. It will not happen. Everything is going to be all right. She'll see me graduate.*

A lesson she'd learned months before about the fragility of life came to mind. It didn't pay to become complacent. On any given day, the situation could change drastically. For years they'd been a happy family. Then her father had mysteriously disappeared, and her mother became distant and withdrawn so that Charlie had to take on most of the household responsibilities.

She'd suffered through a turbulent period when she was often in trouble at school and lost many of her friends. She'd only recently learned to soften her tough exterior and show some degree of vulnerability. Charlie 2.0 was an improvement, but still a work in progress.

She popped open the trunk of her car and slung the heavy bag in with a loud thud. The stadium lights were still shining over the rolling campus, which was buzzing with activity. Music, high-pitched screams, and cries of joy emanated from the mostly inebriated student body as the victory celebration continued. The blast of a car horn nearly made her drop her keys. Then she noticed one of the tires on her classic BMW convertible had gone flat. "Damn it," she muttered, pulling her suitcase out of the trunk. "Can anything else go wrong tonight?"

Half an hour later, her knuckles bloodied from struggling with the jack and wrench, she had the spare on, and her luggage back in the trunk. It was raining again, soft drops hitting her hands and face. *Please don't let me be too late.* She said a prayer and hopped behind the wheel. With a turn of the key, the old ragtop's headlights sliced through the gloom.

CHAPTER 3

Charlie darted through the flooded parking lot, slipped through the hospital's glass doors, and hurried down the brightly lit corridor. A code blue warning in the ICU made her pause for a second, then she rushed ahead, picking damp strands of hair from her eyes.

The woman behind the admissions window who rose to greet her was plump, with short, purple hair and coke-bottle glasses. "Do you require medical attention? If so, please go to the next window."

"No. I'm here for my mother. The doctor called me earlier tonight and said she was in critical condition."

"Name?"

"Beverly Jankowski."

"I'll need to see some identification."

"I'm immediate family. I'm her daughter."

"I'll still need to see some identification."

Charlie rifled through her bag for her driver's license.

"The waiting room is on the second floor. I'll page the doctor in charge of her case."

"Do you know how she is?"

"The doctor will have that information."

Charlie ran to the elevator bank, tapped the call button repeatedly, then sprinted up the stairs and found an empty seat in the packed waiting room.

The décor was functional, designed for efficiency rather than comfort. A family sat lined up beside her, and two of the children stared at her, as though they expected to be entertained. On the other side of the room, a young man with bare tattooed arms studied his phone, and an older woman dozed, muttering in Spanish. On one wall, a dated television set blasted an infomercial for a kitchen gadget.

Charlie picked up a magazine and tried to focus on an article about organic gardening, but she couldn't concentrate and drifted off to sleep. Minutes later, she awoke to the sound of her name.

"Charlene Jankowski?"

The man in the white lab coat was attractive, with a dark, neatly trimmed beard and thick brown hair laced with gray.

"Yes, I'm Charlie."

"I'm Dr. Manolas. Come with me."

She plopped in one of the two thinly padded metal chairs in the consultation room.

"How are you holding up?" he asked.

"I've been better. How's my mom? Can I see her?"

He settled in across from her. "Your mother is in surgery. As I mentioned on the phone, she suffered significant trauma in the accident. Both femurs are broken. Her spleen is ruptured and possibly a femoral artery, as well. She's lost a lot of blood."

"But she's going to make it, right?"

"Dr. Stein is an excellent surgeon. We're doing everything we can for her."

"I understand and I appreciate that. But in your opinion, is she going to make it?"

"According to her medical records, she was in good health prior to the accident. But so much depends on her injuries, and we won't know the full extent until Dr. Stein gets in there. She may be on the table for a while."

Charlie's lips trembled. "So, there's a chance she could die?"

"I'm sorry. I know this is upsetting news. Take a deep breath and try to relax."

"Thanks, I'll try."

"Do you need to notify relatives? Your father?"

"He disappeared a long time ago."

"Sorry to hear that. Any siblings?"

"No, just me."

"Aunts? Uncles?"

"My mother has a sister, Viv, who travels a lot for work. I think she's in the Australian outback."

He smiled. "My brother hasn't been home in years. I got an actual postcard a few months ago from Fuerteventura, but that's the last I've heard from him. He's a freelance journalist, always working on a story."

"That's amazing, Dr. Manolas. That's what I want someday. A career in journalism."

"Why is that?"

"People deserve to know the real story behind the news. So much of what's out there today is sugar-coated. People need to be held accountable for their actions. Nobody should get a pass."

"Well, if my brother ever comes home, I'll see that he gives you a call."

"It would be great to talk to a real journalist."

"What did you do to your hands? Those cuts and bruises look nasty."

"Yeah, not pretty. A not so pleasant experience changing a tire."

"I'll ask one of the nurses to take care of that for you."

The doctor's pager beeped. "Excuse me. I need to get back downstairs, but I'll be here all night. This is my number. Text me your contact info and I'll forward it to my brother."

Charlie studied his card, then dropped it in her bag and found her way back to the waiting room. The thought of a horrible outcome was too much to bear. In despair and overwhelmed, she cried silently. "Help me, Dad. I'm scared and don't know what to do."

On the grainy TV, a celebrity was selling late-night viewers a boxed set of classic tunes from the '50s, '60s, and '70s. Charlie watched for a few minutes then drifted off again. Shortly after two in the morning, her phone buzzed.

"Hey, Amanda."

"Girl, where are you? You are missing everything."

"I'm at the hospital."

"Hospital? We have a hospital on campus? I didn't think you were that sick."

"I'm not on campus. I'm in Parish."

"Parish? What the hell are you doing way out there?"

"My mom was in an accident."

"Your mom was what?"

"I can barely hear you."

"I'm at the party. Oh, man, you won't believe it. Tyrell is here. I caught him looking at my extremely perky boobs, thank you very much. I think he loves me! When are you coming?"

"Amanda, try to focus for a second. I'm not coming to the party. I'm at the hospital in Parish because my mom's been in an accident."

"Say that again. I can't hear you over the noise."

"I said I'm at the hospital in Parish."

Amanda paused. "Well, okay, if that's how you want to spend your weekend."

"Look, I'm trying to explain—"

"I've suspected it for a while, but I thought I'd give you the benefit of the doubt. You've just confirmed it."

"What are you talking about?"

"You've never quite fit in with us, have you? Not only did you wuss out on your pledge, but now you've dumped your friends to visit, let me get this straight, a hospital in Parish? Honey, that's just weird, even for a freak like you. Face it, you've got one big L on your forehead. Check you later, loser!"

"Amanda? You don't understand. Amanda? Are you there?"

Charlie looked distraught. Gaining acceptance had been an uphill battle, and her mother's accident couldn't have come at a worse time. Why had the social scene at State been so difficult to navigate? She knew Omega Chi hadn't been a good fit. Now she wondered if she was suited to any part of the college experience.

Dr. Manolas popped into the room, still looking fresh. Charlie studied his face.

"Good news! Your mother is out of surgery and recovering. She'll be in the ICU for a bit so we can keep a close eye on her. She's not out of the woods yet, but this is a step in the right direction."

"Thank you so much." She leaped up and hugged him.

"She's lucky. Her femoral arteries weren't comprised. Unfortunately, Dr. Stein was unable to save her spleen."

"Oh, no."

"Don't worry. It's possible to live a normal life without a spleen. She'll be more prone to infections and may require a course of antibiotics from time to time. We'll have to see."

"That's a relief. When can she go home?"

"She'll be here for at least a week."

"That long?"

"After a major operation, we worry about sepsis and blood clots, so we'll be monitoring her very closely. Another surgery may be necessary. Your mother has a long road ahead. It won't be easy. She'll need physical therapy to regain mobility. Can she rely on you?"

"I just started at State, and I have a lot of catching up to do. Can I see her?"

"For a few minutes. She's still groggy from the anesthesia, so don't expect her to be coherent. Follow me."

Inside the unit, a nurse was adjusting an IV and a cardiac monitor beeped softly. Her robust mother had transformed into a fragile figure mired in a mass of tubes and wires.

"Mom. It's me. How are you feeling?"

Beverly opened her eyes. "Hey, sweetie. Did you finish your homework? You're in big trouble with your dad, you know."

"Mom, I'm in college now. And Dad—"

"Don't argue with me, young lady. You'll never get into State with those grades. And if you don't get into State, you won't have a chance to pledge Omega Chi. You need to buckle down."

Charlie took a moment to realize there was no point in correcting her mother. "I'll do better. I promise."

"Tell your dad not to worry. I'll see him tonight."

"Mom?"

"Yes?"

"About Dad."

"What about him? Did you catch him smoking again? He is in bona fide deep trouble." She muttered, then nodded off.

Her mother, who had always seemed invincible, was ensconced in the stark white reality of a hospital bed. A wave of guilt overwhelmed Charlie. She had been rebellious, often sullen, and lately, less than a pillar of strength, shunning responsibility with a cavalier attitude towards life. *What was I thinking? Why wasn't I more supportive?* For so long she had fought against it, never wading into the deep end of the pool. But tonight, the battle was over. Her mother needed her. It was time to step up.

CHAPTER 4
MARCH 14, 2017

McKenzie's was a landmark in downtown Parish, the preeminent watering hole for military personnel, a short walk from the Camp Conrad gates. The building, which had once housed a tobacco warehouse, was spacious with solid oak flooring, checkered tablecloths, and gas lighting. Neither the decor nor the menu had changed in sixty years.

A large, European-inspired bar dominated the room. Behind it, mirrors flanked an expansive chalkboard displaying the daily specials. More than a dozen padded stools provided seating, and ancient ceiling fans hung from the exposed beams. Strategically placed glass globes flickered softly, their soft blue light creating a cozy, retro atmosphere.

Since World War II, local and national personalities had frequented the establishment, and each visit had been ceremoniously documented with a photograph hung on the wall of fame in the tiny vestibule. The list included entertainers, politicians, and captains of industry, but the most treasured of all featured a young, beaming McKenzie posing with General George S. Patton, whose signature authenticated the photograph.

Johnson checked the crease in his pants, then returned to

gawking at the faded images on the wall, making sure they were perfectly aligned.

Tyrell shook his head. "Do you have to do that? Every single time?"

"I'm just going to ignore that. Hey, I can't believe we got these passes. How cool is it to be out on a weeknight? I mean, even if it's only for a couple of hours?"

"Very cool, and we deserve it. Blanton is stoked about our progress on the Tangent project. It's his way of saying thanks. What time do the ladies arrive?"

Johnson eyed his watch, then carefully repositioned it on his wrist. It was a keepsake from his father, one of his most prized possessions, and a constant reminder of the importance of punctuality. "Seven o'clock on the dot. They've got less than five minutes."

"Great," Tyrell exclaimed. "I can't wait for you to meet her."

"So, this week it's Alicia? You sound excited."

"Yes I am. She's nice. I think you'll like her."

"Hold on. Is this your second date?"

"Yeah. So?"

"So, wow! Let us take a moment to consider the significance of this unprecedented event. Two dates with the same woman! Could the great Tyrell Cornelius Brown be settling down?"

"Come on. Two dates hardly qualify as settling down."

"Oh, Ty, I'm so proud of you," Johnson said in a bad falsetto. "Can I be your best man?"

"Dude, please. That's so funny coming from you. I wouldn't be the least bit surprised if your girlfriend showed up in wedding attire, veil and all. She's not exactly the queen of subtlety."

"Roger that. Patience is not one of Cam's strong points. She's been dropping hints like crazy, but four months isn't enough time to know someone. What do you think?"

"How the hell would I know? I've never dated anyone longer than four days, much less four months."

"How stupid of me. Mr. Downtown is always on the prowl."

"That's not to say I couldn't date a woman for longer than four weeks. You know, if the right one came along."

Johnson checked his watch again. "How do you know the right one hasn't already come along and you were too busy prowling to know it?"

Tyrell scoffed. "Oh, stop it. You overthink everything."

The big glass door swung open and a woman rushed in, damp and slightly out of breath. She flipped her long auburn hair over a shoulder as she leaned over to kiss Johnson on the cheek. "It's starting to rain," she said. "The lot here was full, so I had to run all the way from Second Street. Hi, Ty."

"Hey, Cam. Let me look at you. I'm disappointed. I thought you'd wear something more formal. Like a flowing white gown."

Johnson punched Tyrell's arm. "Shut up."

"You don't like my dress? It's new!"

"Just ignore him," Johnson said. "He's just yanking his chain."

Cameron giggled. "That's not how it goes, silly man. You meant to say he's yanking *your* chain."

Johnson was flustered. "My chain? Why would he be yanking my chain? He's got his own chain."

"Oh, god, Johnson," Tyrell said. "Stop talking about yanking. That's disgusting."

"Why is that disgusting? I'm confused. So you weren't yanking your own chain?"

"No, you dimwit. I was yanking hers. And just to be clear, I have never yanked yours."

"I get it. Cam, it's your turn to yank *his* chain."

Cameron turned red. "Honey, let's drop it."

Another woman dashed through the door. Flawless caramel skin complemented her shiny, black leather pants. Tyrell greeted her with a kiss. "Excellent timing, babe. Say hello to Johnson."

"It's so nice to meet you. I'm Alicia."

Entranced, Johnson shook her hand. "Wow. Now I know why Ty was so excited."

"Thank you. Such a gentleman. Why haven't I heard more about you?"

"That's because there's nothing to tell," said Tyrell. "My friend here is about as exciting as an Army training manual."

Johnson's stare continued. "Alicia, do *you* have a formal white dress?"

Tyrell glared. "Now *you* shut up."

Johnson faked a sad face, then burst into tears. "Oh, Alicia, he's so mean to me!"

Cameron sighed. "Really? Am I going to have to separate you two?"

Tyrell signaled a timeout. "Okay. That's enough. I'm starving. Let's get something to eat!"

* * *

Cameron and Alicia ordered white wine. Tyrell asked for a beer. Johnson fiddled with something under the table.

"What's he doing?" Alicia whispered to Tyrell.

"He's leveling it. It *has* to be perfect, or he'll freak out."

"Sweetie," Cameron said, "have a drink with us. Okay?"

"No thanks. I'll have water."

"Are you sure? Remember how we talked about becoming more sociable?"

Tyrell shook his head. "You can always count on two things at McKenzie's. Johnson not drinking, and Johnson sending his fries back to the kitchen. Am I right, buddy?"

"So," Alicia said, "Ty tells me you two are working on a big project together. That must be exciting."

"It sure is," Johnson said. "Let me tell you about the programming. Last week, we had to write more than ten new subroutines. That's hundreds of lines of code. Yesterday, I was in the middle of a bubble sort but kept getting an error. It took a lot of digging, but I finally found the problem. It was a Boolean operator with less than instead of less than or equal. Can you imagine how silly—"

Cameron cleared her throat. "Honey, are you sure you don't want a beer? Please want a beer. I can't tell you how desperately I want you to have a beer."

Alicia tried again. "I heard you and Ty used to play football."

"They sure did," Cameron said. "At State. They were quite the duo in the backfield. Senior year they made it to a bowl."

Tyrell pointed to Johnson. "You've got to give my teetotaling friend here a ton of credit for our success. We were a pretty good team, but without his blocking, I would have been dead in the water. Remember the A&M game?"

"Oh, yeah," Cameron said, "That was amazing. You guys were unstoppable. Ty rushed for 162 yards. And the option play—Johnson threw a 46-yard pass for a touchdown. It fooled everybody!"

"Wow, Cam!" Alicia said. "You certainly know your stuff."

"That happens when your boyfriend is a walking Wikipedia of football," Cameron said. "He remembers everything."

Missing Cameron's facial cues, a suddenly animated Johnson launched into a lengthy discourse detailing his history on the college gridiron. He spouted an impressive array of facts and figures up to the point of his final game against Tech, then fell silent. After Tyrell jumped in to describe that drama-filled day, the football conversation ended.

Cameron seized the opportunity. "Moving on, Alicia, I understand you have some exciting news."

"Absolutely. I found out yesterday I made the final cut. I'm going to be a flight attendant."

"Congratulations!" said Tyrell. "When do you start?"

"Soon. I'll be going all over the world—London, Paris, Madrid. I'm psyched."

"You should be," said Cameron. "That's quite an opportunity. I'm happy for you. Johnson, isn't that great?"

"Huh? Oh, yeah. Sure."

"You'll have to excuse him," said Cameron. "He's on another

planet at the moment. On that note, please excuse me, gentlemen. Alicia, care to take a little break?"

"Yes. I need to make a mid-course correction in my coiffure."

* * *

In the ladies' room, Alicia fussed with her curls, reapplied her lipstick, then adjusted her top. "I'm glad we're doing this. I needed a break after all the weeks of training."

"I agree," said Cameron as she reapplied her eyeliner. "And you finally got to meet Johnson. So what do you think?"

"He's a hottie! And so nice."

"Too nice. And man, is he ever wound tight—straight as an arrow and naive about so many things. I keep trying to get him to loosen up, but it's been an uphill battle."

"I take it he doesn't drink."

"Not a drop."

"Well, good for him. How did you meet?"

"A friend from the base set us up. I have a thing for men in uniform. Especially those on the fast track to becoming a high-ranking officer. His grandfather is a famous general, you see."

"So I've heard. Are you getting serious?"

"Not yet. Believe me, he knows how I feel, but I'm not making any headway. He and Ty are up for a promotion. It hinges on the project they're working on together. If that goes well, I think we'll be in a good place. What about Ty? Do you think he's a keeper?"

"This is only our second date, but so far, so good. I've heard he has quite the reputation with the ladies."

"Yeah, and you can see why. He's gorgeous!"

"No argument here."

"I'll let you in on a little secret. He and I dated for a while but it was some time ago. Johnson doesn't know, and I'd rather he didn't find out."

"What happened?"

"Ty wasn't looking for anything serious at the time, and I was.

We had some laughs and that was it. But I'm sure he's absolutely perfect for you."

"Thanks for the vote of confidence," Alicia said. "We'll see how it goes."

* * *

The women returned with fresh glasses of wine. At the same time, a disgruntled Johnson sent his less-than-perfect potatoes back to the kitchen. When the dinner conversation came to a lull, Tyrell lightened the mood with comical anecdotes from his past. The tales grew more outlandish as evening wore on.

Johnson played along for a while but eventually reached his limit. "Please, not the dog episode again," he begged. "I've heard it a million times." Tyrell wasn't about to stop. With Cameron and Alicia now fully hooked, he launched into his next story with a sly grin.

While refueling his car at a mini-mart one balmy day, he emerged from inside the store to find his tank full but the pump spewing gasoline everywhere. By the time he shut off the nozzle, the fluid on the pavement had pooled into a huge puddle. A thirsty dog appeared out of nowhere and began to lap it up.

Tyrell recounted in great detail his attempts to snag him. He was always a step behind the little mutt as it darted back and forth before returning for more of toxic liquid. At the end, it made one big circle around the area before keeling over.

Johnson rolled his eyes. "No kidding? What happened then?"

"He died, didn't he?" Alicia asked. "That's so sad."

"Nope," said Tyrell. "He was fine. He just ran out of gas."

Alicia wasn't sure how to react as Tyrell doubled over with laughter.

"I can't believe we fell for that!" Cameron shrieked.

Johnson wasn't laughing. "I can't believe it either. Hey, I was going to tell a statistical joke but it's just average."

"If you must," Cameron groaned. "Go ahead."

"That was it! Oh well, it's not funny if you have to explain it."

No one cracked a smile.

* * *

After dinner, Tyrell disappeared with Alicia while Johnson escorted Cameron to her car. As they strolled along amid the clamor of traffic and pedestrians, she leaned in and rested her head on his arm. "This feels nice. I wish you didn't have to get back to the base so soon."

"Me, too."

"Did you have a good time tonight?"

"Of course, Cam. I was with you."

"Are you sure? You got quiet there at the end. Is everything okay?"

"You mean you weren't captivated by my self-defecating charm?"

"That's really gross, Mister Smooth. You mean self-*deprecating*! But seriously, please don't keep secrets from me, mister. That makes me crazy."

"Roger that. But it's all good. I promise."

"I'm sorry I pressured you about drinking. It's not your thing."

"I know it's the convention. I just never developed a taste for the stuff."

"I promise not to do it again. Hey, it's chilly tonight. Don't you have a jacket?"

"No. I should probably get one."

"We can go shopping this weekend! What did you think of Alicia? I think Ty has met his match."

A line of motorcycles rumbled by as they waited at a cross-walk, and Johnson took her in his arms. "Yeah, she's nice. They make a great couple."

"And what about us as a couple? You know how I feel about you, but sometimes I think it's one-sided. What's going on?"

Her intense stare unnerved him, and he began to feel shaky. "Nothing's going on. I want us to continue." He kissed her.

Cameron smiled. "That's a good way to continue. You're full of surprises tonight. A brazen, full-on, public display of affection."

"Well if you liked that, I've got another shock for you." He took her hand.

"Oh, please. It was funny the first time. Do *not* ask me to pull your finger again."

"This is not a joke. I promise."

She froze. "Are you serious? Is this what I've been hoping for?"

"Cam?"

"Yes, Johnson?"

"I've been wanting to ask you something for a long time now. I don't think I can wait any longer, so here it is… I'm thinking of switching my PC operating system from Windows to Linux. What do you say?"

* * *

Walking back to the base, Johnson felt guilty. He needed to work on his lack of sensitivity. Worse, he hadn't been truthful. He'd meant to tell Cam he wasn't ready for a serious relationship, but at the last minute, he'd lost his nerve. He hadn't realized she'd get so upset.

The dinner conversation had been troubling, too. He could instantly recall the details of every football game he'd ever played. But his memory of that last Tech game was sketchy. He had no recollection of the winning play, Tyrell's tussle with the linebacker, or anything that happened that day. What was going on?

CHAPTER 5

After the morning inspection, Johnson met Tyrell at the computer center. They were the envy of the unit, hand-picked for the Tangent project, developing a cutting-edge application. They had been given an ambitious timeline, and still had to do significant testing, but both were confident they could deliver the product on time.

Tyrell sat at a large table, printouts spread in front of him. "Hey, did you have a good time last night? I did. You seemed quiet."

Johnson was focused on the monitor at his workstation. "Are you kidding me? I had a great time. But between your motor mouth and Cam's, I couldn't get a word in edgewise."

Tyrell laughed. "I know. I tend to dominate the conversation. Alicia said you and Cam make a great couple."

"I'm not sure about that, but I was super impressed with her. She's different than most of the women you've dated. I can't believe I'm saying this, but I like her."

"That's good. So, what was wrong with the others?"

"You're kidding, right?"

"No. Please tell me. Start with Jasmine."

"Let's see. She was the one at Stransky's wedding, right?

Something about the way she talked drove me crazy. Her enunciation was weird."

"Weird how?"

"She kept commenting on how much she liked the Justice of the Peace, but she pronounced it Justice of the *Peas*. I kept picturing the Jolly Green Giant. Moving on to Danielle, an extremely well-proportioned young woman but not exactly a rocket scientist."

"So?"

"So, she called the proctor who monitored her GED exam the proctologist. Who knew a rectal was one of the requirements?"

"Oh, shut up. What was wrong with Tamika?"

"She snorted when she laughed."

"And Faye?"

"Noisy eater."

"Veronica?"

"No sense of humor."

"Brianna?"

"A tongue clicker."

"Shannon?"

"She was a three-sigma."

"What the hell is a three-sigma?"

"Ninety-five percent of a normal distribution is contained within two standard deviations, or two sigma. Over ninety-nine percent is contained within three-sigma. So, when you're a three-sigma, you're out there."

"Dude, that's you. You are at least a three-sigma. You may be a four-sigma."

"Hey, that's mean. Anyway, Alicia is smart and attractive."

"You're right. She's amazing. But I'll have to survive on your company for a few weeks. She's on another trip to Europe and Asia."

Johnson looked up from the screen. "Like you don't rely on my company already? How long have I been babysitting you? I'm always trying to keep you out of trouble."

"And I appreciate that. Anyway, right now we need to focus on launching Tangent."

"Speaking of which, the simulation is almost complete. Let's run it a few more times to check for glitches. This thing will blow people away."

Tyrell rolled his chair to Johnson's computer and peered at the screen. "It's a war scenario. It's supposed to blow everyone away."

"I'm serious. This could represent a real seed change for the military."

"What kind of change?"

"A seed change."

"Like a sesame seed?"

"I'm not sure."

"A poppy?"

"What the heck is that?"

"I think you mean a *sea* change."

"No, Ty. This has nothing to do with the climate—or the Navy."

"Never mind. I know it's a big deal. They're flying in reps from all over the country for the launch. Does that make you nervous?"

Johnson removed a microscopic piece of lint from the screen with his fingertip. "I guess a little. I was thinking we could open it up with you giving the background and then I'd do the demo."

"So, I soften up the sharks for you. Tell me, Specialist Telling. Why should I do that?"

"Well, Specialist Brown, you could sell steak knives to a vegetarian, life insurance to a zombie, underwear to—"

"Okay, I get it, I get it. *I'll* do the intro. Let's make sure it syncs up correctly with the simulations. We can show them the first three scenarios, don't want to overwhelm them."

"Great idea. Who's handling the A/V?"

"Our man Dutch. We should be good to go."

"I've got a good feeling about this. Blanton will love it. And if

Blanton loves it, that can only mean good things for us. He's never come out and said so, but we may be up for a promotion."

"I hope you're right. Let's run more scenarios."

* * *

Weightlifting was a ritual for many soldiers in Johnson's unit. It relieved stress, boosted morale, and provided a sense of camaraderie. Friendly competition and small wagers were the hallmarks of these spirited sessions, incentivizing the men to stretch their limits. Very few could match Johnson's strength, but newcomers often tried.

Carson Brooks thrived on competition. Square-jawed, brash, and unflappable, his edgy demeanor complemented his overt distrust of most humans. He compensated for a below-average stature with an arrogant strut. His facial features were not off-putting, but he appeared to have no neck as if his clean-shaven head and broad shoulders had been melded into one unit.

He was considered annoying, but harmless, and was guarded in his interactions with the unit. Over time, some of his comrades developed a visceral reaction to his presence, but the onslaught of sour looks and slurs didn't faze him, Instead, his rude retorts spewed forth like pellets from a Pez dispenser.

Brooks studied the men with intense curiosity, made mental notes about each, then put them into good or bad buckets. The assessment of Johnson was more difficult. Brooks admired his physical prowess but questioned his authenticity. He'd need more information before he could decide.

As Tyrell and Johnson entered the locker room, Brooks greeted them, flexing his arm with a dumbbell. "Hi, guys. You're looking so lovely today. Jesus, it's about time you showed up! Ready to get smoked on the bench press?"

Something in the man set Johnson off. He was more than a nemesis. He was the anti-Johnson, an existential parasite of negativity created for the sole purpose of draining the life force from its host. His primary tactics were simple—begin by attacking the ego and creating doubt. Then rinse and repeat.

Tyrell scowled as he unbuttoned his shirt. "I can't figure it out. How is it that you're always so damn confident about everything? And what happened to your neck?"

Brooks peered blankly at Tyrell. "Bite me, Brown! Hey, where the hell is Dutch? I thought he was joining us."

"Double duty today," Johnson said as he changed into his sweats. "You know some of us have been prepping for the big presentation."

Brooks continued his bicep curls. "Oh, yeah. Project Tangent. Still waiting on my clearance for that. I hear all the VIPs will be there. Try not to embarrass us."

Tyrell snatched the weight from Brooks. "Listen to me, no-neck. Why don't you shut up? Thank god you won't be there. If anyone could embarrass the unit it would be your sorry ass."

Brooks peered out the window. "Oh, precious, now don't get your panties in a wad. I'm sure you'll muddle through it some-how. So, what's up with the band over there?"

Johnson finished tying a double knot on his shoe. "I think they're practicing for the ceremony to honor Jennings. My grand-father is scheduled to give a speech. It's a big deal. Captain says they'll be at it on and off for the next few weeks."

"Oh, great. I hope those cretins don't suck. Wait, did you say your grandfather? *The* General Thomas Telling? It all makes sense now."

Johnson stood within inches of Brooks' face. "Excuse me? Exactly what did you mean by that?"

"Hey man, just calm down. I just meant—"

Tyrell dropped the dumbbell and inserted his lanky frame between the two men. "Guys, guys! Let's save this energy for the weight room. Chill out for a minute."

Johnson eyed Brooks in silence for a time then backed away, and the three headed to the weight room. *I can't stand this creep. One day I'll wipe that stupid smug look right off his face.* Insinuating that his grandfather was paving the way for his career had been insulting.

They warmed up with a series of stretches and light aerobics, then spotted each other at bench pressing. Brooks matched Johnson's weight rep for rep on the first three sets. On the fourth set, Brooks loaded the rack with four hundred pounds.

Tyrell looked skeptical. "Seriously? Good luck with that. I'm going to grab a shower."

Johnson was on the bench. "Roger that, Ty. See you in a few after I embarrass this guy. I don't need a spot." He lifted the bar slightly, then quickly lowered the massive load to within an inch of his chest, where it remained, though his face turned purple, and he grunted like an animal.

Brooks took great pleasure in witnessing Johnson's predicament. "Having trouble getting it up, Johnson?"

"Brooks, I, need a little help over here."

"Come on, you pansy. I know you can do it."

"I'm not kidding. I need your help."

"Are you sure?"

"Yes. Now!"

Brooks sauntered over to the bench, performed a quick stretch, then helped Johnson return the bar to its starting position.

"You are one sick individual!" Johnson screamed. "Did you like that? Let's see you do it, you creep."

Brooks smirked. "Oh, hell no, Johnson. I could never lift that much weight. I just wanted to see if *you* could!"

Johnson snatched his towel and shot off the bench. *This guy is a bona fide psycho.* "See you later, man. Don't forget to re-rack everything. Oh, did anyone ever tell you you're an ass?"

* * *

In the shower, Johnson's mind raced. He was still on edge and disturbing thoughts bounced around in his brain like a pinball. His discord with Cam was troubling. She was appealing and having a steady girlfriend fit in perfectly with his world order. Her exit would force him into a new paradigm. Such a thought was panic-inducing, even worse than the unholy terror of, say, breaking in a new pair of shoes. Living in the shadow of a famous grandfather caused much grander angst and a constant reassessment of his own worth. Underlying every accomplishment were doubts about its authenticity. His role in the Tangent project had been a boon. But was it good enough, and had he made it this far on his own?

His thoughts were interrupted by a taut sensation in his groin. *What the hell is going on?* Horrified, he stepped out of the shower and wrapped himself in a towel, hoping to conceal his protuberance. But as he tiptoed through the steamy air, a grinning figure confronted him.

"Why Johnson," Brooks said. "What an appropriate name for someone in your condition. What's with the full salute? At ease! Hey, guys. He likes us. At least one of us."

During his walk of shame to the locker room, Johnson felt all eyes on him, while Brooks led the men in a chorus of hoots, jeers, and whistles. The die had been cast. This man was the devil, and he vowed to get even no matter what the cost.

CHAPTER 6

"Mom! You're supposed to use your walker. I swear, it's like dealing with a four-year-old. Can you talk to her, Aunt Viv?"

"I can try. I'm not sure it will do any good, though. Bev, you need to listen to your daughter."

Charlie's mother was perturbed. "I don't need that damn thing anymore. I'm not disabled, I'm not in a nursing home, and I'm not old."

"Maybe so, but the doctor wants you to use it for at least another month," Charlie said.

Beverly scowled as she continued down the narrow hall. "What does he know? I can't wait until I can drive again."

Charlie groaned. It hadn't been easy. She had been at her mother's side since the accident. They'd sold the family house to cover the medical expenses, and she'd moved their furnishings and possessions into a rented apartment so that it would be ready when her mother finally came home. After two surgeries, extended stays in the ICU, and months of rehab, Beverly Jankowski was finally on the road to recovery and longing to return to normalcy. She met her daughter's attempts to baby her with callous dismissals.

Vivian was unloading the dishwasher. "You've been so good to her, so caring. I dare say your mother would still be in that wheelchair today if not for your persistence. She's lucky to have a daughter like you. She doesn't realize it now, but she will someday."

Charlie eyed the linoleum tabletop, then began to scrub it with a wet sponge. "Well, thanks. I have to bite my tongue sometimes. I try to be respectful, but she's so stubborn."

"Is she ever!" Viv said. "Even when we were kids she always thought she knew best. I'm surprised she didn't wake up during surgery to tell the doctor what he was doing wrong."

"That's funny. I wish I had her confidence."

"Oh, you will one day," Vivian said as she closed the dishwasher and sat down on a rickety chair. "I guarantee it. You've barely had a chance to get out in the world. It takes time. You should think about going back to school. Reconnect with friends. Join Omega Chi. Date. Have some fun while you're young."

"Man, would I love the opportunity to go back to State," Charlie said. "But not Omega Chi. The sorority scene isn't for me."

"Really? Your mother and I loved it. And when you start looking for a job, you'll have a built-in network of contacts all over the country."

"That would be nice. Unfortunately, things have changed since you and Mom were in school. It's gotten a lot more competitive. And the stuff they had me doing was insane. I'm not cool and they knew it. I was drinking a ton just to cope with everything."

"Too bad. It's supposed to be fun."

"I did enjoy parts of my one semester at State, though."

"Well, we've got to get you back there. Time's a wastin,' young lady."

"I can't leave Mom right now. And she's been out of work so long the bills are piling up. I need to get a job."

"What if I helped out? I could stay with Bev a few evenings a week and take care of some of the bills."

Charlie finished wiping down the table. "That would be fantastic."

"I want to help any way I can. It's the least I can do now that I'm back in town."

"I'll bet I could get a weekend job and take a few classes at State in the evenings. I can't believe it. This is happening!"

Beverly shuffled into the kitchen without the aid of her walker. "What's this?"

Charlie broke into a dance as Vivian explained the plan.

"Are you sure about this, Viv? It's a big commitment."

"I sure am. It'll give us a chance to catch up. I can tell you all about the detective I met in Australia."

Charlie's eyes widened. "This I've got to hear."

"Those Aussies can be surprisingly naughty. His name is Dylan. I met him at a place called The Shady Pines Saloon. . ."

* * *

In the late afternoon, Charlie scanned the classified ads. She found a few part-time positions, but none of them looked promising. An online search returned one result. *Kiss and Tell* had an opening for an exotic dancer to work the lunch shift but she couldn't imagine herself gyrating seductively in pasties. She stroked the frayed, faded nap of the sofa where she sat beside her aunt. "What are you watching?"

"Commentary. Followed by an interview with the mayor."

"Gross. Politics. I never pay attention to that stuff. So boring. Can't you find something else?"

"I'll find a movie in a minute. But you should be better informed. Do you know anything about your local elected officials?"

"Nope. Don't care."

"Well start caring. Any luck with the job search?"

"I'm afraid not. If only I were a nurse, a bricklayer, or a long-distance truck driver. I'd be all set. Apparently, there's not much call for people with no experience and less than a semester of college."

"Don't get discouraged, kiddo. I've got some connections in town. I can make some calls."

Charlie sprang up. "That would be great. I'll do anything. Listen, would you mind staying with Mom while I drive into town? I need to get one of her prescriptions refilled."

"Take your time. I'm in no rush. Besides, I'm primed with a few more Dylan stories."

* * *

After her stop at the pharmacy, Charlie wandered around, enjoying her newfound freedom. The town's once bustling commercial area had been in decline for many years, but a local civic group was directing the initial stages of a facelift. Main Street was lined with magnolia trees in full bloom, and flower boxes brightened every corner of the historic central square. She visited the old courthouse, which stood in genteel splendor, authentically refurbished in the spirit of its antebellum roots with ornate details in every crook.

She window-shopped until the irresistible aroma of fresh pastries lured her to the bakery for a blueberry scone. As she sat on a bench enjoying the last bite, a woman passed by pushing a wobbly cart full of bric-a-brac and stopped to catch her breath.

"I'm Emmaline," she said, adjusting her tattered wool skull cap. "Mind if I sit down?"

"No, not at all. If you'd been here three minutes ago, I'd have given you half a scone. I'm Charlie Jankowski."

"Thanks, Charlie, but I'm not hungry. The kitchen over there on Second was open today. Got me a nice hot meal. What are you doing out here? I don't believe I've ever seen you before. And I know most everybody."

"I'm looking for a job. It's been a while since I've been down here. I live with my mom over on the east side."

"Job, huh? I had a good one before they shut down the factory. Now I'm too old. Nobody wants to hire a 69-year-old woman with arthritis. I ain't qualified for nothin' but runnin' that press. Honey, take my advice and get an education."

"That's what I'm trying to do. Part-time, anyway. But I need to help my mom pay off some bills. That's too bad about the factory."

"Sure was. Never understood it, myself. We were doing so well. Then one day we all got pink slips. No warning. No severance. No nothing. It was just… see you later, alligator."

"That doesn't seem right."

"It wasn't. I guess I was lucky because I just had me to worry about. No family to support."

"That's terrible. If I had time, I'd love to talk about it. But I've got to get going. I need to check a few more places."

"Don't waste your time down here. There's not much available, except maybe at the restaurant. I know 'cause I'm here every day. Did you say your name was Jankowski?"

"That's right."

"I thought you looked familiar. I never forget a face. You look a lot like your dad. And I mean that in a good way. He's quite a looker."

"You know my father?"

"Sure do. I met him when he visited the plant. How's he doing?"

"I don't know. We haven't seen or heard from him for quite some time."

"That's funny. Could've sworn I saw him down here not too long ago."

"Are you sure about that?"

"Pretty sure. But I'm old and my memory ain't what it used to be."

* * *

Charlie brushed off the revelation as a case of mistaken identity. She didn't recall her father ever mentioning the factory, and it was unlikely that he'd turn up in Parish without contacting his family.

She made inquiries at the hardware store, an antiques boutique, and a fast-food establishment. Then she saw a help wanted sign in the window at McKenzie's, bounced into the lively restaurant, and asked to see the manager. A portly man with a goatee and silver hair approached her extending his hand. "Hi, Gavin McFadden. Nice to meet you. And you are?"

"Charlene Jankowski, but you can call me Charlie. I'm here for a job. Is it always this noisy in here?"

"No. It's usually way noisier than this. Mondays tend to be slow. Did you say you're here for a job?"

"That's right. I just happened to be passing by and saw the sign."

"Oh, I'm terribly sorry, Charlie, but we don't hire anyone who isn't of Scottish descent."

Charlie looked confused. "Seriously?"

"I'm afraid so."

"What if I told you I'm a big fan of Scotch tape?"

"Nice try."

"What if could play the bagpipes?"

"I don't think so."

"Well, sorry to bother you."

McFadden's eyes lit up. "Gotcha."

"Huh?"

The man's smile disappeared. "To be honest, we're always looking for qualified people. Especially those with a sense of humor. We try to create an atmosphere of fun around here. Do you have any experience?"

"Absolutely I do, and I have references. Most recently, I spent several months as an exotic dancer over at *Kiss and Tell*. My stage name was Bitta Honey. I've got to tell you, those military guys just loved me. Maybe you've caught my act. Come to think of it, you look familiar."

McFadden cleared his throat. "Are you sure about that?"

"You know, a lot of guys think dark sunglasses make them invisible but guess what? It's not true."

"I'm not sure I—"

"Gotcha."

McFadden smiled. "Wow. I don't get fooled very often. Good for you. You would fit right in here. Have you ever worked in a restaurant?"

"No. And I can only work weekends. I'll be taking classes in the evening at State during the week. But I'm willing to do anything. Wash dishes, bus tables, you name it."

"I see. Sounds like you're ambitious. We have an opening for a server on the weekends. You may have to alternate between the day and evening shifts. Would you be okay with that?"

"I sure would. I'm grateful for the opportunity."

"Super. Let's go back to my office and I'll have you fill out an application. If it all looks good, you can start this weekend. You'll be shadowing Lydia for the first couple of weeks."

"Excuse me for asking, but oh my gosh, did you say I'll be working with Lydia?"

"That's right. Lydia Cornwell."

"I may need to sit down for a moment. Please, not Lydia Cornwell. Not her!" Charlie put on her most horrified expression, then burst into tears.

"Is there a problem? I'm sorry, I didn't mean to upset you. You see, Lydia's one of our stars. She's been here a long time and I wasn't aware of—"

"Gotcha again."

McFadden broke into laughter. "Charlie, that was excellent. You fooled me. I can't wait for you to start. We'll get along fine."

"I'm sure we will. And if there's ever a problem, just let me know."

"I'll do that," he said with a wink.

* * *

Later, in his tiny office laden with stacks of boxes, McFadden studied a worn canvas-bound ledger as Charlie filled out the employment application. "You know this is just a formality. You're local, and you're taking classes at State. And since you don't have any relevant experience, I have no references to check."

"There, I'm finished." Charlie handed him the form. "I hope everything looks good."

McFadden glanced at the information for a second then looked up. "Jankowski. That name sounds vaguely familiar. Where have I heard that before? You're older than I guessed. What did you do after high school?"

"I took some time off after graduation and traveled around the country alone. That was an amazing experience."

"Alone?"

"Yes. I couldn't talk any of my so-called friends into going."

"I see. Then what?"

"Then I came back here and went to community college for a year. I was at State for a semester but had to drop out to take care of my mom."

"That's too bad. What happened to her?"

Charlie's lengthy narrative was sincere and passionate, revealing a depth of character she seldom showed.

"Thanks for that, Charlie. Glad she's doing better. Sounds like you've been busy. You know, if you take this job, you'll be even busier. Do you think you're mature enough to handle the added responsibility?"

"Absolutely, Mr. McFadden."

"That's what I like to hear. And please call me Fad."

"Okay, Fad. I'll level with you. I need this job. My mom has insurance, but it only covers so much. The accident has wiped us out financially. We're not destitute, but it's been very tight. If you hire me, you won't be sorry. I'll give you one hundred percent."

McFadden nodded. "Believe it or not, I know what you're going through. Your base pay won't be much, but tips usually make up for it. That is, if you're good. With experience, you'll learn how to interact with our clientele. As you know, most are in the military, and they have come to expect a very high level of service from McKenzie's. Are you up for the challenge?"

"I sure am. After dealing with my mother's rehab, I'm up for anything. It'll be nice to get out of the house for a while."

"Can you start on Saturday?"

"Does that mean I'm hired?"

"Yes. But only for a trial period. We'll have to see how it works out."

Charlie leaped out of her chair. "Thanks so much! I promise you won't be disappointed. What time should I be here?"

"Three o'clock on the dot. And be sure to dress appropriately. Nothing outrageous. McKenzie's is a family restaurant. Oh, and before I forget, take this personnel manual with you and memorize it before Saturday. We have a strict code of conduct here and zero tolerance for offenders."

"Yes, sir." Charlie stuffed the thick binder in her bag. "Thanks again and see you Saturday. I'm super excited."

As she hurried back through the central square, Emmaline waved her down.

"Hey, Charlie. Any luck with the job hunting?"

"Oh, yes! I start at McKenzie's on Saturday. Isn't that great?"

"McKenzie's, huh? Well, good for you. You're a smart one. I sure hope it works out."

"Thanks. I need to get back to Mom. Do you need a lift anywhere? My car is just around the corner."

"Thanks, honey, but I'm fine. Just another block or so to the shelter. You go on back to your ma. And tell her I'm praying for her."

"Yes, ma'am. I will. Thanks."

Emmaline labored to push the heavy cart across the street, then stopped to gab with the occupant of a vehicle parked at the corner. She turned towards Charlie and waved, then hobbled up the avenue, greeting everyone she met.

* * *

As she drove home, Charlie felt invigorated. The challenge of a new job excited her, and it couldn't have come at a better time. The rent for the apartment would soon be overdue and their credit cards were already maxed out. With her aunt's help, she could get their financial house in order. Life would be hectic but surely she could manage working two days a week for the very nice man.

Just when she was a few blocks from home, the car stalled at a red light. None of her begging or cursing could persuade it to restart before the signal turned green. She banged on the steering wheel as other motorists maneuvered around her, took a deep breath, and turned the key one last time. Miraculously, the engine came to life. She'd launched into a soliloquy of sincere contrition when she saw a warning light on the dashboard flash red.

She banged on the steering wheel again. "Damn you, Dieter! Whatever's wrong, it'll just have to wait."

CHAPTER 7

In the early morning hours, Johnson tossed and turned in his bunk. Once again, the dreaded rodent in green had invaded his sleep, paralyzing him with fear. This time, the animal had a condescending tone and spoke French.

"*Bon soir, mon amour. C'est moi.*"

"Go away," Johnson pleaded.

"You and I both know that will not be happening," the squirrel said as it preened its handlebar mustache.

"Why do you wear a spandex suit? You know it's very weird."

"It highlights my glutes, and why should it matter to you what I wear? It would change little about our relationship."

"What do you mean?" asked Johnson.

"You're afraid of me. Would *au naturel* be better?"

"No, I guess not."

"And do you know why I frighten you so?"

"Because you're a big, fat annoying rat."

"*Au contraire, monsieur*. I may be a rodent as you say, but I am not obese. I represent the sum of your fears. Someday, like it or not, you will have to confront me."

A woman in a flowing white gown appeared and scowled at

Johnson. "Hey, you over there. Man up! Don't let that disgusting ball of fur get away with it!"

Johnson gulped. "Cameron?"

"Oh, please. Who else is going to save your ass? Let me show you how it's done." She flashed a fierce look of disdain at the squirrel, and it vanished.

Johnson woke up and began a painful self-psychoanalysis in the dark. *Man, this is so bizarre. I need to shake it off and move on.* He fell back to sleep and slipped into a dream sequence of faint but powerful images.

His friends and family were gathered for a formal celebration on a misty mountain top, and the mood was joyous. Ahead, a garden path lined with lilies and pale roses led to a clearing where a tall figure in a football uniform stood waiting beside an altar.

Laughter and upbeat chatter faded as organ music commenced. Gramps, Grandmother Annie, and Aunt Julia watched beaming as Johnson drifted effortlessly down the path. His feet never touched the ground, and his army green tuxedo and camo helmet sparkled in the early evening light. When he reached the altar, a breathtaking vision in white appeared at the end of the path. His bride-to-be's veiled face and silky torso floated ever so gently towards him accompanied by a flock of doves, while angelic voices filled the air with song.

The figure in uniform spoke. "Friends, we are gathered here today in this surreal setting for a celebration of love. Not just any love, but that of the highest order: eternal love. Remember this day, as we witness a union of the purest kind, a union of souls. George Eliot wrote 'What greater thing is there for two human souls than to feel they are joined for life?' By professing their love and devotion to each other in the midst of their families and friends, these two will be joined together forever in holy matrimony. I can't think of two people who are better suited for each other."

"To the bride—do you take this person to be your wedded husband, to have and to hold from this day forward, for better, for worse, for richer, for poorer, in sickness and in health, to love and to cherish, until death do you part?"

"I do."

"And to the groom—do you take this person to be your wedded wife, to have and to hold from this day forward, for better, for worse, for richer, for poorer, in sickness and in health, to love and to cherish, until death do you part?"

"I do."

"Say what?"

"I do."

"Dude. Are you sure?"

"Well, I think I'm sure."

"Okay, close enough. By the powers vested in me, I now pronounce you married. You may kiss each other. But please, no tongues. This is a family occasion."

As Johnson lifted his bride's delicate veil with the utmost care, the dream abruptly ended. He cried out in the dark, jolted awake. Gazing back at him was not Cameron's exquisite face but the ghastly countenance of Carson Brooks, batting his eyelashes and puckering his lips.

What did this nightmare mean? He wasn't ready for a long-term relationship with Cameron, but could he be subconsciously attracted to Brooks? Had his feelings for him surfaced in the shower? Or was he temporarily insane? He convinced himself to get it out of his head. He was fine and just needed to move on.

* * *

Later that morning, Johnson and Tyrell chatted over coffee.

"So, are you going to talk about what happened at the gym last week?"

"Oh, you mean what Brooks did to me in the weight room? He is one sick animal."

"No. I meant what happened in the shower. That must have been weird. What were you thinking?"

"Nothing in particular."

"You can tell *me*. Were you having sexy thoughts about Cam?"

"You have no idea how much I wish I could say that. But no."

"All the guys have been talking about it."

"Oh great. Not only is Brooks demented, but he's got a big mouth."

"Well, don't worry about it. It's not a big deal. Could have happened to anybody."

"You think? Has it ever happened to you?"

"Are you kidding me? Never. That kind of stuff's messed up."

At that moment, Brooks entered the canteen and Johnson sank in his seat.

"Good morning, Brown. And a very special good morning to you, Telling. Have you missed me?"

Tyrell scowled. "Brooks, who said you could join us?"

"Why, Brown! I'm so disappointed in you. Where's your esprit de corps? We're all in this together, right?" He leaned in and adjusted his shirt collar. "Look, Telling. I wore my new green fatigues especially for you."

Johnson heated to a slow boil. "Let's pretend the whole thing never happened, okay?"

Brooks grinned and whispered. "Oh, I get it. Don't ask, don't tell?"

Johnson pounded his fist on the table. "Listen to me, Brooks. Go ahead and make your jokes today. Have fun with the guys. Get your jollies at my expense. But that's it. Tomorrow we go back to square one. I don't want to hear any more of this crap. And I am not gay!"

"Oh, good. Does your grandfather know that?"

Johnson lunged forward in a rage but Tyrell restrained him. "Holy crap! Knock it off you two."

Another soldier interrupted. He was tall with striking green eyes, and he wore a look of amusement as if he were privy to a lewd limerick. "What have we here?"

Tyrell loosened his grip on Johnson. "Dutch, my man, just the guy I wanted to see! You caught us in the middle of an impromptu therapy session. Johnson here was about to show Brooks how not to be an asshole!"

Dutch adjusted his dark-framed glasses. "I'm not sure that's possible."

Brooks feigned a laugh. "Very funny."

"What is wrong with you?" Dutch asked. "Why the preoccupation with the behavior of others? Is it a deep-seated defense mechanism masking your own inadequacies? Have you considered therapy?"

Brooks grabbed his crotch. "Hey, analyze this!"

"Be happy to," Dutch said with a straight face. "But I'm not sure your junk has ever been visible to the naked eye, or a naked woman, for that matter."

Brooks scowled.

Tyrell laughed, then took a sip of coffee. "So, Dutch. Now that we have that out of the way, Johnson and I need to make sure we're good for the Tangent presentation. When do you need the draft materials?"

"If you can get them to me by this afternoon, that would be great. I'll need to copy everything to the server and test it. Then we'll need to get approval from the brass. It should take a few days. Brooks is my backup, just in case. But I don't foresee any issues."

Johnson looked aghast. "But he doesn't have clearance for Tangent!"

Brooks beamed. "I do now."

"Not to worry," Dutch said. "He might be a douche, but Brooks knows his stuff when it comes to A/V. By the way, Johnson, you still seeing Cameron?"

"Yeah. How did you know?"

"You guys looked pretty tight at that Christmas thing. But I wasn't sure you were still together, you know, given recent events."

"Well, we are!"

"We'll see how long that lasts," Brooks muttered under his breath.

Dutch headed out. "Great. Just be sure you get me the materials this afternoon."

* * *

The remainder of the day was productive. Johnson was only mildly distracted by suspicious glances and stale jokes at his expense and managed to complete the final edits of the Tangent presentation. He figured most of the men were too absorbed in their own dramas to care about his. Brooks was the exception. He took every opportunity to needle his favorite target. Johnson managed to ignore the steady stream of accusations and innuendos.

Later, during their habitual weightlifting session, Brooks was surprisingly subdued. Tyrell and Dutch devised an elaborate alien abduction theory to explain his uncharacteristic behavior, which gained credibility in the locker room. In the shower, Johnson relaxed as he mulled over the events of the day. The Tangent materials had been delivered, and a successful presentation could springboard him to the elite status he so desperately needed. The thought of last week's incident was no longer a cause for concern. Surely, he, a Telling, could handle any adversity.

And then it happened again.

CHAPTER 8

After McKenzie's dinner service ended, Lydia counted the money in the register. "You might want to think about investing in a more comfortable pair of shoes. They look good but I wouldn't last two hours in those torture chambers."

"Oh, man," Charlie said, massaging a foot. "I have *so* been meaning to do that. How am I doing so far? Any complaints? Suggestions?"

Lydia scribbled numbers onto the backs of two envelopes, then began stuffing them with cash. "You're doing fine. Just remember the first rule is to smile a lot. The guys love it, and you'll get bigger tips. And make sure to push the specials. There's a bigger markup on those. Fad likes it when we sell out."

"Thanks for the advice. And speaking of guys, I don't know if you remember, who was that couple at table eleven in your section earlier?"

"Let's see… He's a big guy, athletic type, and she's an uptight chick with an attitude."

"Have they been in before?"

"Oh yeah. They're regulars. Why?"

"I could hear them talking while I was waiting on another

table. Didn't recognize her voice, but he sounded strangely familiar."

Lydia grabbed her keys and headed for the door. "Hmm, I'm sure he's from the base, but that doesn't help much. Half our customers are from there. Not sure about her. She seems conceited to me. That's all I know. Hey, can you do me a huge favor?"

"Sure."

"I'm late again and my sister has the kids. I need to roll. Can you take these envelopes to Fad before you leave?"

"No problem. But why two envelopes? Why not combine the money in one?"

Lydia shrugged. "Beats me. I just work here. That's the way Fad told me to do it. It has something to do with the bookkeeping." She waved on her way out.

Charlie stood outside McFadden's office, listening to muffled speech drift through the door. The tone was vile, vicious, the language threatening, and she heard repeated, vulgar references to a name she couldn't quite make out. After a minute she heard him hang up the phone. She waited a few more seconds, then knocked.

"Come on in, Lydia."

Charlie stepped in. "Hi, Mr. McFadden. Here are tonight's receipts."

He snatched the envelopes. "Where's Lydia?"

"She had to scoot out and asked me to drop these off for her. She didn't think it would be a problem."

McFadden studied Charlie. "Oh. Okay. I usually prefer her to do it, but I'll let it go this time. So how do you like it here? Lydia tells me you're doing great."

"So far, so good. She's coaching me, and that's been helpful. I can recite the menu in my sleep, and I'll be sure to push the daily specials. I didn't realize how tired I'd get from being on my feet all night."

McFadden smirked. "The first few weeks are the hardest. You'll get used to that. Just keep doing what you're doing, and you'll be fine. It's late. Now get out of here before you turn into a pumpkin, young lady!"

* * *

Charlie's trip home was delayed when she became stuck in McKenzie's deserted parking lot. Even after implementing her usual bag of tricks the car wouldn't start, and she feared her beloved ragtop had finally met its demise. While wondering what she had missed, a nondescript truck rumbled in and stopped in the back of the storage area.

She sat entranced, watching men with hand carts fill the vehicle with dozens of small cardboard boxes, moving load after load like robots, barely speaking. After a few minutes, a man dressed in black appeared out of nowhere and tapped on her window. His droopy eyes and scarred face gave him the look of something from a horror movie. She rolled down the window slightly, trying not to appear shaken.

"Need some help?" he asked.

"Thanks, but I'm just waiting."

"Waiting for what?"

"For my car to start. He's so temperamental. I usually have to give it a minute, then try again. There are so many possibilities— the fuel pump, the starter, the battery, who knows? I just went inside to have a few drinks at the bar before it closed, and wouldn't you know, I missed last call. So, I came out here for a smoke, but I'm out. You wouldn't happen to have one, would you?"

"No, I don't. You shouldn't either. Those things will kill you."

"Well, something's going to get you. Pick your poison, I say."

"Slide over," he said. "I'll see what I can do."

As the man reached for the door, Charlie locked it, turned the ignition key and the engine roared to life. "There he goes. I'm fine, thanks. Have a good evening." She glanced in the rear-view mirror and saw the man watching her drive out of sight. *Good riddance, Mr. Creepy.*

As she drove home, she imagined a horde of maniacs in vehicles tracking her every move, ranging from a hearse-like station wagon to a sputtering sedan driven by someone's doddering grandmother. When a flashy, hopped-up sports car got too close, she took another route.

The events of the evening disturbed her, yet she was riveted by the intrigue. Why would anyone be moving restaurant stock at that time of night? What could be so valuable? A story was developing, and she was a budding reporter. She had to investigate.

CHAPTER 9

Cameron trudged up the third flight of stairs, stepped inside, and slammed the heavy oak door behind her. She never took the elevator, preferring to maintain her trim figure with aerobics, yoga, and a vegetarian diet. Her part-time job as a fitness instructor left her with ample time to pursue her other passions—home decorating and the latest fashions. She purchased most of her clothing out of town since she found the options in Parish abysmal.

She'd recently installed new marble countertops and stainless-steel appliances, and she kept the place immaculate. So, she was horrified to find her breakfast dishes in the sink. She picked up the phone to connect with her most frequent contact.

"Maid-to-Order, where we never take you to the cleaners. We bring the cleaners to you. This is Eduardo."

"Yes, Eduardo. This is Cameron Woodson on Glendale Boulevard."

"Hello again, Miss Woodson. What seems to be the problem today? Did we forget to steam clean your exotic frog figurine collection again?"

"You forgot to clean my condo."

"How do you know it wasn't cleaned?"

"Because there are dirty dishes in the sink. What happened to Camilla?"

"Let me check. Oh, sorry, I see she called in sick."

"Sick? That is not *my* problem. What am I supposed to do? Clean this place myself?"

"We can get someone out there early next week."

"Next week? That's not acceptable."

"I'm afraid that's the earliest we can do it."

"Excuse me? Oh, just forget it. Next time I'll hire a cleaning service that's not incompetent!"

She dove onto the sofa, squirming on the plush Italian fabric. Her condo needed attention. The once pristine hardwood floors had lost their shine and the elegant end tables were no longer a perfect complement to the European motif. The matching imported lamps, once the pride of her domain, looked tired and outdated. The paneled wainscoting needed a makeover.

She eyed a copy of *Bride's* magazine on the glass coffee table and began to leaf through the pages. *Ugh. Not in a million years. Yuck. I wouldn't be caught dead in that. A veil? No. Gross. Who designed this dress? Carpet World?* She settled back against a pillow and picked up the phone to connect with her second most frequent contact.

"Hello, Daddy? It's me."

"Hi, cupcake. How are you?"

"Awful. The cleaning service didn't show up today. I'm going to have to live in filth until Monday. Honestly, can you believe that?"

"Is that what you called about? I'm in the middle of a meeting."

"Well, that, and something else. It's important."

"Sweetheart, can this wait?"

"Daddy, do you realize it's been more than six months since I had my place painted? And this furniture is starting to look ratty. The whole thing needs a major facelift."

"That furniture is less than a year old, and the last time your mother and I were there your condo looked fine."

"But that was weeks ago. You should see the way it looks now. It's so depressing. I'm thinking pewter gray in the living room and—"

"Cam, if it's that important to you, go ahead. I give you a generous allowance every month. Have you been saving like we talked about?"

"Oh, Daddy. You know how expensive clothes are. A girl has to keep her wardrobe up."

"Did you fly to New York again?"

"Only a couple of times last month. But it was so worth it. I found some gorgeous outfits."

"Keeping your wardrobe up to date is not in our agreement. Much less flying all the way up there to do it. I don't have time to get into this now. We'll have to talk later. Bye."

"Daddy? Daddy? Did he just hang up on me? Ooh, that is so infuriating!"

Cameron padded into the kitchen for a late lunch of spinach salad and white wine. Then she poured herself a second glass and drank it in the tub. Paint swatches swirled through her head as she soaked. She had finally settled on the perfect palette when her phone buzzed.

"Hey."

"You again? Look, I'm busy right now."

"Come on, you're never that busy."

"Why do you keep calling me?"

"I wanted to hear your voice."

"In case you've forgotten, we broke up months ago. Besides, you have a girlfriend."

"I know, but I can't stop thinking about you."

"Well, this has got to stop. I can block your number, you know."

"You could, but then you'd miss out on all the information I have for you."

"Okay, I'll bite. What information?"

"Information about your boyfriend."

"Johnson?"

"He *is* your boyfriend, isn't he?"

"Listen, if this is some kind of joke, I'm hanging up right now. I've got way more important things to think about."

"Like whether to go with pumps or flats?"

"You shut up. I never wear flats. Tell me what you know."

"Okay, but you've got to promise you'll think about giving me a second chance."

"Okay, I thought about it. Now, what's going on with Johnson?"

"Come on. I'm serious. Okay?"

"All right, all right. I'll give it some thought. Now, what do you know?"

"Let's just say Johnson may not be the man he pretends to be."

"What does that mean?"

"Recent events indicate he might be a little light in the loafers."

"You're crazy. What evidence do you have?"

"I've seen it firsthand. I won't go into the gory details, but he obviously likes being around guys. It's all over the base."

Cameron silently processed the news.

"Are you still there?"

"Johnson *likes* being around guys? Wait. Do you mean—?"

"Yep, *that* kind of like."

"I still say that can't be true. There's been no indication. Johnson's never, I mean he's just way too normal not to be straight."

"Cam, I wasn't the best boyfriend when we were together, but I never lied to you. And I'm not starting now. Sorry, but it's the truth. Thought you should know."

She fell silent again.

"You okay?"

"I think so. Sorry. Thanks for letting me know."

"No problem. I promise to keep you updated. Have a good evening."

"Okay. Bye."

Cameron ran a finger over the rim of her wine glass. The idea of Johnson being gay or even bisexual seemed absurd, but she had no reason to doubt the evidence. She had read stories about men in denial who led double lives, deceiving their partners for years.

What a total creep! Acting all macho and everything. I should have known better than to trust him. She grabbed her phone again to connect with her third most frequent contact.

"Alicia. Hey. Can you come over? I'm in crisis mode."

"I'm trying to finish packing for Europe. I leave tomorrow."

"I need some girl talk. I mean, *really* need."

"Well, okay. Just give me a minute. What's going on?"

"We'll talk about it when you get here. Oh, and bring wine. Lots of wine."

CHAPTER 10

A few minutes before six in the morning, Johnson battled drowsiness as he prepared for his unit's routine inspection. His sleep had once again been disrupted by unsettling dreams, causing him to wake up in a cold sweat. Brooks was continuing his merciless assault with a barrage of faux sweet talk and incredibly bad puns. A few of the guys engaged in the fun, but most simply acknowledged his presence with a cursory turn of the chin. He felt like an outcast. Tyrell seemed unfazed by it all, laughing it off. But Johnson detected a slight hint of wariness in his attitude. *He must think I'm weird. Everybody thinks I'm weird.*

"Earth to Johnson," Tyrell said. "How long are you going to stand there? You might want to get dressed sometime this morning."

The faraway look in Johnson's eyes drew stares from the other men.

Tyrell snapped his fingers. "Johnson!"

He jumped to attention, then fell at ease. He still seemed disoriented, and the men were still staring.

"Welcome back," Tyrell said. "Missing something?"

Johnson reached into his locker, then drew back, panicked by the sight of his uniform. He slammed the metal door shut at the sound of approaching footsteps. *Oh, Crap. What should I do?* Standing in his underwear and hoping for the best, he braced for the wrath of his commanding officer. Stifled laughter echoed across the room.

"What the frack, Telling?" Blanton demanded in a Southern drawl. "Why aren't you in uniform? You've got exactly two minutes to correct this situation."

"But sir."

"Now!"

Johnson reluctantly began to dress. As Blanton continued the inspection, the men's wide-eyed expressions evolved into amusement and disbelief.

"Telling, is this some kind of a joke? If it is, it's not very funny."

"No, sir. It's not a joke."

"Then tell me, why is your uniform pink?"

Behind the captain, Brooks stood in tears, trying to maintain decorum. Then Johnson broke the silence with a sudden inspiration. "Sir, you should know it's breast cancer awareness month. I'm trying to do my part to spread the word."

Tyrell gave Johnson a stunned look.

Brooks could no longer contain himself. "Oh, shit. That's funny."

The captain, trembling in anger, glared at Brooks. "Double duty for you, mister. And that's for a week. Still think it's funny?"

"No, sir."

"Good."

He turned back to Johnson. "Telling, while I appreciate your concern for our women in uniform, and for that matter, all women in this great country, your beautiful pastel outfit is not standard issue. I'd be willing to overlook it, except for the damn ruffles. You need to take care of this ASAP! Got it?"

"Yes, sir."

Blanton dismissed the unit, and the men's chatter dissipated into a soft murmur. Johnson confronted Brooks. "Okay, I know it was you. Do you have a vendetta against me?"

"Why no, not at all. Your new fatigues are very becoming. They fit your persona so well. Why are you upset? I'm the one who got double duty."

"So, you don't deny you planted this thing in my locker?"

"Hell no, Telling. I wouldn't be caught dead near your locker."

Johnson inched closer. "That's a lie and you know it. I've had it with you. If you so much as—"

"Good grief," Dutch said. "Enough is enough. Even if he *is* gay, why does it matter? You must know there are other gay soldiers on this base. It's not a big deal."

"Of course. I'm well aware of that."

"Then why are you against them? What's the problem?"

"I'm not against them. In fact, I have absolutely no problem with them. In the military or elsewhere. If you're gay, so be it. But come on, be upfront about it. The trouble with Telling is he's gay but he won't admit it!"

"For the last time Brooks, I am not gay," Johnson insisted.

"Oh, sure you're not. I'm sorry, but the evidence speaks for itself."

* * *

After the morning inspection fiasco, Johnson felt even more self-conscious than usual. His pink outfit drew the expected quota of stares and many of his regular contacts on the base seemed uneasy around him. Elaborate visions of revenge percolated through his mind and he vowed again to get even with Brooks. He'd render his adversary vulnerable and defenseless for all the world to see, reducing him to a blubbering mass of humanity. His virtual joy was soon replaced by an overwhelming sense of guilt for having thoughts so dire.

Johnson lunched alone, half-heartedly picking at a lukewarm

dish of beef pot pie. A passerby congratulated him on finally attaining regulation attire.

"Did someone tell you pink is the new green?"

"Yeah, that's it exactly."

"I thought so. Maybe you should think about dyeing your hair, to match. The captain would love that."

Before Johnson could respond, his phone buzzed.

"Hey, Cam. I was just thinking about you."

"Is this really you? Why didn't it go straight to voicemail like it always does?"

"Yes, it's me. Blanton's given Tyrell and me a few perks because of our progress on Tangent. Accepting personal calls during lunch is one of them. How goes it?"

"Situation normal. Can you say the same?"

"Yeah, pretty much."

"Are you sure?"

"Of course. Why?"

"So, nothing you want to tell me? No new developments?"

"Cam, what are you talking about?"

"Oh, nothing. I just thought, as your *girl*friend, and I'm assuming I still am your *girl*friend, there might be something you needed to tell me."

"Why are you being so weird? Of course, you're still my girlfriend. I'm not interested in anyone else."

"Okay then. That makes me feel better. I heard a rumor that— well, never mind. I should know better. So just a couple of things. Wanted to know if we are still on for Friday night."

"Absolutely. McKenzie's. Seven o'clock sharp."

"Good."

"What else?"

"Daddy wants to take us out for a celebration dinner. Some-place fancy. Details to follow. Okay?"

"Well, I'm not sure about that. I'll see. What are we celebrating?"

"Your promotion, of course."

"Cam, that's not a done deal. There's a lot that has to happen before it's official."

"Nonsense. All you need to do is blow them away with your presentation next week. A lot is riding on this for me so *please* don't screw it up. I want Daddy to be impressed. Got it?"

"I'll do my best but—"

"Sorry, I'm getting another call. Got to go. Bye."

Johnson slumped in his seat with an exasperated sigh. The added pressure from Cameron put the upcoming presentation in a new light. He'd only been slightly nervous about it, but now facing a hundred or more of the top brass raised his anxiety to the level of panic. Bright red welts erupted on his face and neck and inched their way down his torso. He eyed his tray. The remaining beef pot pie seemed to look back, daring him to eat it. His stomach rumbled. *Ugh. No more for me.* On his way out, he passed Tyrell.

"There you are. Holy crap! Dude, you look awful. What's up with your face?"

Johnson launched into a series of bizarre contortions, trying to relieve the torment of his itching lower back. "Oh, that. Just a small case of hives. No big deal. I'm fine."

"Are you sure? You don't look fine. Hey, want to grab some chow?"

"That's a negative. Already eaten. Look, I'll check in with you later. I'm heading over to the auditorium to check on the presentation."

"Good idea. We have a few days, but we should see if Dutch has any questions. I'll meet you over there in a bit."

"Roger that."

Johnson paced back and forth for a few minutes before taking a detour outside. The fragrant spring air invigorated him as he strolled along a tree-lined walkway, then stopped, transfixed by the adjacent field. There, the camp band had just finished rehearsing, their brass instruments glinting in the bright sunlight. In a flash, a daydream took him back to the football field. Vivid images appeared and instantly vanished. The Tech game. Halftime.

Excited by this fleeting memory, he pumped his fist in the air, startling a flock of pigeons. *Kupert! The linebacker who hated him. I can picture that creep.* Though most of the events of that day remained shrouded in mystery, recalling even the slightest detail was a win. Other pieces of the puzzle would emerge over time. With newfound confidence, Johnson sprinted to the auditorium.

He opened the large double doors to A-10, took a seat in the front row, and savored the quiet. The dull whirring of a projector fan relaxed him as he examined the layout of the dark room. On stage, a small wooden table and chair had been placed beside the podium. In the background, a massive screen displayed a bright blue slide with the words "Project Tangent." Johnson took a deep breath, imagining the tense atmosphere awaiting him in a packed auditorium.

His thoughts were interrupted by the outline of a figure watching him from the dimly lit control room above. He rose to get a better look. Suddenly, lights illuminated the seating area, and his itching returned. His stomach rumbled again, as a familiar voice boomed over the PA system.

"Hello, Telling. I thought it was you. Are you ready for your big presentation? You look awful."

Brooks soon joined him in the seating area, dabbing his forehead with a handkerchief. "Man, it's warm in here. The A/C must not be operational yet. I hope it's not like this next week."

Johnson gave him a sour look. "What are you doing here? Where's the other guy?"

"Nice to see you, too. Dutch has been reassigned, so I'll be handling the A/V for Tangent. But don't worry, I have everything under control."

Johnson frowned. "I'm not exactly brimming with confidence."

"I can see that. Do you want me to hold your hand?"

Johnson turned red. "I meant I'm not confident about *your* abilities, you moron!"

Brooks faked a wide-eyed, frightened look.

Tyrell strode into the room, grimacing. "Oh lord, not you. How did we get so lucky?"

"Calm down, Brown. I was just telling your buddy here that Dutch is on a new project, so I'm taking over for him. Everything will be tested and be good to go by next week. You'll use the remote to advance the slides from the podium. I'll be in the control room in case there are problems. But trust me, I know what I'm doing."

Johnson sank in his seat and contemplated his fate, which now rested in the hands of an incorrigible jerk. With Brooks in the picture, any number of things could go wrong. He wanted to please Cameron, but more than anything, he wanted to make Gramps proud. Anything less than a stellar performance would be unacceptable. Scenarios of doom raced through his head. His confidence was waning. With only a few days until the presentation, he needed to snap out of his funk. His career and his identity depended on it.

CHAPTER 11

Shortly before her shift began, Charlie scurried around the apartment. Juggling school, work, and her responsibilities at home had been challenging, leaving little time for anything else. Still, she loved her classes and was grateful for the opportunity to further her education. "Mom, have you seen my heavy coat? It's supposed to cool off tonight, and I'd rather not freeze my butt off on the drive home."

Beverly looked up from her newspaper. "I think it's at the cleaners with mine. Why don't you get that car fixed, anyway?"

"Because they want over five hundred for the parts and we can't afford that right now. And no, I'm not asking Aunt Viv for the money. She's already done enough for us."

"Five hundred dollars? Good grief. That car isn't worth a hundred. Why don't you take the bus?"

"I won't be home until after one, and the buses stop running at midnight. Even Uber is too expensive. Oh well, I guess I can get by for a night."

"I'm sure we can find you something. Have you checked all the travel bags? I'll bet there's stuff in there we never unpacked."

Charlie dragged a large suitcase from the coat closet and

rummaged through it. "Holy moly!" she said, holding up a huge green jacket. "Was this Dad's?"

"I don't think so. I've never seen it."

"I don't recognize it, either. How did we even get this?"

"Not a clue, honey. It's your stuff. A friend from college?"

"I don't think so. Oh, look at this. Somebody put their phone number in the lining. Who does that? A fifth-grader with a pituitary problem? I guess it's mine now."

* * *

Driving to work, she felt comfortable swaddled in warmth. Something about the oversized garment seemed familiar. If it didn't belong to her dad, how did it wind up in her stash? Was it Amanda's? A former boyfriend of Amanda's? Some trophy from one of her binges? Her car slowed to a crawl. She pressed the pedal to the floor, but nothing changed. "Oh, come on, Dieter. Please don't do this. I can't be late."

A horn blasted behind her. She checked the rearview mirror. The driver looked menacing. She waved him on, and his rusty sedan passed her in an instant, its engine hemorrhaging smoke and clanging like pennies in a dryer. Dieter, her used-to-be-red convertible, limped along for a few seconds, then came to rest as she turned into the parking lot of a liquor store.

She took a moment to orient herself. She was stuck in one of Parish's least desirable neighborhoods, a magnet for illicit drug activity and petty crime. Most of the merchants there had long since fled to the suburbs, leaving behind a bleak panorama of boarded-up storefronts and empty warehouses. Vagrants roamed the area, a tragic complement to the progressive urban decay.

She called the restaurant.

"McKenzie's. This is Gavin McFadden."

"Hi, Mr. McFadden. This is Charlie."

"Hey, Charlie. I thought I told you to call me Fad."

"I would never call you fat, Mr. McFadden."

"No, no. Not fat. Fad."

"I'm sorry. I've got a weak signal. Can you repeat that?"

"I was saying I want you to call me fat. No, not fat. I mean call me Fad. Never mind. What's up? You're not sick, are you?"

"No, sir. I'm not sick. But I will be late. My car just died."

"That's not good. Chelsea just called to tell me she's not coming in. I need you here tonight. Where are you?"

"I'm at a liquor store on South Street."

"South Street? What are you doing over there?"

"I always come this way. Saves me some cash every week. The highway has those nasty tolls. Anyway, I'll have to get my aunt to drive me. Be there as soon as I can."

"You need to get out of there as soon as possible. I'll come and get you. Are you sure you're okay?"

"Mr. McFadden, you don't have to do this."

"Call me Fad. And it's no bother."

"Well, okay. It looks like the cross street is Jackson."

"I know where it is. Hang tight. See you in a few."

Charlie jumped out of the car and opened the hood. As she pored over the engine, a slightly built man with a ruddy complexion dashed out of the store. His colorful tie clashed with the bright geometric pattern of his shirt, and his pants, precariously held by a mammoth leather belt, sagged dangerously low.

He stood there, scratching the dark stubble on his chin. "You can't park that thing here. That is, unless you was planning on buying something."

"What?"

"This ain't no parking lot for the public. You got to buy something. You know, like make a purchase from my store."

"Oh. Sorry. My car broke down and I needed to get it off the road."

"Well, that ain't my problem, is it? This lot's for paying customers only. Were you planning to buy something?"

"What if I just wanted to look around?"

"That don't do me no good. Like I said, you need to make a purchase."

"Funny. I don't see any sign that says that. What if you don't have what I need? Are you saying I have to buy something, anyway?"

"Don't get smart with me. I got anything you want."

"Okay. Do you have any imported products from France? I'm looking for a rare Pinot Noir."

"A pinto what?"

"Pinot Noir. It's a type of wine."

"Lady, I got red or white table wine. Take your pick."

"Neither. I want the Pinot Noir."

"Suit yourself. I'm calling the police. They'll bring a truck, and your precious little convertible will be towed at your expense." He shuffled back inside, wiping his hands on his trousers.

Charlie turned back to the machinery under the hood, hoping for a sudden insight. She knew it would be impossible to rule out all possibilities without tools, so she hopped back into the driver's seat and turned the key. Nothing. "Damn!"

A stranger with a stocky build and a man bun peered into her passenger window. "That won't help," he said. His shabby T-shirt had once displayed the phrase, "I'm With Stupid." Now, the vital preposition in the middle was too faded to see. "Damn, you're a pretty thing, aren't you? You want to take a ride with me?" He pointed to a pickup truck in the next parking space.

Charlie got out of the car and stared at him. "Excuse me?"

"I said you want to take a ride with me?"

She clapped her hands together. "Oh, sir, I would love to take a ride with you. I do that all the time with complete strangers."

"Well, good. I just bought a fifth of my favorite bourbon. You can help me finish it off tonight." He walked over to his truck and opened the door.

Charlie shoved down the hood of her convertible. "Oh, fantastic. Then maybe afterwards we can have sex."

"Hell, yeah. Now get your pert little ass over here."

"Are you out of your mind? I'm not going anywhere with you."

"Now come on darlin'. I'll show you a good time. You don't want to hang around here all day. You may not have noticed, but all kinds of creeps come to this liquor store."

"Oh, you are so right. I don't want to meet anyone like that. We'd better get out of here right now." She took a few steps toward the truck, then stopped.

The man's expression turned sour. "I said let's go."

"No way."

He ran over to her. "Why you teasin' little bitch. Somebody needs to teach you some manners. I'll throw you in the truck if I have to."

Charlie stood her ground. "Go ahead and try." He grabbed her arm. She gave him a swift kick in the crotch, knocking him to the pavement, where he lay squirming and muttering under his breath.

A patrol car screamed into the parking lot and a police officer emerged. The liquor store owner came out to meet him. He pointed to Charlie.

"There she is, Bert. That's her car right there. She's taking up space for paying customers. And I seen her kick Junie here. You got to do something. That girl is a menace!"

"Now just calm down a minute, Carl. Miss, is this your convertible?"

"Yes sir, and this is my license and registration. I hadn't planned on stopping here, but my car broke down and I needed to get it off the road."

Junie hobbled to his truck. "She kicked me where it hurts, offi-cer. That's assault and battery. Now do your job and run her in."

Bert gave Charlie a curious look. "Is that true, Miss Jankowski? Did you kick him?"

"Yes, sir. He was trying to drag me into his truck. I thought I made myself clear when I said no the first time."

"Junie, were you harassing this girl? Did you touch her?"

"No. Not at all, officer."

"So, you didn't provoke her at all?"

"No, sir."

"Come on Junie, I know you. Tell the truth."

"Well, okay, I may have touched her a little. But she had no right to kick me."

Bert rolled his eyes. "That's what I thought. This isn't the first complaint I've had about you, mister. Miss, do you want to press charges?"

Charlie took a moment to study Junie. He looked like the kind of man who had weathered more than his share of adversity in life. She knew people like him who never caught a break. A line from one of her mother's favorite movies seemed apt— *Some of us drink because we're NOT poets.* Her kick had done enough damage to his physical and emotional well-being for one day. "No, officer, I won't be pressing charges."

Bert looked disgruntled. "I've got a mind to run you in anyway, Junie. But here's what I'm going to do. I'm letting you off with a final warning. Miss, you're free to go."

Carl raced over. "Wait a minute. What about her car? I want that thing off my property. Now."

"Be reasonable, Carl. Give her a chance. It's not like you have scads of customers. Miss, can you have the car removed by this time tomorrow?"

Charlie nodded. "Absolutely, officer."

"Good. Have a good evening. And Junie, try to stay out of trouble. I don't want to hear any more complaints about you."

Carl turned to glare at Charlie as he swung open the creaky door to his store. She returned the favor by making a face at him as a late model silver Mercedes pulled into the lot. She hopped in. "Nice car."

"What was that all about?" McFadden asked.

"Long story. But I've to get my car out of here by tomorrow afternoon."

"Okay. Anything else?"

"Yeah. Are you familiar with *The Nutcracker*?"

McFadden stared at her blankly. "Huh?"

She reached for her seat belt. "Never mind. I appreciate the ride."

"No problem at all. I have a feeling we'll be slammed tonight, so you might need to stay late. And don't worry about your car. I'll take care of it. It'll be my way of saying thanks."

"Mr. McFadden, I can't ask you to do that!"

"It's Fad. And like I said, no problem at all. Hey, I need some tequila. Stay here a second. I'll be right back."

Charlie checked her phone for messages while she waited. The sun was dwindling and business at the store was picking up. Soon, vehicles of all sorts were jammed into the tiny parking lot. Most were luxury models that seemed out of place in the austere surroundings. Some customers carried small briefcases into the bland, weathered building. Engrossed in the odd promenade of well-dressed men, she barely heard the rear door open.

She tensed as someone slid across the back seat. A quick glance in the mirror showed a clean-shaven face with dark glasses and long dreadlocks. One silver earring projected an attitude that bordered on edgy, but in a non-threatening way.

She laughed nervously. "You have the wrong car. I can see how it would happen. A lot of these vehicles look alike. But some stick out like a sore thumb, for example, that convertible over there looks like it used to be red. Now it's the color of a day-old grapefruit. The inside, not the outside. I mean the inside of the grapefruit, not the inside of the car."

"Don't freak out," he said softly. "I just want to talk to you."

"I'm listening. What do you want?"

"This is about McFadden. Just hear me out. I'll make it worth your while."

"You know him?"

"Yeah."

"Then you must know he's inside the store. He's likely to be here any minute."

"I know exactly where the dude is."

"Is that so? What does he look like?"

"Fat, thinning gray hair, thinks a lot of himself. Does that sound like him?"

"I would say his hair is more silver than gray."

"Gray, silver, whatever. Do you like working for him?"

"Who says I work for him?"

"I just know. Trust me."

"Why should I trust you? I don't even know you."

"Fair point. You don't have to trust me. But I think we can come to an understanding that could be beneficial to both of us. I need information. And I think you can provide it."

"Why me?"

"You work for him. I need a pair of eyes on the inside. Someone smart, but also someone he wouldn't suspect. Someone he trusts. You fit the bill, Barbie doll."

"I'm confused. Are you some kind of detective?"

"No. I used to work with him. But after he screwed me more than once on major deals, we parted ways. Now I want to get even with him."

"What on earth are you talking about?"

"McFadden is not your friend, honey, he's a slimeball. He's a drug dealer, an embezzler, and a cheat. He may seem nice, but he'd sell out his mother to make money. Been doing it for years. Take my advice—do not trust him. He's got a temper, so whatever you do, don't cross him."

"I don't believe that. He's such a nice man. He came all the way down here just to give me a ride to work."

"Yeah, sure. Out of the goodness of his heart. Do you think he gives a shit about you? No doubt he has another motive. Like I said, he's evil."

"Let's pretend that's true. You used to work with him. What does that make you?"

"I'm no saint. I admit that. But I was just the middleman. At least I was always honest with him. This man has no principles whatsoever. I, on the other hand, am trying to reform." He pointed to a small bible in his shirt pocket.

"So that's how you reform? By getting even with him?"

"I said I'm trying. I'm not totally reformed. Look, I need an answer. Are you in?"

"Let's see if I've got this straight. A total stranger with an admittedly dubious reputation hops in the car and asks me to spy on my purportedly slimy boss so I can help him get even for an ill-fated drug deal. Yeah, that sounds right up my alley. What do you think?"

"I think you're smart. He's not. And you don't strike me as the type to trip over your own feet. You'll be fine."

"I never said yes. You seem sure of yourself, and you know a lot about me, but I know nothing about you."

"What do you want to know?"

"For starters, do you have a name?"

He took off his glasses. "Reggie."

"Reggie what?"

"For now, it's just Reggie."

"Okay, Just Reggie. Let's assume I agree to help. Not that I am, mind you, but let's just assume so for the moment. I'd be putting myself at serious risk. I'm no genius, but I'm smart enough to ask what would be in it for me."

"Time's up, baby. I've got to bounce. Stay in touch." He tossed a wad of money on the console, jumped out, and sped off in a black SUV. Charlie gasped. He'd left five crisp, one-hundred-dollar bills and a note.

Let each of you look not only to his own interests, but also to the interests of others. Philippians 2:4. Call me. 555-3421.

She stashed Reggie's offering in her purse.

Shortly, McFadden returned to the car, empty-handed. "Sorry it took so long. Man, they are doing business tonight. I've never seen it so busy."

Charlie fastened her seat belt. "Yeah, I noticed. They were out of your stuff, huh?"

"What stuff?"

"Tequila. That's what you wanted, right?"

"They didn't have my usual brand. I'll have to come back later."

Charlie felt uncomfortable. She was usually a good judge of character, and she had pangs of doubt. She made small talk with him during the drive, looking for subtle signs of the monster Reggie described. They talked about the weather, sports, and the new menus soon to make their debut at McKenzie's. He was upbeat and pleasant—even joked about his weight. When he voiced concern about her coursework and her mom's progress, she felt more relaxed. He was not the demon to be feared.

"So, what's up with Chelsea?" she asked.

"She wasn't specific. My guess is too hungover to work. I've been told that girl likes to party. I hope you don't have that problem."

"I hate to admit it, but during my one semester at State, I got pretty wasted on a regular basis. I was pledging a sorority and they had me doing some ridiculous stuff. It was my way of coping. It all came to a head when I was supposed to—"

"Go on." As he waited for her to continue, their eyes met.

Charlie looked away, feeling his searing gaze, and huddled in her huge jacket. "Forget it. Boring story, anyway. Hey, do you think I could take my break a little early tonight?"

"We'll see. It depends on how busy we are. Any particular reason?"

"I need to make a phone call."

CHAPTER 12

They arrived at McKenzie's in short order. McFadden let Charlie out near the side entrance and she rushed inside. In the locker room, she found Lydia brushing her hair. "Cutting it kind of close today?"

"Yeah, it's been one of those days."

"I'm glad you're here. Chelsea is so unreliable."

"Oh, yeah? This happens a lot?"

"Yep. Last time was when we had a special on drafts. Fifty cents. Guys were lined up around the block to get in here all night. We finally ran out of beer around midnight. She never did show up."

"Man, how did you keep going?"

"Lots of caffeine. Like today. I've been at it since seven this morning. I've learned to love double shifts. My youngest has a birthday coming up and I want to get her something special."

"That's sweet. You work hard for them. It'll be all I can do to cover my station tonight, let alone half of Chelsea's."

"Oh, you'll be fine. I've seen you work. You're an excellent server. You have a future here."

"I hope so. At least in the short term. Eventually, I want to go back to school full time. I want a career in journalism."

Lydia smoothed a wrinkle in her top, then sat down on a bench beside Charlie. "Good luck with that. I barely finished high school."

Charlie changed into her work shoes. "And you're doing okay working here?"

"I was doing fine until a few weeks ago. Alimony check from my ex bounced, my kid got sick, furnace died—you name it. I've been having trouble making ends meet."

"Sorry to hear that. I'm in the same boat. Trying to help pay off hospital bills for my mom since she's been out of work."

"If you want help, make sure you're nice to Fad. He paid my rent last month."

"That was very generous."

"All I know is I'd be out on the street without his help."

"Interesting. Hey, can I ask you a personal question?"

"Sure. Hit me."

"Has Fad ever made you feel uncomfortable, in any way?"

"Uncomfortable. How?"

Before Charlie could respond, they heard a knock on the door.

"Are you decent?"

"Yes, Fad," Lydia said.

McFadden poked his head in. "Ready? I have a feeling we're going to be rocking and rolling tonight. Who knows, we may have a record take. Oh, by the way, Charlie. I'm having your car towed to my mechanic. He specializes in German imports."

"You're a lifesaver, Mr. McFadden. Just let me know how much I owe you."

"Don't worry about it. You just focus on the customers tonight. We can work something out later."

"Fine with me. I'll check in with you at some point. That is, if it ever slows down."

"No problem."

Charlie felt guilty for thinking the worst of McFadden. Courteous and respectful, he didn't seem like the drug dealer type. Had she simply overreacted to his creepy stare in the car? Still, the money from Just Reggie meant business. People didn't throw around that kind of dough unless they had a serious axe to grind. She wanted to press Lydia for more details, but as the evening wore on, non-stop droves of ravenous customers gave her little time to dwell on anything but waiting tables.

* * *

After the dining area closed for the evening, Charlie and Lydia prepared to leave.

Lydia grabbed her purse. "See, that wasn't so bad now, was it?"

"I guess not. You were right. I had a good haul tonight. How did you do?"

"Fantastic. I should be able to make rent this month. I waited on the mayor and he gave me a humongous tip."

"That's cool. I wouldn't know him from Adam. Anyway, I did okay, too. I think I can make a down payment on getting the parts for my car."

"What happened to it?"

"Broke down on the way here tonight."

"Bummer."

"Yeah, but Mr. McFadden, I mean Fad, gave me a ride."

"Well look at that. Fad to the rescue again."

"Yeah, he is good to us. Speaking of Fad, I've been meaning to talk to you about something."

McFadden poked his head in. "Great work tonight. I appreciate it. I hate to tell you, but Chelsea was supposed to cover the bar area until closing. Since she's not here, I'll need one of you to do it."

"I can stay," Charlie said. "It's not that busy anyway."

"Girl, you are a lifesaver!" Lydia exclaimed as she headed out. "Catch you guys later."

McFadden stepped out, then returned a few seconds later. "Charlie, come see me when you get a minute."

"Absolutely, sir."

* * *

Charlie checked in with the bartender. "I'm here. Any orders from the late menu?"

Pete held a glass up to the light, inspecting it for water spots. "Nope. It's slowed way down. We might get out of here semi-early tonight."

"Awesome. I'll be back in a few. Fad wants to see me."

"What are you in for? Did you get caught with your hand in the register? That kind of behavior is usually frowned upon."

"Very funny. I'm not in trouble. He probably wants to give me a raise. That's what happens when you're a star."

"There it is. I should have known. That's how it all starts."

"How what starts?"

"Your inevitable rise to fame."

"Excuse me?"

"Let me explain. You'd always been one of us. Just a regular Joe. Or in your case, a regular Josephine. Approachable. Likable. A good friend. Then one day, the boss notices you. He sees you're a cut above. You make Employee of the Month. But do you stop there? No. Next, it's assistant manager. Then manager. The next thing you know, you're the owner with a chain of McKenzie's across the country. Your livin' the dream. Mansion in the hills. Premium wheels. Designer clothes. A string of hunky lovers. Now it's years later, and I'm still slaving away here behind the bar. So, what do *I* get? Nothing. Not a damn thing. Not even a stinking hello when you walk by. You rat bastard!"

"I was just kidding about Employee of the Month."

"Oh. Okay. Never mind."

"Pete, did anyone ever tell you that you have a warped imagination?"

"Once, I think. Hey, since you're going down there, do you mind taking him his brew? He's usually wanting one about now."

"I'd be glad to. You stay here and think happy thoughts."

* * *

"Where would you like your beer, Fad?"

"Put it on my desk. Are we busy?"

"No, sir."

"Good. Have a seat."

"Thanks again for taking care of my car."

McFadden shut the door. "Sure. About that, it was two hundred to have it towed to my dealership. It's all the way on the other side of Parish."

"Holy moly. That's a lot of money."

He returned to the seat behind his desk. "It is. Even more than I was expecting. Now I know you've been struggling with finances lately. So, if you want, I can float you a loan, and you can pay me back later."

"That would be great. But it might take me some time. Is that okay?"

He stared at her for a few seconds. "Of course. That's under-standable."

"Anything else?"

He eyed her again. "There's another option."

"Such as?"

"Such as this. I'd like to get to know you, Charlie. Ever since that day you interviewed with me and joked about being an exotic dancer, I've had fantasies about you. It'd be great if some of them came true."

She studied him cautiously. "Is this a joke? You're my boss. It would be better if we kept our relationship strictly professional."

"Like I give a shit about that. Come on, I thought you said you needed this job. If you can make me happy tonight, and I'm certain you can, then we're all good."

The vulgar monster Reggie described had emerged in full, taking raspy breaths and preening his silver goatee. His face wasn't repulsive, but the eyes staring back at her were cold and dark. Razor-thin lips curled into a perverse smile when he rolled his chair next to her. As he caressed her leg, the smallest of his tentacle-like fingers lay apart from the rest. With each stroke, the cold, lifeless member dragged awkwardly over her skin. She felt sick.

She struggled between fight and flight, and as her rage intensified, fight seemed the more satisfying option. She spied a letter opener on the desk, easily within reach. One plunge into his carotid would bring sweet revenge. The attendant gush of blood would be horrific and messy, like the inevitable murder trial and its not-so-rosy outcome. A firm slap might subdue him temporarily, but Reggie had warned her about his temper. Retaliation might result in unexpected consequences. She convinced herself to stay calm.

"Well, Fad, this is certainly unfamiliar territory for us. I'm flattered you feel that way about me and so glad you let me know. It's not good to keep emotions like that all bottled up. You might explode one day. We certainly don't want that."

He nodded slowly, his face flushed, his dewy forehead gleaming.

Charlie stood up, maintaining her intense eye contact with him. "I don't think we should rush into anything. Here's your beer."

He gulped nervously as she poured the ale into the frosty glass. "So, just to be clear. If I perform certain acts for you tonight, then I get to keep my job?"

"Yes, that's the deal."

"What kind of acts did you have in mind?"

"You know that already. Cut the crap. You can start by taking off that top." As he sat back, eagerly anticipating her next move, there was a knock on the door.

"Hey, sorry to interrupt your meeting, but we just got a party of seven."

Charlie groaned. "Okay, Pete. Be right there."

McFadden looked devastated. "Of all the rotten luck. We'll continue this later."

"Of course. I wouldn't want you to be disappointed."

"I could give you a ride home tonight."

"Thanks, but I've got that covered. Enjoy your beer."

* * *

Charlie clocked out. She headed down the street to a public parking lot where a run-down Eldorado sat idling. A missing grill, multiple dents, and faded blue paint adorned its classic exterior. As she peered inside, the passenger window lowered. The lone occupant stared at something on his phone.

"Nice car," she said.

"Thanks," Reggie replied.

"What are you doing?"

"Streaming a movie."

"I see. Which one?"

"None of your business."

"Don't be like that. Let me see. What is it? An action flick? One of the Jason Bourne films?"

Charlie caught a glimpse just before he switched off the phone. "That looked like Gena Rowlands. That ain't no action flick."

"What? Just because I'm a guy I can't be watching something a little more cerebral than violence?"

"Sorry. You don't seem like the romantic type."

"Are you saying I can't have feelings?"

"Oh, you absolutely can. At least tell me what was so captivating."

"It's not important. Why did you call? Are you ready to work with me?"

"No. But you were right about McFadden. He's a perv."

"That figures. What happened?"

"When he picked me up from the liquor store, I got a weird vibe from him. Then I caught him staring at me. More than once.

Near closing time, he asked me to come to his office, and that's when it went downhill."

"He came on to you?"

"He threatened me with my job if I didn't make him happy."

"That miserable SOB. What did you do?"

"A lot of things ran through my mind, some of which involved retaliation with a sharp object. I decided to play it cool. Luckily, we had a pile of late customers, so I had to go before anything happened. I should have quit on the spot, but I need this job. My mother is counting on me. He's so creepy. It's infuriating."

"I get it. All the more reason to work with me and pay him back."

"Tempting, but it ain't gonna happen."

"You'll change your mind. Did you notice anything peculiar about his office?"

"No. Boxes of condiments and other stuff stacked everywhere. Extra stock, I assume. An old file cabinet, a ledger, and oddly, no computer. How is that possible?"

"That's because McFadden is still living in the stone age. He doesn't even have a cell phone. The dude is massively challenged by technology. Again, good for us. Everything must be on paper. Somewhere."

"What do you mean 'us'? I never agreed to anything. Look, here's your money back." She dropped the cash through the window. "It's late. I'm going home."

"Need a ride?"

"No thanks. I'll manage."

Reggie stuffed the bills in his shirt pocket. "At this time of the morning? Are you crazy? Didn't you read about what happened in that cab last week? I can't let you do that. Come on. Hop in."

"I'm not getting in the car with you."

"Nothing's going to happen. I promise. I'll even let you drive."

* * *

Minutes later, immersed in self-doubt, Charlie sat behind the wheel. She barely knew Reggie and wasn't on board with his plan. Even so, the thought of sticking it to McFadden was exciting. Anything she could use against him was a bonus.

As they cruised through the empty streets of Parish, Reggie thought out loud. "We need to figure out a way to get into his office and nose around. He's got to come out of there sometime."

"You keep saying 'we.' I haven't agreed to anything."

"Are you sure? Don't you need to get your car fixed?"

"I do, but I can work overtime at the restaurant."

"That'll take weeks. What would you say if I doubled your take? To start."

"That's a lot of money, mister! How can you afford that?"

"Because I'm diverse. Back when I was in the business, I made a ton of dough. But unlike most of the dawgs I knew, I invested it. Large caps, small caps, exchange-traded funds, bonds—you name it."

"You must have done well."

"I'm doing okay. One more big score and I'll be set. And speaking of scores, do me a favor and take the South Street exit."

"No way. That's not a great area of town."

"I'll make it worthwhile if you do."

"And then what?"

"Nothing dangerous. We'll just be observing. I promise."

"Triple my take and you've got a deal."

"Done."

* * *

Soon she was parked behind a vacant building next to the liquor store while Reggie busied himself with a task behind the car. "I can't believe I'm doing this," she muttered. "What was I thinking?"

Reggie hopped in next to her, license plate in hand. "That's finished. Got to make this old Caddy look abandoned."

Charlie chuckled. "Excuse me, but are we on a stakeout?"

"Sort of. I have a hunch there may be some activity next door. I just want to see if our man shows up. Do you have a mobile?"

"Of course."

"Switch it off. Let me see you do it. Now."

"Seriously? We're nowhere close to that building."

"I know. Just to be safe."

Charlie took out her phone and shut it down. "I think the liquor store is closed."

"I noticed."

"Then why are we here?"

"You'll see."

They sat in silence, staring into the darkness. Then McFadden's Mercedes rolled into the adjacent lot. Within seconds, a van appeared and parked next to him, followed by another car. McFadden jumped out, as did the other drivers. They chatted under the dim light of a lamppost, before surveying the vicinity.

Reggie and Charlie watched the men briefly, then ducked out of sight, in time to avoid a flashlight checking out the Eldorado.

"You were right," she whispered. "That's him."

As she eased back up, Reggie grabbed her shoulder. "Stay down. And don't move again until I tell you to."

She brushed his hand aside. "Screw that. I'm watching. What are they loading into McFadden's car?"

"My guess would be contraband. Or drugs. Or both."

Charlie gasped. "I saw that van at McKenzie's well after closing the other night. They were loading it with boxes. One of the goons saw me, but I got out of there before anything happened."

Reggie flinched. "Holy shit! I can't believe it. That looks like Scolina. Enrico Scolina."

"So?"

"That means McFadden is in over his head. Scolina is a big-time crook. A kingpin. He's been indicted for everything under the sun but never charged. He always pays everyone off and gets away with it. Good thing he doesn't know we're here."

"Yeah, I suppose he wouldn't like it too much."

"If he did, we'd be dead."

Charlie sank in her seat. "Great. I wanted to finish college, get my degrees in journalism and computer science, have a distinguished career, get married, have kids. . ."

"Will you chill? All we have to do is lay low for a little while longer, then you can drive home."

"Fine. I'll try not to freak out. But while we're sitting here, answer one question: Why would Enrico Scolina do business in a one-horse town like this? Wouldn't his market be bigger elsewhere?"

"It would, and I'm sure he hits other places, but don't discount Parish. It's small and forgettable. Flies under the radar. The police force is a joke, so the risk is minimal. I'm guessing the demand for high-end recreational drugs must be decent these days. From what I understand, it tracks right along with opioid use. That's a soaring market on its own."

"Seriously? Even in Parish?"

"Unfortunately, yes. After that factory closed, lots of folks fell on hard times. I know people who lost their homes. Then their savings dried up. Desperation has a way of testing people. Some turn to drugs to get by. Once they get that high, they'll do anything to support the habit. I mean anything. Then on the other side of the tracks, you have your high society crowd with money to burn. In their circle, meth parties are all the rage. Not just in Parish. All over the country."

"I had no idea. Guess I've led a sheltered life."

"Well, look at that!" Reggie's eyes never strayed from the activity next door. "Another car. Somebody else has joined the party."

"Who?"

"I don't know, and I can't make out the license plate." He reached under the passenger seat for a pair of binoculars and scanned the scene. "Looks like initials. RM something. Here, you try."

"That's all I can make out, too," Charlie said. "You know, this operation isn't so bad after all. I'm spying on my no-good boss, which makes me a first-hand witness to corruption. Now there's a mystery man. Color me intrigued."

"Me too, baby. We can make life miserable for McFadden. If his buyers think for one minute he's screwing them, he'll be sorry."

"Yeah, but if *we* screw up, think of the trouble he'll make for us. This is not just one guy, you know. It's bigger. It may be an entire crime syndicate."

Reggie smiled. "Did you just say 'we'?"

"Maybe. I'll have to—"

"Quiet! I think an animal is roaming around the car. If I can still smell McKenzie's Special on that jacket of yours, it can, too. Let's lay low for a while."

Charlie squirmed. "I need to adjust my position here. These seats suck." Her elbow poked the steering wheel, setting off the horn.

A dog whined and snarled in response as it sprang against the door. They heard footsteps on the pavement.

Reggie's eyes widened. "We're in trouble."

In an instant, the car's throaty engine roared to life. Charlie backed out at full speed over a curb, then lurched forward, leaving sparks and a cloud of dense smoke as gunshots erupted in the distance.

Careening down the dark street, she swerved into an abandoned field. Wildflowers, saplings, and months of accumulated debris were no match for the metal-clad mammoth as it churned and bounced its way through the mire. She plowed into a battered fence at the edge of the property, then plunged back on the road, wooden fragments dancing off the fenders.

At the next intersection, she maneuvered the beat-up Cadillac through a hairpin turn onto Lake Street, notorious for its derelict row houses and ramshackle motels. After a near-miss with a slow-moving minivan, she eased up for a second, then resumed the heart-stopping pace as she charged through stop signs and blinking traffic signals.

Reggie looked around, trembling.

Charlie grinned. "You okay?"

"Are you kidding me? Hell, no. I am *not* okay. You're a maniac. We could have been killed."

"You're welcome. I'd say we got a good head start, but we're not out of the woods. Any ideas?"

"In just a few more blocks there should be—look out!" Reggie screamed.

Directly ahead, a large family of geese was strolling across the road. Charlie braked hard and skidded into the oncoming lane, then veered back to avoid a lumbering diesel-powered street sweeper making its early morning rounds. She pumped her fist triumphantly and slowed down as the odor of burnt rubber wafted into the cabin. "See? Piece of cake. And no animals were harmed in the making of this film."

"Girl, you are not funny. We've got thirty seconds, if that. Can you make us invisible?"

Charlie looked in the rearview mirror. "No sign of them yet. Hang tight. I know the perfect place." In the next block, she spotted a used car lot and eased into a space flanked by pickup trucks in the back row. Soon after, they watched the three cars from the liquor store streak by, then vanish into the night.

Reggie bowed his head in prayer briefly, then sighed. "Okay, we lost them. Let's wait a few more minutes, then we can go. I'll ditch this car tomorrow. It'll be like we were never there. Where did you learn to drive like that?"

"My dad."

"Well tell your dad he taught you well."

"I will, if I ever see him again."

"Sorry, girl. That's rough. Do you want to talk about it?"

"No."

"Message received. Listen, I liked the way you handled your-self tonight. You're a real badass, you know?"

Charlie scoffed. "Not really. Inside, I was petrified. Still am. I'm not the best fit for this job."

"I disagree. You're a great fit. This will be good for you."

"Oh, yeah? What's so good about pursuing something that scares the absolute crap out of me?"

"It's real life, baby, good training."

"What are you talking about?"

"You said something about pursuing journalism. Last time I checked, most reporters cover stories based on reality, not fiction. How are you going to write about real-life if you never experience it? Don't get me wrong. A college degree? That's dope. I'm all for it. I wish I had that sheepskin. But you can't just *read* about shit all the time. Sometimes you've got to get your hands dirty. Come on, girl. We can do this together. I have been to the mountaintop. I have a dream. That one day—"

"Very impressive, Dr. King. Are you finished?"

"For now."

Charlie fired up the engine while Reggie hummed a gospel tune. On the way to her apartment, she glanced around nervously, checking for signs of McFadden and the others. When they rolled into the parking lot of her building, she was still on edge. He grinned at her.

"Stop doing that," she said through gritted teeth.

"You ain't fooling nobody, honey. You're in."

"Let me sleep on it."

"Oh, please," he said with a laugh. "Stop pretending." He dropped a roll of bills on the console.

Sneering, Charlie grabbed them. "Damn you. Okay, so you're right. I'm freaked, but I'm also invested. I want this. I need the money, and I want to see that turd get what he deserves, but this could also be a great opportunity."

"What opportunity is that?"

"Are you kidding me? To uncover the truth. To hold these

people accountable. I'm writing a kick-ass story that will shock the citizens of this sleepy little town. We're talking Pulitzer Prize quality. It's going to blow people away. And I'll need your help."

"You got it, Barbie doll. What can I do?"

"Just make sure *we* don't get blown away in the process, okay?"

"No worries, princess. I got your back."

CHAPTER 13

When a pleasant spring morning in Parish quickly devolved into a steamy afternoon, creatures of all types were caught off guard by the searing heat. At Camp Conrad, industrial-sized fans roared, providing scant relief to the streams of officers filing into the stuffy auditorium. The packed crowd buzzed with anticipation.

Despite Brooks' relentless annoyances, Johnson felt prepared. He'd forgone his daily workouts at the gym so there'd be no more embarrassing incidents in the shower. And he'd worked diligently, considering and addressing every detail of the Tangent project, proofing, and reproofing visuals. He'd honed his delivery until it was smooth and professional. He was ready to answer any questions. His confidence soared.

Tyrell gave him a few last-minute reminders. "Remember, just like we practiced, Blanton will introduce us, then I'll open with the overview. You'll be sitting here at the table. When I'm done, you'll come up and walk them through the scenarios. Are we good?"

"Roger that. Let's do this!"

After the introduction, Tyrell stepped up to the microphone. "Distinguished guests, we are very excited to show you today the culmination of over six months of work. It has been an extreme honor to be associated with Project Tangent, the next phase in wartime management. As you know, in the heat of battle, having good information is crucial. Today, with the benefit of drone technology, we can get real-time information on enemy location, troop strength, artillery, air support—you name it, not to mention data about our own troop movements. Officers, what if I told you all this information could be collated in real-time and displayed dynamically on your military-issued smartphone, using state-of-the-art encryption? Yes, we have an app for that."

As Tyrell continued with the presentation, Johnson followed along, feeling relaxed and focused. Doors were opened to improve ventilation. Outside, the band was practicing, and the sound crescendoed, adding a dramatic effect to the proceedings. As the music continued, Johnson began to feel strangely apprehensive. Perspiration trickled down his face, and hives erupted on his back and chest. He scanned the audience for reactions. Everyone seemed mesmerized by Tyrell's silky delivery. Blanton seemed equally entranced and unaware of Johnson's comical attempts to subdue his incessant itching.

As Tyrell neared the end of his overview, Johnson readied himself for his turn at the podium. *I know I can do this.* Then panic set in as the unmistakable sensation below his belt returned. *Think of something else. Soil. Dirty socks. Dust.* He sat frozen at the table, mortified by his predicament as Blanton implored him to move. Marching across the stage in his current condition would be humiliating, but he couldn't wait indefinitely. The poorly timed biological urge raged on, and his hellish hives created a heightened sense of agony.

Tyrell looked bewildered as Johnson maintained his awkward silence. "While my colleague here collects his thoughts, were there any questions on what I covered?"

During the impromptu Q&A, the veins pulsing in Blanton's scarlet face grew larger. Meanwhile, Johnson undertook a desperate act to save face. Still seated, he inched across the stage using a noisy process that involved sliding his chair across the floor while simultaneously dragging the heavy table with him. The squeaks and groans drew baffled looks from the attendees followed by howls of laughter. Brooks, looking down from the control room, was in tears. A befuddled Tyrell paused before continuing the discourse. Blanton, now fuming, shook his head in disbelief at the embarrassing spectacle.

When Johnson finally reached the lectern, Tyrell greeted him with a wide-eyed expression of shock. "What is wrong with you? Are you having a stroke?"

"I've got this. Just go take a seat. I'll fix everything with a joke."

"Dude, no! You are not a comedian. Don't try to become one now."

After another awkward pause, Johnson began, interspersing his remarks with bouts of furious scratching. "Sorry for the delay, officers. I want to continue by showing you exactly how this application works. But first, does anyone know the technical jargon for a missile failing to penetrate the enemy target?"

The audience was silent.

"Come on. No guesses? It's obviously a case of projectile dysfunction. Get it?"

After the tepid response, he scrapped the remaining jokes and launched into his talk. He felt his mojo returning. Tyrell seemed pleased, the crowd engaged, and even Blanton gave a nod of approval. *Maybe I can salvage this day after all.* He thought about his upcoming promotion, the excited look on Cam's face, and his grandfather bursting with pride. *Tellings always persevere.* Then the microphone failed. Without the benefit of amplification, Johnson's low-key voice couldn't fill the void. The hall again became morbidly quiet. After a brief hiatus, the music from outside the auditorium resumed.

The next few moments were chaotic. Brooks rushed down from the control room but couldn't revive the defective device. After a mad dash turned up no replacements onsite, a dispatch was sent to retrieve one. Johnson was ordered down from the stage and closer to the audience.

"Belt it out so they can hear you," cried Blanton.

But Johnson was again held captive by the impulse over which he had no control. He stood like a statue, too terrified to move. Seconds passed. Blanton's face exhibited a new, disturbing level of contortion. Sensing disaster, Tyrell hopped off the stage to take control.

"Sorry about the audio problem, sirs. I hope everyone can hear me okay. Let me continue."

As Tyrell proceeded with the presentation, Johnson stared blankly ahead, barely listening, trying to comprehend what had transpired. Today's fiasco had undoubtedly earned him pariah status with both Blanton and the unit, if not the entire base. At some point Brooks would pay for his tactical maneuver, but at the moment, other worries took precedence. His star was fading and his career track was swaying far off course. Self-doubt invaded his psyche like a virus, sapping his drive and weakening his resolve. He desperately needed recourse. For the first time in his life, he felt lost.

CHAPTER 14

After the presentation was over and the room had cleared, Blanton approached the podium as Brooks joined Tyrell and Johnson. "Excellent job, Brown. A-1 in my book. You had them eating out of your hand today."

"Thank you, sir. They were impressed."

"Absolutely. I'll be talking to you later about next steps. Dismissed."

After a crisp salute, Tyrell headed for the exit, avoiding eye contact with the others. Blanton then turned his attention toward Brooks and Johnson. For a while he said nothing, pacing back and forth, alternately staring at the two men. Then he halted, eying Johnson, but remained silent. After another pause, he concentrated on Brooks, squinting, studying his face like a road map, looking for a twitch or quiver that might betray guilty feelings.

"Brooks?"

"Yes, sir?"

"What do you know about the audio snafu today?"

"Nothing, sir. I don't know what happened."

"Terrible answer. You're on official notice and will be reprimanded. Dismissed."

Brooks saluted the captain, then walked off, turning to glare at Johnson.

Johnson stood solemnly, still dumbstruck by the preceding events and the re-emergence of his random, inexplicable desire. This was his own miserable ordeal, yet he couldn't help laying some of the blame elsewhere. At that moment in his life, he had never despised any human as much as Brooks.

Blanton looked at Johnson with an almost sympathetic expression. "Telling, up until recently, your work and reputation have been stellar. And that's exactly what I expect from you—always. I don't know what the hell you were doing on stage today, but that's not the kind of behavior that gets rewarded. I understand you're going through some personal issues. Whatever they are, get some help and address them. I have to be able to count on you. For now, you're off the project. Dismissed."

"Yes, sir."

* * *

Back in his quarters, still reeling from the sting of Blanton's criticism, Johnson slumped down next to his locker.

Dutch was waiting there. "Heard about the presentation today."

"Yeah, so?"

"I heard it didn't go so well."

"I don't know what you heard, but it went fine."

"Oh, so you're still on Tangent?"

"Of course, I am. Why would I not be? And while we're on the subject, why do you care so much about what happens to me?"

Before Dutch could answer, Tyrell stepped in, glaring at Johnson. "It did not go fine. Between this guy acting all weird with some demented affliction and his sudden onset of stage fright, it was a freaking disaster. What in the hell is the matter with you?"

Dutch crinkled a smile. "Big ol' Johnson with stage fright. That's funny."

100

Tyrell's fierce brown eyes were still fixed on Johnson. "One of the worst cases I've ever seen. And Blanton was not amused."

"I was fine until the mic died," Johnson bellowed. "Obviously Brooks had something to do with that. And he lied about it to Blanton."

Dutch chuckled nervously. "You just can't trust that Brooks. He's an eel." He snickered, then slipped quietly into the background.

Johnson and Tyrell continued their hostile stare down.

"The microphone worked fine for me," Tyrell said.

Johnson inched closer, infuriated, one hand clenched in a fist. "Yeah, funny thing about that. What are the odds it would pick that moment to malfunction? You and Brooks were in on it together, and you paid him to do it. Anything to keep you in the spotlight. Don't try to deny it."

"What? Me and Brooks in cahoots? Dude, are you crazy? Do you even hear what you're saying? You need to calm down." Amused by the absurdity of a possible alliance with Brooks, Tyrell's stern expression melted into a smile.

"This is not funny, and I will not calm down!" Johnson screamed, unleashing his wrath with a powerful right cross. Tyrell swerved, and the blow landed on his locker, denting the gray metal and loosening a hinge as it clanged shut.

The two stood in stunned silence, eyeing each other, adrenaline surging, each waiting for the other to make a move. Then, turning pale, Johnson dropped to his knees. Bright red retribution oozed from his mangled hand. "I think it's broken!" he shrieked.

"Aw, don't worry about it," Tyrell said, examining the dented door. "I think they can get me a new one."

CHAPTER 15

The next morning at breakfast, Johnson was still a physical and emotional wreck. The craziness had gone on long enough. He needed help. It was time to heed Blanton's advice and get his life in order for the sake of his sanity, if not his career. But how could he discuss his problem openly with anyone? Cameron would quickly disown him as a pervert, and the thought of explaining it to Gramps was too scary to imagine.

"Nice cast," said Tyrell, taking a seat at the table. "Want me to autograph it?"

"No thanks." Johnson examined the white plaster shrouding his right hand. "Got it done last night. I'd like it to stay pristine, at least for a while."

"Fine. Suit yourself. Hey, you're not going to take another swing at me, are you?" He ducked playfully under the table.

Johnson smiled halfheartedly. "Maybe."

"Does it still hurt?"

"Not with the meds I'm on. They've got me feeling a little out of it. Listen, about what happened."

"Yeah, about that. What is your deal these days? You're acting like a complete ass."

"Maybe so, Ty, but you and Brooks deserve some of the credit."

"Unbelievable. So, you still think I had something to do with that?"

"How else do you explain it? All I know is I'm off Tangent, and you came out smelling like a rose."

"Dude, that was on you. I had nothing to do with it."

"That's a load of crap and you know it."

"Will you listen to yourself? That's crazy talk. What possible reason would I have to make you look bad?"

"I have my suspicions. Funny, but I get the feeling Cameron suspects something is up with me. Like she knows about my episodes. I wonder how she could have gotten that information. Any ideas?"

"Episodes?"

"Don't play dumb with me. You know exactly what I'm talking about."

"Is that what happened during the presentation?"

"Yes. I don't like to talk about it. It's so weird. I'm just sitting there and the next thing I know, boom."

"So, this was the third time? Twice in the shower and then during the presentation? That is warped."

"I know. And even worse, Brooks is the only thing common to all three events. Can you believe that? I hate that guy. Why would he turn me on?"

"So what if Brooks was there? It doesn't mean he's the trigger. It's just a coincidence. Come on, we're analysts. Let's think about this for a minute. What else did the events have in common besides Brooks? There must be something. What are we missing?"

"Well, let's see. All three occurred about the same time of day. Late afternoon. All unusually warm days. Not sure what that means."

"And twice in the shower at the gym and once in the auditorium. But the gym and the auditorium are right next to each other.

So that might mean something. What happens at the gym and the auditorium?"

"People congregate. But I've been in that shower before and it never happened until a few weeks ago. And it hasn't happened since. Add the auditorium to the mix and none of this makes any sense."

"Then maybe it's something in the air. Some weird spring fever. You should see a doctor about this."

"I guess I should, but there's no way I'm going to one on base. I can just see the look on his face when I try to explain this. He'll have me committed."

"Good point. I'm not sure I would believe it, either. Let's keep thinking about it."

Both men sat in silence, sipping coffee, while the unmistakable aroma of fried bacon and sausage infused the air around them. Johnson put down his mug. "I've got nothing. At least nothing that could have any connection. But why are you so interested in all this anyway?"

"Because I'm trying to help you!"

"Oh, sure you are. Listen, I know you and Cameron used to date. And now suddenly she suspects I have a problem. If you wanted to get back together with her, you could have just talked to me. But instead, you go behind my back. That's low. That's a great way to treat a friend. Just stay the heck away from her. And you know what? While you're at it, just stay the heck away from me, too."

"Gladly," said Tyrell as he stormed away. "You know what? I didn't think so at first, but you *are* crazy."

* * *

Routine tasks filled the remainder of Johnson's morning. After the daily stand-up, he submitted his standard weekly reports, solved a runtime issue with the mainframe, and added a software patch to the security suite. He stared out his office window at the light rain trickling down the glass and thought about Cameron and his falling out with Tyrell. He tried to recall more details about the Tech game, but his memory remained as cloudy as the ominous gray sky.

Later that afternoon, a welcome respite arrived in the form of an ASAP report request from Blanton, necessitating a trip across the base to the Major's office. On the way back, he soaked up the late afternoon sun, his boots squeaking rhythmically on the damp walkway. In the distance, music from the camp band resonated through the air. Another rehearsal for the memorial service was in full swing.

As he strode alongside the auditorium, the soothing sounds grew louder, triggering a powerful and strangely familiar emotion. A distant memory flashed and then vanished instantly. *The Tech game. Halftime.* Pausing, he tried to comprehend the connection between the music and this new insight. Then, as the buoyant notes of the melody continued, an all too familiar sensation grew stronger. Feeling both alarm and a slight sense of closure, Johnson quickened his pace. *No one will ever believe this. I'm not sure I even believe this.* It seemed a bizarre concept, that music could have such a powerful effect on a person. But why this particular song? Why the National Anthem?

CHAPTER 16

Charlie sat in the break room at McKenzie's, wolfing down a turkey sandwich brought from home while she studied her notes from last week's lecture. English literature was one of her favorite courses. The Renaissance poets easily captured her imagination, and something in Professor Shelton's seductive delivery made them come alive. The rakish instructor had developed a huge following at State. His suave demeanor and crushingly charismatic persona both entranced and aroused many of her classmates. Tall and fit, with just a touch of gray at the temples, he had an irresistibly sexy air of maturity. She often thought about him and wasn't the first to notice the lack of a ring on his left hand.

She turned off her laptop, stood, and checked herself out in a mirror. *I'd look older if I could do something with these bangs. Who am I kidding? I am such a nerd.* She shrugged and made her way back to the dining area, arriving just as her first customer was seated.

"Hi, I'm Charlie and I'll be taking care of you. We just started serving lunch. Can I get you started with something to drink?"

The woman's face was hidden behind the large, colorful menu. "I'll have unsweetened iced tea. How's your seafood? Is it fresh?"

"Yes, ma'am. Fresh from the Gulf every morning."

"I see. What's the catch of the day?"

"Today we're serving red snapper. You can have that grilled or fried."

"I see. Which do you recommend?"

"I prefer grilled myself. But either way is good."

"I see. According to the latest health inspection notice posted over there by the door, this restaurant got a score of 99. Why not 100 percent?"

"That was due to a minor inconsistency in the daily temperature log for one of our refrigerators."

"I see. What was the inconsistency?"

"I believe the date on one entry was incorrectly recorded as last year, instead of this year. It's since been corrected."

"I see. You believe that was the issue, but you don't know?"

"That was my understanding."

"I see. Do you have crabs?"

"I beg your pardon?"

"It's a simple question. Do you have crabs?"

"If you're inquiring about my personal hygiene, then no. If you're asking about our menu, then the answer is yes. Lady, are you going to order anything, or do you plan to sit here and waste my time for the rest of the afternoon?"

The woman laughed as Charlie grabbed her menu. "Nice try, Aunt Viv."

Vivian looked up, still laughing. "When did you figure it out?"

"Right after you were seated. I saw your car in the parking lot. Nice touch with the New York accent. It was very convincing. So, what brings you to McKenzie's?"

"I just dropped your mom off for therapy, so I thought I'd treat myself to a little lunch. You know, I haven't been in this place in years. It still has that 1940's film noir vibe. Say, where does Mugsy sit? Be careful, I'm certain he's got a heater."

Charlie did her best gangster imitation. "Mugsy and the boys hit the streets, ya see? And he took his heater with him. Someone told him the jig was up."

"So I heard."

"Thanks for helping out with Mom. I don't usually work on weekdays, but we're short-staffed. And I've got class tonight. You're the best."

"No problem. Happy to do anything. And, I'll have the shrimp salad."

Charlie scribbled the order on her pad. "I'll get that in right away." She started for the kitchen, then turned around. "Sorry, but I need another favor. Can you create a diversion?"

"That's an odd request. For how long?"

"Just for a few minutes. I need to get my boss out of his office."

"Oh, okay. I'm good at diversions. Any particular reason?"

"We're trying to plan a surprise for him, so we need to plant some stuff in there for later."

"That's nice. I think I can handle that. Tell you what. Wait until after I get my entree, then tell him a customer has asked to speak to the manager. I'll take it from there."

"Sounds like a plan! Thanks so much."

Charlie soon brought Aunt Viv her iced tea and salad, then made a beeline for McFadden's office. She knocked. "Excuse me Fad, it's Charlie. Do you have a minute?"

"Yep."

She cracked open the door and peeked in. "Sorry to bother you, but a customer has asked to speak to the manager."

McFadden stood up at his desk. "What's the problem?"

"She wouldn't say. But she didn't appear to be upset."

"Okay, I'll take care of it."

Charlie waited until he was out of sight, then tiptoed in. She glanced around the room, looking for anything suspicious. Nothing stood out. Same desk and file cabinet, the extra stock of condiments, and boxes of napkins stacked in the corner.

She riffled through a pile of invoices and business correspondence on top of the desk, all legitimate. Each drawer of the file cabinet contained more paperwork, arranged neatly in folders by date of receipt. Standard office supplies occupied three drawers of the desk, but the fourth was locked. She tried to force it open with no luck. On a wooden rack behind the door hung McFadden's coat, dripping with clandestine potential. A quick search of its pockets produced only a single crumpled candy wrapper and a handful of lint. Frustrated, she grabbed a box of napkins from the corner stack and stepped out.

Lydia caught up with her near the kitchen. "Hey, I've been looking for you. Where have you been?"

"I went down to get Fad. A customer asked to speak to the manager. And while I was in his office, I picked up some napkins. Not sure you'll have enough here for the dinner shift tonight."

Lydia grabbed the box. "This is from Fad's office?"

"Yes. He's got a ton of them in there. The lunch crowd is sparse today, so I thought I'd start on dinner prep."

"Yeah, well don't do that. Don't ever take another thing from Fad's office. Got it? If he finds out about this, he'll be furious."

"Whoa! What's going on? I didn't think it would be a big deal. They're just lousy paper napkins."

Lydia clutched the box tighter. "All I know is we have strict orders never to touch that stuff. I made that mistake once and almost got fired. If we need more, we're supposed to get them from storage."

Charlie giggled. "Oh, I get it. You're funny."

Lydia eyed her, expressionless.

Charlie looked surprised. "Holy moly. You're serious? Let me see that for a second." She grabbed the box from Lydia. "This looks like it's been opened, then sealed up again." Taking a pen, she broke the top seal and rummaged inside, then snapped it shut. "Here, do me favor. Take this back to his office and seal it back up. Now!"

Lydia gave her a curious look. "What did you find?"

"Something we weren't supposed to see."

"What something?"

"We'll talk later. Now go."

Charlie looked around nervously as her oblivious co-worker

hastily retreated, hoping that McFadden was still occupied. Reggie had been right. Her boss's extracurricular activities were expanding, but who would have guessed the evidence would be right there under her nose? Now she understood why he was so guarded about his office. Knowing where the drugs were stashed was a breakthrough, but intuition told her to keep digging. Her ground-breaking story would be nothing without solid documentation—the names of contacts, suppliers, and schedules. And all the incriminating evidence lay locked in a drawer she'd need to access at some point. She brushed her bothersome bangs aside, took a deep breath to calm herself, and went to check on Aunt Viv.

"Ma'am, is everything all right?"

"Absolutely. I was just telling Gavin about my travels in Australia. Turns out he and I both went to Walker High. I had the biggest crush on this guy."

"That's adorable."

McFadden grinned, adjusted his necktie, then moved closer to Vivian. "If I had known that, I would have been on you like white on rice. You look so much like a homecoming queen; I don't know how I didn't notice you."

"Back then I was way too shy to talk to you. I was just a mousy little first-year student, and you were a senior. You're still a handsome devil. Look at me. I'm blushing!"

A delivery truck rolled into the parking lot, catching McFadden's attention. "Of all the luck. I'd love to chat with you some more, Viv, but I've got a shipment to tend to. Now don't be a stranger. I'd love to take you to dinner some time."

Vivian locked eyes with him as he stumbled awkwardly on the way out. "That sounds great, Gavin."

"Wow, you're full of surprises," Charlie whispered. "That's unbelievable. You know my boss."

"Oh, hell no, dear. That was complete bullshit. I've never seen that man before in my life. But he bought it."

"No way."

"Yes. And so predictable. Men and their egos. I swear. I could write a book."

"You're amazing. Thanks for keeping him busy."

"You're welcome. And you should know I have no intention of going out with him. He went on and on about how hot I am. That jerk spent more time staring at my tits than talking. Are you sure he deserves this surprise you talked about?"

"Oh, he deserves a surprise all right. A big surprise. And he's definitely going to get it."

* * *

After her shift, Charlie primped in the ladies' room, playing with various hairstyles. An updo made her look older and more sophisticated, but her unblemished face was boringly cute. She'd brought along makeup borrowed from Vivian and tried applying dark shadow and eyeliner, practicing the techniques she'd seen on a YouTube video. Lydia walked in as she was finishing the look.

"Good, you're still here. I've only got a few minutes. Wow, you look hot. Do you have a date?"

"No, just class."

"Oh. Okay. Are we alone?" Lydia checked under the stalls.

"Yep. Just you and me."

"Good. So, I've got to know. What was in the box?"

"I'm not completely sure," Charlie whispered. "But I have a fairly good idea. Can I trust you?"

"Of course. I'm not a kid. Tell me what's going on. I can handle it."

"The truth is, I've never dabbled in pharmaceuticals myself, but what I saw was a baggie of white crystals near the bottom layer of napkins. It's probably methamphetamine. Our boss is a drug dealer."

Lydia peered into Charlie's eyes, then smiled. "Now you're the one being funny. Fad? A drug dealer? Come on. What did you see in the box?"

Charlie looked back at her, stone-faced. "I'm not kidding. He really is a drug dealer."

"Oh my god. Fad's a—"

"Hush! There's no telling what he'll do if he thinks we know. Understand?"

Lydia nodded in agreement. "How's he even doing it? I mean, where does he get the stuff?"

"I'm working on that. My guess is he's been skimming off the restaurant to buy it. What I don't understand is why McKenzie doesn't suspect anything. McFadden must be making a small fortune at his expense."

"That's easy. The old man rarely comes into the restaurant anymore. He's eighty-nine and has early dementia. He trusts McFadden to run everything. This is sad."

"Taking advantage of someone like that is not just sad, it's despicable. Payback's going to be hell."

"What are you talking about?"

"Okay, here's the deal. I was going to tell you eventually. I'm working with a former associate of McFadden who wants revenge because he was cheated out of a lot of money."

"Revenge? How?"

"I'm not sure, but he needs my help to gather information."

"Charlie, this sounds scary and dangerous. How do you know you can trust this guy?"

"I have to admit, I was skeptical at first, but he seems legit. He's paying me a boatload of cash, and I'd be willing to share my take with you. We could use another pair of eyes on McFadden. Interested?"

Lydia looked away. "I'm not sure."

"What's wrong?"

Lydia's tortured face was awash in misery. Like an infection, the conflict had festered for months. She tumbled to the floor in a heap, exhausted by the weight of her terrible burden, and poured out a tirade punctuated with guilt and shame.

A newly single mother of two, she'd been struggling to stay

afloat. A series of unfortunate events had led her to the brink of financial collapse, and her landlord threatened eviction. The job at McKenzie's was her lifeline. With so many people in Parish out of work, she was grateful to McFadden for the opportunity.

At first, he'd been sympathetic and supportive, going out of his way to make her feel welcome. But as she became distracted by a messy divorce, her attention to her work began to slip. She was late too often and botched orders. Customers and co-workers complained. McFadden was furious and gave her an ultimatum: she could sleep with him on demand or walk.

"It was a stupid thing to do," Lydia said sobbing. "But otherwise, me and the kids would have been out on the street. That man scares me."

Charlie thought of her own demeaning experience—McFadden's smarmy touch, her visceral reaction, the fleeting thoughts of homicide. She boiled over with contempt. Thousands of women in similar situations were victimized every day. "We're not letting him get away with this abuse," she said. "Now try not to worry. Everything's going to be fine." *I hope.*

* * *

In class that evening, Charlie had trouble focusing on the lecture. Life had suddenly become complicated. Between her instructor's gorgeous eyes and Lydia's revelation, she was in over her head. The mere thought of being around McFadden made her squirm, but nailing the bastard to the wall would be supremely satisfying. On the other hand, fantasizing about Dr. Shelton had its own special rewards. In the middle of a lurid daydream, the sound of his silky voice snapped her out of it.

"Charlie?"

"Yes, Dr. Shelton?"

"Do you have a few minutes? I'd like to discuss something with you."

"Of course." She stashed her laptop in her bag, then strolled over to his desk, trying to appear nonchalant as her classmates filed out of the room.

"Please have a seat."

Charlie sat down stiffly, avoiding eye contact. Blushing, she shifted her position a few times and cleared her throat.

He smiled. "Thanks for taking the time to talk to me. I wouldn't normally keep you after class, but this is important. I want to discuss your last assignment. I've started grading the essays, and yours—"

"Oh, no. I'm so sorry, Dr. Shelton. I've been a little distracted lately, and what I sent you is not my best work. Think of it as a rough draft—a very rough draft. I can do much, much better. I know all of us has distractions, so please don't think I'm trying to make excuses. Or should that be all of us *have* distractions? Which one is correct? This is embarrassing. Indefinite pronouns always trip me up."

"Charlie, calm down. I was just going to say I liked your essay. It's truly remarkable."

"Are you sure you're talking about *my* essay, Dr. Shelton?"

"Very sure, Charlie. And please, call me Bruce. You displayed great thought and insight in your narrative. Most students misinterpret Donne's 'Negative Love.' Not you. Your analysis was both innovative and provocative. I'm impressed. Would you be interested in writing a scholarly article with me about it?"

She took a moment to examine his face. *He looks sincere. Holy moly. He's serious.* "Dr. Shelton, I mean Bruce. I'm flabbergasted. Of course, I would. This is awesome."

"Wonderful. I think this calls for a celebration. How would you like to have dinner with me tonight? We can brainstorm ideas for the article. There's a new place with tapas just a short walk from here. What do you say?"

I can't believe this is happening. He is so hot! "Well, let me check my messages. I got several texts during class. Let's see what's going on."

"If you're busy, I certainly understand. I'm springing this on you with no notice. We can do it another time."

Charlie picked up her phone and noticed the recording app running. "Okay, just one second while I save tonight's lecture. I'll check my messages later. There, I'm all yours! I mean, thanks, I'd love to go."

* * *

At dinner, the food was bold and exciting. Charlie especially liked the *gambas al ajillo.* But the award-winning cuisine was no match for the pure splendor of an evening with an idol. After two hours with Dr. Shelton, she was even more taken with his amazing intellect and larger-than-life personality.

He was not only an expert in his field but also surprisingly conversant in popular culture, effusive and animated. She was captivated by his insights into every subject. She tried to mask her eagerness with an air of maturity and sophistication but couldn't help staring at his rugged features and permanent stubble.

When she got home, she was still in a daze. A black and white movie was on the television. She tossed her bag aside and plopped down on the sofa beside her aunt. "Mom gone to bed?"

"Yep. About an hour ago."

"What's this?"

"It just started. *The More the Merrier,* starring Jean Arthur and Joel McCrea. It's about the housing shortage in Washington during the war. Jean Arthur's character sublets half her apartment to a couple of men. Hilarity and romance ensue."

Vivian muted the TV and sat up. "Okay, who is he?"

Charlie stared at the screen. "Huh?"

"You come home late with your hair up and my makeup on your face. I'm guessing you've met someone older. Not too much older, I hope. Someone in your class?"

"Yes, someone from class."

"Oh, god. I know that puppy dog look. You're in love."

"Maybe."

"So, tell me about him, kiddo. Spare no details. Is he hot?"

"Oh, yeah. Tall, articulate, accomplished. The list goes on."

"What does he do?"

"He's got a great sense of humor. And the most beautiful eyes."

"Great. But what does he do for a living?"

"He's so polished. A great dresser. And he listens to what I have to say."

"He's your professor, isn't he?"

"I never said that!"

"Sweetie, not too many twenty-something guys fit that description. Please tell me my sister has had *the talk* with you."

"Yes, Aunt Viv. Years ago. I know all about sex."

Vivian laughed. "Oh, honey. You're twenty-one years old. You may think you do, but no. And this is not just about sex. I'm talking about being in a relationship."

"Why are you treating me like a child? I know what I'm doing."

"Really? Your mom tells me you've hardly dated at all."

"She doesn't know everything. And while we're on the subject, what do you know about being in a committed relationship, anyway? Go back to your stupid movie and leave me alone."

"Not so fast. Did you say committed? Let me ask you a question. Is he married?"

"Of course not," Charlie said. "What kind of person do you think I am?"

"They usually are."

"Well, he's not."

"Fine. For your sake, I hope you're right. But I'm telling you, for your own good, he's not right for you. So don't come running to me when it all goes south."

"See, that's it right there. That negativity. That unabashed negativity. It drives me crazy. You've never met him, but you're convinced he's not right for me."

"Unabashed? Impressive. That's a high-class insult. At least you're putting your education to *some* use."

"Let me ask *you* a question. Why do you always assume the worst will happen?"

"Because in my experience, it usually does."

"Oh, I see. In *your* experience. In *your* experience it usually does. But right now, we're talking about *mine. My* experience. *My* life. And I'm a glass-half-full person. I like to think I won't wind up alone in my forties like you."

"That's a little harsh, don't you think?"

"Maybe. But it's true, right?"

"Sweetheart, news flash for you. In case you haven't figured it out, and I guess you haven't, I'm alone because I choose to be. I'm fine with that. I'm sure your Prince Charming is everything you ever wanted. That's wonderful. Good for you. Go out with him. Have some laughs together. But don't get serious. And if you do, don't be surprised when he walks out on you like your father did."

As Viv's dagger sunk in and ripped its way through her heart, Charlie eyed her aunt in astonishment, then sprang up from the sofa, a tear clinging to her cheek. "Damn. Talk about being harsh. Leave my father out of this!"

"I'm sorry," Vivian said. "That was uncalled for. But I don't want to see you get hurt."

"It's a little late for that now," Charlie erupted in bitterness and stormed out of the living room. What did her aunt know about life, anyway? She was certainly no expert. Dr. Shelton was too nice to be a rat, and their age difference was irrelevant. He was accomplished, intelligent, and attractive. Sparks flew in his presence. If she wanted a serious relationship with him, it didn't matter what anyone thought. She was old enough to decide.

In her room, as she undressed and climbed into bed, doubt seeped in. It was all a fantasy—another case of wishful thinking. The man hadn't shown the slightest romantic interest in her. Surely there was a university code prohibiting professors from pursuing students. His intentions were strictly professional. How could she have been so naïve? Did she think a hopeless nerd like her could attract someone like him? Shortly after she fell asleep, a text message appeared on her phone.

Charlie - Absolutely loved spending time with you tonight. You are a remarkable woman. I can't wait to see you again. Sweet dreams.
Bruce

CHAPTER 17

Retired General Thomas Telling whistled an upbeat melody as he traversed the familiar grounds of Camp Conrad. His robust stride and huge presence were the envy of men half his age. Gregarious and fun-loving, retirement had not slowed him down. He traveled often and networked with an extensive circle of friends acquired over his forty years in the Army. To the amazement of his loving wife Annie, he was immune to the ravages of excess, rarely suffering from his frequent overindulgences.

His cavalier attitude had been fueled in part by the wild escapades and legendary antics of Major General "Wild Bill" Jennings, with whom he'd enjoyed an adventurous synergy that took outrageous behavior to a new level. When Bill passed away, many expected the general to become withdrawn and sedate. Instead, he carried on with the same vigor and panache, undaunted by the loss of his closest friend.

"HiYo, Maggie," Thomas said with a grin as he stepped into the executive suite of headquarters. "How goes it?"

Maggie jumped up from her desk, sending a neatly stacked pile of paper to the floor. "TT!" she squealed. "I can't believe it's you."

Thomas bent down. "Here, let me help you with that."

"Oh, don't bother, you big lug." She sprang into action, returning everything to its place in an instant. "Come here and give me a hug. You look wonderful."

Maggie's petite form disappeared into the huge frame of her former boss.

"So how are Dale and the girls?"

"He's fine, and you wouldn't recognize them. They're almost through high school."

Thomas winced. "Geez, you know how to make an old man feel older. But you, young lady, still don't look a day over thirty."

"Oh, you shut up. How's Annie?"

"Hasn't changed a bit. Still gets on my case every day, and still as pretty as the day I married her."

"You're a lucky man, TT."

"Don't I know it. Hey, is Doug around? I need to talk to him about the ceremony for Bill."

Maggie bounced back to her desk. "Let me check. He's in a meeting but should be back in a few. Have a seat and tell me what you've been up to. I was so sorry to hear about Bill, although I have to say I wasn't too surprised. That kind of partying catches up to you after a while."

"So Annie keeps telling me. Anyway, Bill didn't have any regrets, that's for sure. He led one hell of a life."

"And together you raised a little hell, too. Do you miss him?"

"Haven't had time," he said with a chuckle. "Just got back from a fishing trip down the Amazon with a bunch of my buddies. It was amazing. That reminds me, I got you something when I was in South America. A box of *alfajores* and a bottle of wine from Argentina. You can't get that in the States."

"You remembered! That is so sweet of you. The girls will love it. The cookies, I mean."

"Now if I had just thought to put them in the car. You know what, I'll have them sent to your house. Let me make sure I have your address." As Thomas checked his phone, he felt a tap on his shoulder.

"How are you doing, you old buzzard," said Doug. "Long time no see! I'm glad you're here."

"Sure as hell good to see you, too," Thomas said. Maggie gave him a thumbs-up as he followed the younger man. He walked around Doug's spacious, wood-paneled office, examining each picture and plaque on the wall. "This is nice. You've spruced up the place."

Doug looked up from the computer where he was checking his email and laughed. "Well, it was a bit overdue for a facelift, don't you think? The last one happened when you were in charge."

"I'll be damned. Who would have thought the decor in here would ever be anything except Army green? Listen, how are things set for next week?"

Doug leaned back in his seat. "We finalized the program about an hour ago. And let me tell you, it hasn't been easy. With the POTUS in town, everything gets an extra level of scrutiny. All the major media outlets will be here, and we certainly don't want to be embarrassed on national television."

"For Bill's sake, I hope not," Thomas said, easing into a plush armchair. "He meant so much to this country for so long. And he meant a lot to me. I want everything to be perfect for him."

"I do, too. Have you prepared your remarks? You have fifteen minutes on the schedule."

"I'll be ready. Hell, I could talk all day about Bill's accomplishments. Doug, about the ceremony, I want to ask you a favor. I know the program is set, but it would mean a lot to me if my grandson could participate. Bill loved that kid."

"Johnson? I don't see why not. What did you have in mind?"

"I'd be over the moon to see him in the color guard. You know, front and center with the flag. I think Bill would have wanted it that way, too. It would be a nice tribute to the man."

"Yes, sir. I'll make it happen. Anything else?"

"With all the media around here over the next few days there will be lots of questions about Bill's private life which we both know was on the wild side. This is a memorial to Bill and his service to this country as a soldier, pure and simple. Everyone knows he was a party animal out of uniform. The focus should be on his career."

"Naturally. What are you afraid of?"

"The hyperbole, mostly. You know how it is. Bill might have been a lush, but somehow, his dalliances get blown way out of proportion. If he had one drink, he had six. If he was drunk for a weekend, he was drunk for a week. I don't see the need to dig up all that history. Patton wasn't a saint, either, you know."

"Sure, but on the other hand, you can't just ignore it, Tom. That's who he was. Now be honest. That's not what you're afraid of."

"Look, I knew the man for over forty years. We were kids when we went to 'Nam and I was scared to death. I had no idea what I was doing. He showed me how to be a soldier. For Christ's sake, in Da Nang, he saved the lives of over a hundred men in a single day. That's what I want his legacy to be. Not the personal stuff."

"Tom, I get it. But I can only do so much to control the press now, right?"

"Sure. But you're much better with them than I ever was. I'm counting on you."

"You know it's going to come out eventually."

"So, you were aware of his problem?"

"Yes."

"Well, it damn well better not come out." Thomas pounded his fist on the desk. "You've got to make sure it doesn't."

"You know I can't guarantee that."

"Promise me you'll try."

"Of course, Tom. I'll do everything I can. But in today's environment, nothing stays a secret for long."

"That's for sure. I liked it so much better back in the days before all the twenty-four-hour news channels and social media and the damn internet. Nowadays, if you sneeze, somebody records it, somebody else gets offended, and the next thing you know it's the subject of an editorial."

"Unfortunately, you're right. It's a strange new world."

"Indeed it is. Well, thanks for your help, Doug. I'm off."

"So soon? Where to?"

"Where any self-respecting soldier in Parish would be on a Friday evening," Thomas said with a sly grin. "McKenzie's. Where else?"

CHAPTER 18

Charlie lounged in the bulky leather recliner, sinking her toes into the plush carpet and sipping Pinot. On the table beside her, cloth napkins were strewn over a pair of dinner plates littered with shrimp shells and red sauce, the remnants of *Cacciucco*. An air conditioner hummed quietly in the background as stiff, colorless curtains fluttered above it.

"Hey, you!" she called. "Don't you ever take a break? You know, just chill out?"

Across the room, Shelton pored over his computer, typing intermittently and muttering to himself. "Charlie, to quote Shakespeare, 'The web of our life is of a mingled yarn, good and ill together.'"

"Huh? So what am I? Good or ill?"

"Why, good, of course. What a silly question. Grading papers under a very tight deadline is ill, and that drudgery is currently holding me hostage. Not very stimulating, but it pays the bills. Unfortunately, many of your classmates are not well-versed in verse."

"Do tell. Care to drop any names?"

"No. I do not."

"Wow, you're no fun at all. What good is it to be dating your professor if you're not privy to inside scoop?"

"Sorry, I'd love to banter endlessly with you over this, but I need to focus."

"Okay, I get it, I guess, but to quote Shakespeare, 'The time of life is short; to spend that shortness basely were too long.'"

"Very good," he said, without looking at her. "I see someone's been reading *Henry IV*."

"Yeah, trying to, anyway. I'm not a fan. I find Shakespeare a little daunting."

"Of course. And so it is even for seasoned scholars."

"You included?"

"No. I've only had a few issues."

"Ugh. Lucky you. I've had more than a few—they encompass the entire subscription."

He smirked. "Embrace the struggle, sweetheart. Trust me, it's worth it."

"If you say so. Hey, before I forget, I'm taking off in a few. I'm meeting someone at McKenzie's."

"Are you coming back tonight?"

"No. We're not having that discussion again."

"Why not? Are you meeting another man?"

"As a matter of fact, I am."

This time, he looked up. "Should I be jealous?"

"Maybe. Have you ever heard of Alex Manolas?"

"The name sounds familiar. What does he do?"

"He's a freelance journalist," Charlie said. "Widely published. I'm sure you've read some of his articles."

"Yes, I have. How do you know him?"

"I don't. His brother is an ER doc at the hospital. He took care of my mom after her accident. We were talking, and it came up that I'm majoring in journalism. So, Alex just happens to be in town for a few days and agreed to meet with me. I didn't think you'd have a problem. You don't, do you?"

"Well, not exactly."

"What does that mean?"

"Nothing. It's just that I've always found his writing a bit odd for a journalist—both unintentionally droll and slightly sarcastic. It undermines his credibility."

Charlie put down her glass. "Interesting you have that reaction. Shakespeare is a bit droll, too. But it's the subtle whimsy that elevates him above the noise. In case you're wondering, I'm paraphrasing Bruce Shelton, Ph.D."

"Are you comparing the prose of a second-rate journalist to Shakespeare? You can't be serious, Charlie."

"Excuse me? Did you say a second-rate journalist? The man has won dozens of awards and may be up for a Pulitzer. You *are* jealous."

Shelton scoffed. "Hardly, sweetheart. I'm a tenured professor at a university with dozens of my own accolades. I've written poetry, scholarly books, articles published in prestigious peer-reviewed journals, as well as a collection of critiques of modern literature. My body of work is certainly more encompassing than his. But I don't mean to burst your journalistic bubble. Meet with him. Converse. Let his wisdom soak in—limited though it may be. Marvel at the experience. You have my blessing."

Charlie watched him work for a few minutes. "Amazing. You men are all alike. You think yours is bigger than his. That's a little pedestrian. It's not always about size."

"Oh, don't be so juvenile. You know what I meant."

"I do. But methinks the gentleman doth protest too much."

"Nonsense."

"Whatever. So, to change the subject, I was wondering, when do I get to see this house of yours? Not that this hotel isn't awesome, but it's not exactly homey, either."

"I told you the renovations are still in progress," Shelton said, still typing. "It's in such a state right now, I'd be embarrassed to let you see it. Just a few more days and it should be ready. Then we can christen it properly. In the meantime, since you're not staying tonight, how would you like to go away for the weekend?

Somewhere warm. Nassau, perhaps? We could leave tomorrow afternoon."

"Ooh, the Bahamas. That would be so nice. I've never been. But there's only one problem. Like you, I have bills to pay, so I have to work."

"At that dreadful place downtown? Surely you could find something more suitable for your talents. I have but one response. The time of life is short, to spend that shortness basely were too long."

"And I have but one response to that. The web of our life is of a mingled yarn, good and ill together. The ills help pay the bills. See what I did there?"

"Very clever. But seriously, have you considered doing something other than schlepping bad food and watered-down drinks to the riffraff?"

"For one thing, the food may not be up to your culinary standards, but it's consistently good. The drinks are strong and the riffraff are decent people who are not getting rich while they work their asses off to keep our country safe."

"Now don't get defensive. That job would be fine if you were just an ordinary student. But you're not. I think you should consider other opportunities. Something more suited to your abilities."

"Like what, for instance?"

"Like becoming my teaching assistant. How does that sound?"

Charlie choked on her wine. "What? Are you serious? I would be a TA for Dr. Bruce Shelton? That would look great on my resume. But aren't those positions for doctoral candidates?"

"Generally, yes, but there are exceptions. We just received word our application for a large NEA grant was approved. I'll need to hire someone soon."

She stared into the distance, swirling the remaining contents of her glass.

Shelton bounded out of his seat. "Why the hesitation? Opportunities like this don't come along every day."

"I know I should jump at the chance, but I can't just walk out of McKenzie's. I've made commitments."

"What kind of commitments?"

"It's complicated. I'm not ready to talk about it."

"Well, at least give it some serious thought."

"I will, Bruce. And I'm sorry about Nassau. I'll try to make it up to you."

He hugged her. "Thanks, but the weekend will be dismal without you. How will I ever muddle through it?"

She finished the last of her wine and smiled. "All I can tell you is, embrace the struggle, sweetheart. Trust me, it's worth it."

* * *

Charlie took a seat in a secluded corner of McKenzie's cocktail lounge, checked her phone, then motioned to Pete. "Just sparkling water, please. With a twist." Many of the regulars were engaged in lively conversation around the bar.

Leonard French, a retired widower, looked dapper as always with his cane and houndstooth wool blazer. "Mac" McDonough, a thirty-something bachelor, sat at the far end next to a leggy blonde who squealed on cue in response to his tired jokes. According to Mac, Bluetooth-enabled sunglasses were the next big thing. Twenty-something Charles Dennison sat alone in his usual spot near the exit, drinking his IPA and spouting bizarre trivia to anyone willing to listen. He was always planning his next prank.

Pete appeared with her water. "So, what brings you out on a school night, young lady?" He leaned over and whispered in her ear. "Hey, if you're looking for some action, just belly up to the bar. Mac is here tonight."

"Very funny, mister barkeep. I'm just here to meet a friend."

"I see," said Pete, with a glassy-eyed look.

"You don't believe me?"

"Yeah, but see, that's how it all starts."

"How what starts?"

"You have a few drinks together at the bar, share some laughs. At some point, an innocent glance is followed by a stolen kiss. You feel guilty, but the attraction is undeniable. Then more drinks, and a few more kisses. Pretty soon you're groping each other in the parking lot. You wake up at four a.m. in the back of her minivan, barreling down the highway, wearing nothing but her panties as a hat. Her soon-to-be ex-husband and now your worst nightmare is behind the wheel, setting your clothes on fire and tossing them out the window while singing *"Ain't No Sunshine"* off-key at the top of his lungs."

"I see. That's good advice, I think. Believe me, I won't forget it. And when you get a chance, bring a beer for my friend."

"You got it. And forget what I said. Just have a nice evening." He stood still for a second with a blank look, then sashayed back to the bar.

A text from Shelton begged Charlie to reconsider his offer for the weekend. She imagined taking their relationship to the next level. After tonight's magical rendezvous, she was optimistic about their future. The fine wine and cuisine had made it easy to overlook his flaws. She felt compatible with him on many levels and the intense physical attraction was clearly mutual.

In walked a man who appeared to be Dr. Manolas from the hospital. She waved, then realized her mistake as he approached the table. "Hi. I'm Charlie. I thought you were the doctor! You two could be twins. Nice to meet you."

Alex took off his jacket, draped it over the back of his chair, and sat down. "Nice to meet you, too. We get the twins thing a lot. My usual response is I'm Alex—the better-looking one."

Charlie giggled. "Yep. I can see that. Thanks for agreeing to meet me."

"No problem. I'm sorry I'm a little late. I had a tough time finding a place to park. I was finally able to squeeze in next to an amazing old BMW. You don't see too many convertibles like that."

"I know. It's mine. My dad bought Dieter for me when I was in high school. Two hundred eighty-six thousand, four hundred and twenty-three point two miles."

"That's so cool! Is it a manual?"

"Yep. Five-speed. Manual top. Leather interior. Original everything. Six cylinders. But sometimes only five of them work."

"Too bad. I'm afraid you may also have some leaks."

"I know. Been keeping my eye on them. The front axle, the oil pan, and the top, even in light rain. Dieter has them everywhere. I just had him in the shop for a starter problem I couldn't solve. At least that's been fixed, I hope. I'll be working on the brakes myself."

"Must keep you pretty busy."

"Without a doubt. But enough about Dieter. What brings you back to little old Parish?"

Alex sighed. "I'm way overdue for a visit. My work takes me all over the globe. I love my job, but everybody needs to relax now and then. So far, it's been great. I'm meeting some of my nieces and nephews for the first time."

"That's wonderful. Hey, I read your latest piece on the opioid crisis. It was so good."

"Thanks. It took a lot of research."

"I had no idea how serious it is."

"Yeah. The only good thing to come out of this mess is more donors for organ transplants. That was a real eye-opener for me."

"Wow. I never thought about that."

"I'm learning more about it myself. I'm writing a companion piece. Should come out in about a month."

"That sounds fascinating. I can't wait to read it."

Alex took a taste of the frosty draught beer Pete brought over. "Not bad. So how long have you been working here?"

"A few weeks. Mostly weekends. I take classes at State during the week."

"Well, keep at it. State has a good journalism program. I'm sure you'll do fine."

"I hope so. My dad always wanted me to go for something

more technical. He's in IT. I'm a full-fledged nerd, I admit it. I've always been fascinated with computing, but I love the arts, too. Any advice?"

"You could pick up a minor in computing and write about technology."

"That sounds interesting, but a little too sterile for me. I want to be out there in the fray, rattling the cages."

"You've got lots of time. Don't rush your decision. Anything else I can help you with?"

"Yes. I have a favor to ask. I'm in the middle of an investigation of sorts, and I think it will lead to a huge story. I was wondering if you could help me write it."

Alex took another taste of his beer. "An investigation?"

"Let's just say I have reason to believe this town has a growing drug abuse problem and I'm almost certain my boss is involved."

"And you're doing this on your own?"

"Not exactly."

"Sounds intriguing, but where's your evidence?"

"I'm working on that. But like I said, I'm almost certain my boss is involved."

"I get it, but unless you have direct evidence, there's no story. Only conjecture. Journalists don't write based on conjecture. You need facts. Facts, Charlie. Rule number one."

"I saw the packet of drugs with my own eyes."

"How do you know it was drugs?"

"Clear crystals. Probably crystal meth."

"Probably?"

"Okay, I'll admit I don't know for sure, but my informant thinks so. He used to work with him."

"Your informant? Informants are notorious for stretching the truth. What evidence do you have your informant and your boss ever worked together?"

"He told me so."

"Charlie, you need to be careful here. This so-called informant could just be using you as a pawn."

"But he's given me a lot of money already."

"All the more reason he could be using you. I don't like the sound of this. You're in over your head. Take my advice and walk away. Walk away now, before you get hurt."

"Is that what you would do?"

"It depends. I have a lot more experience. I've dealt with people like this before. I can usually spot a con a mile away. After a while, you develop a sixth sense for the bullshit. But it's not foolproof, even for me. Nothing is ever foolproof. That's why you should get out of this trap before it's too late."

Charlie stared at her glass of water. *It's already too late.*

"Sorry, I know that's not the answer you *wanted* to hear, but it's what you *needed* to hear. Are you okay?"

"Yes, I'm good."

Alex checked his phone. "Look, I've got to run. But I want you to keep in touch. Let me know how you're doing. And for god's sake, don't do anything stupid." He tossed a twenty on the table. "You can get it next time."

Charlie watched him leave and spotted Lydia in the background. *I can't let her down. I can't let my scumbag boss win. If it's evidence I need, it's evidence I'll get.* She knew what had to be done, but Alex was right. She needed corroboration and knew exactly where to start.

CHAPTER 19

Downtown Parish was usually boring and sedate, but tonight it seemed eerily different. Charlie sat alone on a bench in the center of town where only the glint of a flashing traffic signal breached the darkness. A plastic bag dancing in the wind roused her paranoia, as did the subsequent rumbling of a souped-up truck. Later, the dull thud of a jogger's shoes on the gritty pavement startled her again. Minutes crept by. Surrounded by shadows, the solitude was unnerving.

The chime of her phone cut through the silence. "Hey, Bruce. I've been thinking about you."

"Only good thoughts, I trust?"

"Of course. I miss you already. I was even reconsidering my decision to work this weekend. The Bahamas sound so much better than McKenzie's. No schlepping—just the sun, the sand, the surf."

"You get an A-plus for alliteration. But I didn't call to discuss the elements of style. I'm afraid we'll have to postpone our little tête-à-tête."

"What? How come?"

"Something came up."

"That was sudden. Did you get cold feet?"

"No, nothing like that. I have to fill in for a colleague at a conference. He's developed a case of laryngitis, so I'm giving his talk. I leave first thing in the morning."

"Bummer! Of all the luck. I hope it's someplace nice at least."

"The Silver Tray in Atlanta."

"Not too shabby."

"Yes, I think I'll make do."

"If you're away, who's teaching your class next week?"

"I'll get one of my grad students to do it."

"Okay. You have fun. I'll see you after you get back?"

"Yes, I'll call you. I've got to run. Bye."

She caught a young man in a hoodie watching her. He stared for a second, then approached with a self-confident gait. "Yo. You got any money?"

"Yeah, man. I've got a whole dollar in my purse."

The stranger stopped in front of her. "So can I have it?"

"Why should I give you my dollar? What's in it for me?"

"That's not how this works on the street. See, I ask for money, and you give it to me."

"And if I refuse?"

"Oh, come on now. Just give me the money. It's only a dollar."

"I think you should at least give me a reason."

"Hey, I've got to eat. Every little bit helps. And how do I know you ain't got more stashed in that fancy backpack?"

"If you're that desperate, did you ever think of getting a job?"

"In Parish? Girl, what've you been smoking? Ain't nobody got any jobs around here."

"Go on, take it." She took her purse from her backpack and handed it to him.

He snatched it up, took out a dollar bill, then tossed it back in her lap. "Hey, what about those credit cards?"

"Those won't do you any good. I'm maxed out on all of them."

"For real?"

"Yep."

"Well, damn. So, you're broke, too. Thanks for the dollar." As he turned to go, a voice called in the distance.

"Antoine! What are you doing out here? Are you bothering that girl?" A woman appeared, drawing labored breaths with each step. "Charlie, is that you?"

"Emmaline! Yes, it's me. Charlie."

Antoine tried to take off, but Emmaline tripped him and he fell face first in the grass. "Why'd you do that, old lady? I only got a dollar."

"You know better, young man. Give it back to her. Now. And apologize!"

Antoine handed the money back to Charlie. "Sorry about that."

"Thanks, but you keep it."

Emmaline took a seat on the bench. "Now, dear, don't encourage him. I've been trying to get him straight for some time now."

"I see," Charlie said. "So, Antoine, why'd you do it?"

"I told you. I need something to eat. I could get some fries or something."

Emmaline sighed. "I'm getting too old to be chasing you around town. You need to settle down. If you're hungry, I told you to come to the shelter before nine. Charlie, what are you doing down here at this hour?"

"I was looking for you. I stopped by the shelter earlier, but they said you were out. I wanted to see how you're doing, and to ask if you could help me get some questions answered."

"That's nice of you to be so concerned. I'm doing fine for an old lady, as Antoine so elegantly put it. I'm happy to help if I can. What do you want to know?"

"Do you know a guy called Reggie, by any chance?"

"I can't say I do. But I know someone who might know him."

"Who?"

"Her name is Marla. We go way back. Saw her downtown not

too long ago. She talks about a friend of hers all the time. I'm fairly sure she calls him Reggie. He might be your guy."

"I think he might be. Did you happen to mention me to Marla?"

"I'm sure I must have. But honey, I talk about everybody's business all the time. I didn't mean no harm. Did me and my big mouth get you into trouble?"

"No ma'am. I don't think so."

"See, I was bragging on you a little. I was real excited when I found out you were a college girl and had a job at the restaurant. Marla seemed impressed."

"So, I guess a lot of people must know."

"Probably. Marla used to go to my church. From what I've heard about Reggie, he's a wild one who's made some poor decisions. Got into alcohol and drugs and who knows what else. I'd stay away from him if I were you."

"I hear you. Right now he's working through a lot of stuff. Let's call them resentment issues. I'd like to help but I need to know if I can trust him."

"I don't blame you a bit, honey. I wish I could say for sure, but I don't know. I usually try to give people the benefit of the doubt."

"Of course. Thanks."

"Good luck, Charlie, and please be careful. It's late and I'm tired. Antoine, you stay out of trouble, okay?"

"Yes, Miss Emmaline," he said with a groan. "Have a good night."

Emmaline rose slowly, then hobbled down the street and out of earshot. Antoine took her place on the bench. "I know that dude y'all were talking about. I used to do drops for him."

"You worked for Reggie?"

"Yeah."

"For how long?"

"Almost four years. It was all going great until he got religion."

"When was the last time you worked for him?"

"Last year. He was in some kind of deal with a guy at that restaurant down the street."

"McKenzie's?"

"Yeah, that's the one. With the older fat dude. They had a sweet racket going."

"What kind of racket?"

"Drugs, mostly. But he turned out to be just another asshole."

"Who did?"

"That fat dude. Reggie bitched about him a lot. Said he didn't always pony up his share. So, one day Reggie got fed up and just walked away. I'm not sure if he's legit, though. If he stays off the sauce, maybe. But when he doesn't he gets weird."

"Weird how?"

"I don't know. He's like a different person. Gets all emotional and shit. One time we were driving to do this job and a bug flew into the windshield. Reggie must have had a few that day because he started crying about it and couldn't stop. Over a damn butterfly!"

"Antoine, are you making this up just to mess with me?"

"It's the truth. I promise."

"Man. Now I don't know who I can trust."

"That's easy. Don't trust anybody out here on the street!"

"Sound advice." Charlie reached into her backpack, pulled out a ten-dollar bill, and handed it to him. "Here, get yourself something to eat. I think the fast-food joint in the next block is still serving."

He eyed Charlie for a second, then took the cash.

She flashed a sly grin. "I never said it was my *last* dollar. Now get yourself a happy meal or something."

"So what are *you* doing?"

"I've got some business to tend to."

"Okay. But be careful out here. Later."

* * *

After midnight, Charlie watched from across the street as McFadden locked the door at McKenzie's, trudged to his Mercedes, and climbed in. He sat for what seemed like an eternity, fiddling with something on the seat and then the glove compartment before driving off.

Feeling a chill, she zipped up her jacket and took a deep breath. *I'm doing this.* Her task seemed simple enough. Get in, open his office, and find what he stashed in the locked drawer—hopefully something incriminating. In the morning she could give Reggie a concrete report. Her dad would be proud. He'd always encouraged her to honor her commitments.

She and her father had been close. She'd been at his side most days, working on cars, building computers, watching sports on TV. Her mother playfully referred to them as "two nerds in a pod." She missed his unkempt hair, steely blue eyes that saw right through her, and his warped sense of humor.

After he disappeared there'd been a somber investigation, persistent reporters, and interminable questions. She still agonized over it. Where was he? What caused him to check out so suddenly? When would she see him again?

At that hour, the serenity of the deserted town was both reassuring and unsettling. The freedom to move about gave her confidence, but if she got into trouble, her stifled cries for help would go unheard. As she started across the street, a familiar voice cut through the quiet.

"Where you going, girl?"

She whipped around. "Antoine! Holy moly. Man, you scared me. What are you doing here?"

He pulled back the hood from his head. "Checking up on my girl."

"Since when did I become your girl?"

"Since you gave me eleven dollars."

"You need to go home. I don't want you mixed up in my business. This isn't exactly on the up and up."

"Not exactly on the up and up *is* my business. What are you trying to do?"

"I need to break into my boss's office."

"You mean fat dude's office?"

"Yeah."

"Why don't you just do it during the day?"

"Too risky. He's always there, and when he's not, it's locked."

"Okay, I get it. I'm in."

"No. Let me do this. Now go home!"

"How are you planning to get in?"

"Look, Antoine. I'm not an idiot. One of my co-workers wrangled the keys."

He took a step closer. "Cool. But please tell me you got sense enough not to go in the front."

"And why not?"

"Video, baby. They'll ID you in a heartbeat." He pointed to a security camera. "Let's go in the back."

"How do you know they don't have one back there?"

"They do, but it ain't working. It's just for show."

"How do you know all this?"

"I told you. I worked for Reggie. Duh. Follow me."

They crept to the rear of the building which was dark and cluttered with wooden pallets stacked high and wide. The air reeked of garbage. Charlie stepped into the troughed entrance and spotted a camera dangling above. "Are you sure this one is just for show?"

"Guaranteed. Look up here behind it. This thing's not even plugged in."

"Could it be wireless?"

He laughed. "At this place? You're kidding, right?"

"Okay, never mind. Let's get started." She tested every key before kicking the door in frustration. "What the hell? They must have changed the lock."

Antoine pulled a phone from his baggy pants and turned on the flashlight. "Now don't freak out. There may be a spare out here. If there is, it's got to be somewhere close." He paced the grounds, kicking up stones and dirt with his worn high-tops.

"Any luck?"

"Give me a minute!"

He continued searching, then threw up his hands. "Shoot. I don't know how I missed it. Guess we'll have to break a window or something."

"That sounds like a bad idea."

"How else are we supposed to get in?"

"If we break in, McFadden will know something's up. Reggie wants this to be clean."

"Who the hell is McFadden?"

"Fat dude."

"So what? I'm not afraid of fat dude."

"Of course not. You don't have to work with the creep. I do."

"Do you want my help or not?"

"I never asked for your help!"

"Fine with me. You do this shit by yourself. I'm gone!" He stormed away as the compressor for an HVAC unit switched on with a clang. He stopped, wheeled around, and looked at Charlie.

"What?"

"I know where a key might be. Look under that exhaust thingy. Just a few feet to the right of the door."

Charlie scooted over to an air duct. "I don't see anything."

"Put your hand down there. It's hard to see. The case blends in with it."

She ran her fingers under the vent and retrieved a small metal container. "Woohoo! I've got it! Let's go… Wait… Oh, man."

"What's wrong?" Antoine whispered.

"It's empty. Now what?"

"Let me see your set." Antoine picked up a key and inspected it. "This one looks worn. When they get old like this, it's all about technique. You just pull it out slightly and turn at the same time."

"Great, do it."

"Whoa, girl. Hold on. Think about what you're doing here. What about the alarm system?"

"Crap! I forgot about that. I don't know the code, and Reggie never mentioned it. He figured this was an inside job."

"Let me see what I can do." Antoine took out his phone and tapped through a few screens. "Four, six, nine, eight, five, one."

"You have it?"

"Yeah, I have a list from one of my sources. I got codes for half the places downtown."

"Are you serious? How did you get them?"

"Do you really want to get into this now?"

"Okay, right. We'll talk about that later. Here we go."

"There's only one problem."

"No more problems! What is it now?"

"These codes are old. If fat dude changed it, we're out of luck."

Charlie took a moment to think. "You know what? I'm willing to bet fat dude didn't change it. I'm not even sure he knows how to change it. And I'm feeling lucky, anyway. We're doing this."

Antoine jiggled the key in the lock and the heavy door gave way with a loud groan.

"Man, that's crazy. It's like they never bothered to oil this thing. We've got less than a minute to disable the alarm. If it doesn't beep, we get our asses out of here. Fast." Using the blunt end of a key, he tapped in the code. A monotone computer voice announced, "Alarm disabled."

They exchanged high fives and walked down to McFadden's office, unlocking it with another key. Charlie turned on the overhead light. "Wow, there's a ton of boxes in here—even more than usual. Now, for the grand prize." She bent down to open the desk's locked drawer, then cried in exasperation. "This is a completely different kind of lock. There's no way any of these suckers are going to work. I can't believe it."

Antoine walked around the wooden monstrosity, examining it like a used car. "Wow, baby, this thing is old." After poking and prodding at various angles, he slid under it. "Just what I thought." Seconds later, he was up, a dusty key in hand.

She looked at him in awe. "What just happened? Are you some kind of magician?"

"Nope. On some of this old stuff, the furniture company taped an extra key to the bottom, you know, in case you lost the original. Most people don't know about it. I guess fat dude didn't either."

"How did you know that?"

"What can I say? I learned from the best." He opened the drawer, pulled out a thick pile of papers in folders, and spread them out on the desk. "There you go."

"This is so great. Thanks, Antoine!" She gave him a hug, then sat down to immerse herself in the materials.

"No prob. Look, I've got to roll. Are we cool?"

"Yes. Thanks again for everything."

"Good. Now don't forget to re-arm the system before you leave. Otherwise, fat dude will suspect something. Put in the code, then you have about thirty seconds to get out. Got it?"

"Got it."

After Antoine left, Charlie flipped through the contents of the largest folder. Unimpressed, she scanned another set of pages, finding only handwritten notes regarding maintenance contracts, food orders, and annual receipts for an insurance policy. The remaining stacks were filled with the same innocuous information. *I must be missing something.* She skimmed through the mounds of paper again.

As she gathered the materials, she noticed a small gap in the flimsy base of the drawer and pried it out, revealing a worn canvas-bound ledger. "Come to mama!"

The first several pages contained the original hand-written financial accounts of the restaurant, presumably maintained by McKenzie himself. She was impressed with his neatness and remarkable penmanship. As she read on, the handwriting changed to a cryptic style she recognized as McFadden's, highlighted by very creative bookkeeping. Everything else seemed legitimate, incredibly detailed, and boring. The next several pages were blank.

Charlie stared at the compendium of facts and figures in front of her. *The good stuff's not here. It's mostly worthless. What a giant waste of time!* She slammed the ledger on the desk and it fell open to a dog-eared page near the back, but it was merely a list of serial numbers for kitchen equipment installed during the pre-McFadden era. She decided her quest had been for naught.

Taking one last look, she admired the extreme tidiness of the office which was orderly and dust-free. Then she saw it in a corner on the floor, a cluster of debris so minuscule only someone with maniacal attention to detail would notice. It had the texture of grainy fiberglass. *No freakin' way.* Using a chair for support, she hopped up on the file cabinet, removed one of the spongy square ceiling tiles, and onto the desk fell a black binder.

She stepped down and started examining its contents. Nearly every page contained her boss's script and initials, with numerous references to the letters RP. Contact names, dates, locations, and quantities of various drugs were listed with their cash amounts. Recent entries contained multiple references to crystal. The amounts varied, but many exceeded several thousand dollars. The earliest transactions had been registered years ago, and many more were scheduled in the future.

Who was RP? Where did he get the drugs? How could she find out? The investigative journalist in her was begging to know. She took photos of each page with her phone then returned the evidence to its spot above the ceiling. Soon she had secured the rear entrance and was back outside, reveling in her discovery. Reggie would be impressed, and surely with a little more detective work, a dynamite story would all but write itself. She imagined her byline and the look on McFadden's face when he found out.

She had taken a few steps when a van pulled into the adjacent storage area. From behind a massive oak tree, she watched a man get out.

He walked around for a while, then opened the back of the vehicle and set down a ramp. Charlie didn't like her options. If the man came any closer, she'd be seen, and she couldn't explain why she was there at that time of the morning without raising suspicion. She could take cover inside, but if she opened the door now, the raspy squeal would surely alert him to her presence. A tall wooden fence was behind her, but gymnastics had never been her forte.

The man seemed preoccupied with something in the van, so she bolted for the fence and stumbled, falling well short of her target. *Stop freaking out.* Hugging the ground, she scrambled back.

She stood up, taking slow, shallow breaths. For a while, her face and clammy palms were on the rusty metal door. She unlocked it in a panic, but the man was still within earshot. Seconds crawled by as she waited for the right moment to make her move. Then a silver Mercedes rolled in next to the van. *Are you kidding me?* A blinking red light, barely visible through the crusty window above, alerted her to impending disaster. She rushed in a second too late as the shrill security alarm reverberated through the building.

With a shaky hand, she entered six digits on the keypad, but the wailing continued. *What the hell is that last number?* She tried again, then charged forward in search of cover.

The walk-in freezer in the kitchen was one option, but becoming a popsicle was not on her bucket list. At the far end of the hallway, refuge beckoned in the form of the ladies' room. Hurtling forward, she fell flat after a bone-crunching impact with the locked door on which a 'Closed for Maintenance' sign hung. She limped into McFadden's office, cursing under her breath. The ungodly pulsing noise ceased, but the brief silence was interrupted by voices and the sound of approaching footsteps.

"Put that thing away. It was probably a malfunction. You know how flaky this system gets."

"I'm telling you, I heard that back door open. I swear I did. Someone is in here. And if we find them, they're dead."

"For crying out loud! Don't be so dramatic. I've been doing this for years, and I never had any trouble. Our operation is airtight."

Charlie heard the office door open.

"Damn, I could have sworn I locked up tonight. Well, screw me. Look, you hang back here for now. And whatever you do, don't go shooting at shadows. Just so you'll stop freaking out, I'll check around. Then I'll come back and finish up the documents for your cover. The product needs to be there before sunrise."

Crammed beneath the desk, Charlie tried to compose herself. If she could slip past the other man, she might make it out before McFadden returned. She had a minute or two at most. She prayed for a miracle.

She inched forward, holding her breath. The door creaked slightly. A ceiling light switched on. The sound of heavy breathing sent a chill down her spine. The light went off, and footsteps continued down the hallway. She slowly exhaled. Crawling on her hands and knees, she peered out. The mystery man stood nearby, dressed all in black with a handgun tucked into the waistband of his pants. It didn't register at first, but something about him looked familiar. Then she saw his scars and ghoulish face. The same face that had terrified her that night in the parking lot. *Hello again, Mr. Creepy.*

She stood up, her eyes glued to the figure in black. She grabbed a letter opener from the desk. Adrenalin rushed through her like floodwater. She leaned over slightly and nudged the door. At first, there was no reaction to the subtle squeak. Then footsteps approached and stopped, followed by the mechanical click of a silencer as the man crept into the office. She slammed the door on him with all her might.

Stunned by the blow, he stumbled forward, dropping the weapon, which skidded out of his reach. He dove for it but was met with a blow to the head and collapsed on the floor. Charlie was on him, one knee on his back, the other on his neck. She grabbed a fistful of his collar and pulled it tightly around his throat. "Keep your face down or we'll keep it down for you."

The man squirmed.

She grazed the edge of the letter opener across his cheek. "Do you want this in your throat?"

"No," he grunted.

"Good. Don't try to reach for the gun, don't get up, and don't make any noise. If you do, you'll be sorry. Do we have an understanding?"

"Yes."

She tightened her grip with a yank. "Are you absolutely sure?"

"Yes!"

"Okay. You've been warned. Don't do anything stupid. We're watching you." Charlie grazed him again with the letter opener, streaked out the back door, and slipped away.

CHAPTER 20

True to form, Johnson arrived early for his date with Cameron. Sitting in their usual booth, he sipped ice water, perusing McKenzie's familiar menu. *Do I dare try something else?* Options other than steak and fries suddenly seemed absurd. He laughed, and his brief flirtation with heresy was over.

The establishment was more crowded than usual for a Friday night. Waitstaff rushed from table to table, carrying large oval trays of beer, wine, and steaming baskets of the daily special. Cheers interrupted the clinking of glasses as the drama of a baseball game unfolded on a massive flat-screen television.

Familiar laughter caught his attention and he went to the bar. On a stool that could barely support a man his size sat the center of attention, a larger-than-life symbol revered by many. How could any mere mortal ever measure up to such an icon?

"Gramps?"

"Hey, son! I was hoping I'd see you. I'd ask you to sit but there's no room here. Say hello to French."

"Hi, Mr. French. Good to see you again."

"Johnson, my boy, how are you? Last time I saw you, you

were, well, you've always been big," he said, laughing. "How's military life?"

"Not bad. I'm afraid to ask, but what kind of scheme has my grandfather roped you into tonight?"

Gramps interrupted. "I've got a fifty-dollar bet with Frenchy the Yankees don't score this inning."

"I thought you promised Grandma you would quit gambling?"

"Hell, this is nothing. When I said that, I was talking about the casinos. Anyway, this is a sure thing, right Frenchy?"

"No way," said French. "Top of the order's up. And they've been hot lately. The pitcher is awful. Tom, you might as well put the money right here in my pocket."

When the first batter went down on strikes, the bar patrons exploded with thunderous hoots. The second batter's line out to the shortstop brought a louder reaction. When the third batter flew out to center field, the crowd erupted with cheers and high fives.

"Damn, you are one lucky son of a bitch," said French as he pounded his cane on the floor in disgust. "After thirty years, you'd think I'd know better than to bet against you."

"You would think that, wouldn't you," Gramps said, hugging his friend. "Want to try double or nothing?"

French slapped a wad of money on the bar. "Hell, no. Now get out of here before I get violent."

"Such a good loser. Come on, son, let's eat."

Back at Johnson's booth, Gramps downed his drink. "I'm dry. Oh, young lady, bring me another Scotch," he said to a confused patron.

Johnson shook his head. "Gramps, that's not our server."

"Oh, it doesn't matter, son. She'll take care of it. Hey, what happened to your hand?"

Before he could answer, Cameron arrived, sat beside Gramps, and pecked his cheek.

"Well, hello young lady. So good to see you again. She sure looks pretty tonight, doesn't she?"

Cameron frowned at Johnson, waiting for a response.

"Of course, she always looks nice."

Gramps grinned. "Great to see you two together. So, son, how did you wind up with a cast?"

Cameron took Johnson's hand. "Yes. Do tell us what happened."

Johnson turned red. "Oh, nothing to worry about. Just a mishap from a training exercise. It'll be fine in a couple of weeks."

She looked puzzled. "So, the IT unit has maneuvers? Sounds odd to me."

Johnson gave her hand a gentle squeeze. "Yes, we do. Occasionally."

She wrenched her hand from his grip. "Okay. Whatever you say, sweetie."

"Damn, I'm still dry," Gramps bellowed. "Look, there's my girl." He waved to a petite but buxom woman. "Hey, we're dying of thirst over here."

Lydia popped over to the booth. "Sorry, General, we are slammed tonight. Let's see. A scotch on the rocks, a Pinot Grigio, and I see he already has his water. Anything else?"

"No thanks, darling. Isn't she great?" Gramps turned to Johnson. "Son, tell me about your big presentation. Wasn't that last week?"

Cameron fussed with her hair, put her head in her hands, and smiled. "Yes, please tell us all about it."

Johnson gave her an odd look. "It went great. All the brass were there. Captain said we had them eating out of our hands."

Gramps beamed. "That's my boy. I knew you could do it. Any word of your promotion?"

"No, sir," Johnson responded, squirming. "Not yet. But I'm expecting it any day now."

"Well, I wouldn't worry. You absolutely deserve it. I'm sure you'll get it."

Cameron glared at Johnson. "Oh, I agree. He's going to get what he deserves. No question about it."

"Oh, before I forget, I've got a favor to ask," Gramps said. "It would mean a lot to me if you could participate in the ceremony for Bill coming up. I've already cleared it with Doug."

"Sure, Gramps. Anything."

"Great. You'll be in the color guard when the band plays to kick everything off."

"That's it? You don't want me to say anything?"

"No, I've got that covered. I've got fifteen minutes."

"Only fifteen? You could talk all day about your adventures with him. Or should I say misadventures?"

"That's for sure. But I think I'd better stick to the script."

"Not even the trip to Hawaii?"

"Oh, I would love to hear about that," Cameron said.

Lydia brought over their drinks, and Gramps launched into a detailed account of Johnson's favorite fishing story. He became increasingly animated as the tale progressed.

"So, Bill and I decided to play a game. Whoever caught a fish, the other would have to do a shot of tequila. We sat there on that boat for about an hour with hardly any action. We caught some small stuff, but nothing exciting. We were thinking about moving on when a school of bluefish showed up. Between us, we must have caught over twenty of those suckers in the next hour. We ran out of tequila about halfway, so we started doing shots of vodka. We got so wasted, we both passed out in the boat, stinking to high heaven from fish that had been rotting in the sun all afternoon."

"Annie refused to let us in the car after that, so we had to walk back to the hotel like two drunken sailors. Bill walked the whole way without knowing he had two dead little fish stuck to the seat of his pants. One on each cheek, pointing in opposite directions. Whenever he'd take a step and fart, which was a lot, it looked like one would open its mouth just a little as if to croak. I've never laughed so hard in my entire life."

As Cameron squealed, a terrifying thought crept into Johnson's mind. "Hey, Gramps. Sorry to interrupt, but did you say what the band will be playing at the ceremony?"

Cameron scowled. "Does that matter? Can't you let him finish the story?"

"I'm not sure," Gramps said. "The usual stuff, I guess. the National Anthem, 'America the Beautiful,' 'Amazing Grace.'"

Johnson became catatonic. He imagined the nationally televised ceremony, his humiliation captured in viral video clips, forever enshrined in the archives of social media. He needed an excuse to make this go away. Anything would do.

Cameron snapped her fingers. "Hello. Johnson! What's going on with you? It's like you're in a different world over there."

Her annoyed look came into focus. "Sorry about that."

"Oh my gosh, General. Looks like your grandson is blushing. He is *so* turning red."

"No, I'm not. I was thinking about all the good times we had with Bill. I can't believe he's gone."

"Nothing to be embarrassed about, son."

"I'm not. Just a little upset. You see, I've been thinking I might not be the best person for the color guard."

"What are you saying?"

Johnson looked away. "I can't be in the color guard."

"What's this?"

"You see. . . well, um, the thing is. . ."

"Of course, he can. Johnson, tell your grandfather you'll be happy to do it."

"Well, I don't know."

"He'll do it!"

"Yeah, right Gramps, never mind what I said before, I'll be there."

Gramps smiled. "That's the spirit. I knew I could count on you. Well, I'm off. I'd love to spend more time with you two, but I told Annie I'd be home by eight, so I'm already in trouble. You kids have fun. Dinner's on me. Just tell Lydia to charge it to my account. I'll see you at the ceremony, son." He hugged Cameron before making his way out.

Johnson sat in silence, preoccupied with a server at the next table. He leaned forward to get a better look.

"Can you please stop staring at her?" Cameron said.

"Sorry, she looks familiar for some reason."

Cameron glared at him, her heel fiercely tapping the floor.

"What's going on with you tonight?" Johnson asked.

She threw up her hands in disgust. "Are you serious? What's going on with me? The real question is what's going on with you?"

"You're the one in a mood," Johnson said. "And keep your voice down."

Cameron chugged a healthy dose of her wine, then leaned over the table. "I will not keep my voice down. I swear! Refusing to do your grandfather a simple favor. What is wrong with you?"

"Don't make a scene. Anyway, I said I'd do it."

"But only after I pressured you. What's the big deal about being in the color guard? What are you afraid of?"

"You wouldn't understand."

"Try me."

Johnson took a sip of his water. "Well, it might be embarrassing. I can't explain it."

"That's it? That's your explanation?"

"Just trust me. It's not a good idea."

"Oh, I'm supposed to trust you? The man who lied about getting a promotion?"

"What makes you think I lied about that? How do you know?"

"Well, did you?"

Johnson stared at the ceiling.

"Look at me! I know that's not the only secret you've been keeping from me."

"What are you talking about? Have you been talking to Brooks?"

"Who I've been talking to is none of your business. The important thing is I know the ugly, filthy truth. When were you planning to tell me? On our tenth wedding anniversary?"

"Tell you what?"

"Don't you dare sit there and pretend you don't know what I'm talking about!"

Before Johnson could respond, Cameron downed her drink, snatched her purse, and stormed away. He felt he was watching a disaster play out in slow motion. The supple, stunning figure he had once held so close was out of reach.

His life was unraveling. A once-promising career was on life support. He had alienated his best friend. His girlfriend had walked out on him. To make matters worse, the possibility of further disaster loomed. His reaction to the National Anthem would be on full display, with no less than a million people watching.

He needed therapy, or drugs, or both, but the prospect of discussing something so personal with anyone was frightening. Distraught and overcome with doubt, he phoned the only person who might understand.

CHAPTER 21

Julia Chatham had been a child at the time of Woodstock, too young to experience the sixties in all its psychedelic glory. She'd been a typical suburban homemaker until her early thirties when a divorce left her alone and stigmatized. Following a brief stint as a commercial artist, a trip to India changed everything. She met the first of several yogis who inspired her. Back in the States, the years rolled on, but she refused to age gracefully. Her life was a party, and she became a living testament to the peace-love-dope generation and its acute sensibilities. Many years of intense therapy helped shape her unique outlook on life, enhanced by the frequent consumption of an array of mind-altering substances.

In her late fifties, she gained national renown for a series of self-help books. Described as spiritual guides to the inner self, each famously claimed, "Your journey is just beginning." The local community adored her, and she frequently led group sessions on a wide variety of topics. Of these, "Inner-tubing down the river of your being" was the most popular.

For years, Julia fretted about Johnson. Following the death of his parents, she lost a lengthy custody battle to the senior Tellings. From then on, she feared the worst for her nephew's emotional stability. The rare weekends when he visited were filled with group encounter therapy, meditation sessions, and holistic coaching. Each activity was designed to develop his inner being and compensate for a lifetime of spiritual neglect. Gramps had little patience with her "new age crap," fearing it would turn his grandson into "a pacifist hippie, scared of his own shadow, with no sense of right and wrong." Johnson learned not to elaborate on the time spent with his aunt, providing sketchy details about fun games with new friends.

When he told Julia about his plans to join the Army, she tried desperately to talk him out of it. Weeks of intense discourse failed to sway him. She capitulated, but only after gathering hundreds of signatures for a peculiar petition designed to keep him out of the military. Still, he always maintained a soft spot for her in his heart. Although he wasn't fond of her eclectic ideas and offbeat lifestyle, he appreciated her sympathetic ear.

Julia shrieked in delight when she noticed her nephew's name on her phone. "My little Tommy! How are you? I've been so worried about you. I hope they're not brainwashing you over there."

"Hey, Aunt Julia. It's great to hear your voice. How are you?"

"What's wrong? You sound so tense. You're not being sent overseas, are you? I swear I'll speak to your commander, and I know people in Washington. I'll organize a protest if I have to. I can have five hundred people picketing outside that base in no time."

"Please don't call my commander," Johnson pleaded. "And I'm not being sent overseas. I just need a recommendation."

"Thank goodness for that. Can you hold on a sec?" The hem of her paisley bell-bottoms skimming the green shag carpet, she padded across the living room and picked up a glass of Merlot. "There, I'm back. So, what's up?"

"I need help. I've got some problems I've never had to deal with before."

"Poor Tommy. Aunt Julia's here for you. What can I do?"

"I need to see a doctor. Maybe a psychiatrist. I was hoping you knew someone here in town. It's urgent."

"My dear boy, you don't need a doctor. They're a dime a dozen. What you need is a healer. Someone to treat your tortured soul. I can think of a few. But before I do, you have to promise to see me. And I don't mean in a couple of weeks. Soon."

"Okay, I promise. Now, who do you recommend?"

"Well, that all depends. What kind of issues are you having?"

Johnson didn't answer.

"Tommy? Are you still there?"

"Yes. I'm still here."

"I asked what kind of issues you're having."

"I'd rather not say."

Julia sank into a bean bag chair. "Oh my god. It's PTSD, isn't it? I knew it. This is terrible. First football. Now the military. Those fascists have destroyed my little boy."

"It's not PTSD, I promise. I've never been in combat."

"Are you sure? Well then, what is it?"

"It's kind of personal."

"Oh, Tommy. You're so inhibited. Come on, just go with the flow. Keep it real. You need to loosen up and learn to trust people. There's no reason to be embarrassed. I've seen you naked, you know. Now go ahead and bare your inner self to me."

"You've seen me naked?"

"Relax, hon. You were three years old. Now, what is it?"

"Okay. It's sex. It's a sexual problem."

"I see. So, you're having trouble in the bedroom. That's nothing to be ashamed of. I can recommend—"

"It's not a bedroom problem, exactly."

"Tommy? Are you coming out? Is that it? That's perfectly okay with me. You've nothing to be ashamed of. You're a very brave man. A close friend of mine went through a similar experience. I'm so proud of you!"

"No, Aunt Julia! That's not it, either."

"Then are you trying to tell me you're a gender-affirming

procedure candidate? Oh, you poor thing. I bet you've been struggling with this issue for years. Trapped in the wrong body. I know a great therapist who can help you work through those issues. Then we can find you a surgeon. I just had a thought. After the transformation, what would you say to changing your name? I think Thomasina Telling would be fabulous."

"What? Thomasina? No, I'm not a transgender candidate. What I've been dealing with is a very strange problem and I would appreciate it if we didn't get into the details of it right now."

Julia fought back tears. "So, so uptight. Oh, I wish I had pushed harder for custody. My little Tommy has grown up to be a broken man. His life is falling apart, and it's all my fault."

"No, no. It's nobody's fault. I've just hit a rough patch, and I'm not used to rough patches. Especially like this. I need someone to help me understand what's going on."

"All right, dear. I'm so sorry. You're obviously deeply distressed by this. Let me think. Ojo's not bad, but he's out of the country, and Carla's still in rehab. There is a man from Berkeley who's supposed to be exceptionally good. He's a little bit older but has a great reputation. I'll have his assistant call you to set up an appointment."

"That would be great. I appreciate it."

"Happy to help. Now, I expect to see you on my doorstep soon."

"You got it."

CHAPTER 22

Reggie stared at the spreadsheet on his tablet. "I can't believe it. You did good, kid, really good. How'd you get all this?"

Charlie feigned a yawn. "It was child's play. Oh, so simple. A piece of cake."

"I took everything you sent me and collated it. It's fascinating. Have you looked at it yet?"

"A little. It's fairly detailed. Names, transaction dates, amounts. You can see the money ramped up about three years ago. He's got buyers everywhere."

Reggie scrolled through the screens. "I see it. That must be when he started with the meth. And look at these names. It's a cross-section of the rich and famous of Parish. Government officials, business leaders... This dude is making a fortune."

"Looks that way. Thanks to McKenzie's and some creative bookkeeping. I went back and reviewed the accounting records from his journal. He's been under-reporting income. I know because I help Lydia with the register every weekend. Our total receipts are usually five hundred dollars more than he's showing. Any idea where he's getting the drugs?"

"My guess is from Mexico. That's where most of the super labs are now. It's hard to make this stuff in your apartment, you know. Too much toxic waste."

"Sounds dangerous."

"It is. I was out before he got into this."

"Lucky for you, I guess. Now I've got to ask. I didn't see your name listed in that book anywhere. What did you do for him exactly?"

"I was a hustler. I hooked him up with buyers. I knew the market for every drug, and I knew his competition. If things worked out, I'd get ten percent. It was a low-stress way to make a lot of money. At least until he started cutting me out."

"Weren't you worried about getting caught? You know, by a narc?"

Reggie laughed. "In Parish? Not likely. What do we know about his operation?"

"It's pretty straightforward. As we found out, he meets the supplier behind the liquor store for the cash transaction. Based on the records, it's somebody with the initials RP, most likely the same guy you saw that night when I was in the car with you. Anyway, they load the product into McFadden's car and he takes it to the restaurant. It's then stored in boxes in his office until the van takes it to the buyer. Who would suspect packets of crystal meth mixed with paper napkins? It all looks so legitimate."

"So, all we have to do is switch them out."

"You make it sound so simple."

"You can get into his office, right?"

"Well, I could and did, yes. But not anymore."

"What happened?"

"McFadden is always in his office, and when he's not, he keeps it locked. I would, too, if I had a stash of illegal drugs in there. So, I had to break in after hours, and I almost got caught by one of his goons. Every lock in that place was new the next day. But don't worry. I'm quite sure they don't suspect me. I mean, after all, who would?"

"Yeah, I'm pretty sure, too."

"How come?"

"Come on. You know the answer to that."

Charlie turned pale. "Because if they suspected me, I'd be dead?"

"You got it."

"Maybe I should take a vacation."

"Nah, you'll be fine. Just watch your back. Now that I have his records, we can start planning for the sting that will bring your man down. You'll need to be a part of this. I'll make it worth your time."

"Oh, man. I so hope you're right. I'd like not to die."

"You worry too much. This will be easy. You'll see."

Charlie pretended to be enthused, but something told her more trouble was on the way. So far, nothing in this caper had been straightforward. Why would it change now?

CHAPTER 23

Fidgeting as he sat on a tiny brown sofa, Johnson wondered how life had gotten so complicated. Now he had a new list of nits to pick. The starched civvies he wore were stiff, his short hair was a fraction too long, and the slippery synthetic leather beneath him felt strange. Was the sitar music twanging in the background supposed to be annoying?

The office looked more like a flea market than a retreat for analysis, a hippy-dippy place for the enlightened. Across the room, large modern murals were interspersed with strange artifacts in various stages of restoration. A subtle fragrance may have been potpourri, or another concoction with an equally impossible spelling. And he sensed another odor, reminiscent of his university experience, something he couldn't identify.

He was terrified by the prospect of discussing something so personal with a stranger. He sensed his anxiety rising, churning, and gurgling like a steaming teapot. He checked his pulse, fearful of an impending medical event. It felt normal, but the other man's dappled fingers resting on his forehead were disturbing. At last, the hand drew back.

"Dude," said the man. "You are so uptight. Also, you're not chanting."

Johnson fiddled with the stiff polyester tie tucked into his shirt. "Sorry, Mr. Olsen."

"By now you should be at the point of alpha. You're nowhere close. I'm sensing so much fear. You need to disassociate and unravel your mind. Otherwise, our discourse will be meaningless. Let's try another approach."

"Whatever you think is best, Mr. Olsen."

"There's no need for formality here. Call me Lars. And, the accent is on the second syllable. It's Ol*sen*."

"Of course. My mistake."

Lars smiled. He bundled his long gray hair into a ponytail, then slipped out of his Birkenstocks and positioned himself on a rubber mat, legs straight with toes pointed up. "Now, take off your shoes and socks, then get down here and face me so our feet are touching."

Johnson felt sick. *Oh, man. Again with the touchy-feely stuff. This guy is a three-sigma.* "Excuse me, isn't there another way? Why can't I just tell you when I'm relaxed?"

"Because words can be deceiving, my friend. Look, I promise this will benefit us both. The feet are one of the most sensitive areas of the body. They're the gateway to healing. This way, I'll feel what you feel, and can react accordingly. Oh, and don't forget, it's okay to cry."

Johnson slipped off his loafers and mismatched hosiery then settled into position. "Before we continue, I have another question."

"Of course. Ask me anything."

"No disrespect, but I thought this meeting would go a lot differently. Don't you just want to know what my problem is?"

Lars scoffed. "Of course I do. For that kind of therapy, all you need is some stiff with a fat prescription pad."

"Huh?"

"I'm talking about a board-certified zombie trained in traditional Western medicine with a license to kill your soul. Take it from me, you'll lose any sense of self you ever had before it's over.

And it'll cost you an arm and a leg for the so-called treatment. Is that what you want?"

"I don't think so. There's a Dr. Atkins at Camp Conrad who's supposed to be good. I considered seeing him, then decided against it because there's no way I want this on my permanent record. It's got Section Eight written all over it."

"Nothing I can't handle," said Lars. "I once counseled a llama, you know."

"Like the Dalai Lama? I'm impressed."

"No. I mean an actual llama."

Johnson stared at him blankly.

"I can't go into detail because of patient confidentiality."

"Oh, right. Due to the hippo."

"The hippo?"

"Yes. It's like the elephant in the room. You're not allowed to talk about it."

Lars snickered. "I think you mean HIPPA, the federal law that regulates the sharing of personal health information. Regardless, let's just say Sidney is no longer bitter."

"What?" Johnson shrugged it off as outside his domain of expertise but wondered how the animal had made payment. "If you can do that for a llama, my issue should be a breeze," he said. "To speed things up, can you give me something for it? I'm in a real bind here."

Lars sighed. "Why is everyone always in such a hurry? Feeling nervous? Pop a downer. Feeling down? Pop an upper. This ain't no Jiffy Mart for analysis, soldier. There are no shortcuts to therapy. Like all good things, it takes time."

"What if I can't afford to wait?"

"You can't afford not to. Make no mistake, you need the guidance of an experienced practitioner like me. I treat the composite you, not just your symptoms, using all-natural shit. Now, are you ready to commit? The sooner we get started, the sooner we can get to the bottom of this. Remember to keep it real. Are you up for the trip?"

Johnson scowled. "Yeah, I'm up, I guess."

"Perfect. Now lean back, placing both hands behind you for support, and close your eyes."

"Like this?"

"Yes. Now trust the method. Go to your happy place. Think serenity. A stream. A babbling brook. Floating in space. Calming thoughts. Remember the chant?"

"Yeah, something about that opera guy. Plácido Domingo?"

"Close," said Lars. "It's ahma sabba placendium."

"Abma what?"

"No, ahma, not abma. Ahma sabba placendium."

What the heck is he talking about?

"It's from the Graeco-Roman period," Lars explained. "Loosely translated, it means 'I am the master of my place in the universe.' It may also have been a battle cry for those dudes who wrestled in loose-fitting togas."

"So which is it?"

"It doesn't matter, man. I'm teaching you how to relax, to be immune to outside distractions. If you don't learn anything else from me, your time spent on this will be worth it. Now chill for a second while I alter the mood in here."

Lars stood up and soon, the heady lavender scent from a perfumed candle saturated the air. Johnson took in a whiff, made a face, and had a coughing fit.

Lars returned to his position on the mat. "Let's try it again. Take some deep breaths and let go."

Johnson leaned back and chanted, suppressing a laugh. "Ahma sabba placendium." He had to fight through the unnatural sensation of another man's feet and what repose he could manage was quickly interrupted by terror. Sweat oozed from every pore.

"Wow, I'm sensing a major disturbance. You are not in your happy place. Now don't panic. We're cool. It's not always easy to achieve alpha on your first attempt."

Johnson squirmed. "Give me a minute. I can get there." He

made a valiant effort to ignore it but kept wondering. *Why do I notice these things?*

"What is it?" asked Lars.

"It's the window."

"Do you mean the window to your soul? That's really heavy. We can rap about that."

"No."

"The window to my soul? I'm down with that."

"No, sir. I mean the actual window. The one behind you."

"Oh, *that* window. What's wrong with it?"

"I noticed it first thing," Johnson explained. "It's the blinds. There's a slight tilt at the bottom. The right side is about a quarter of an inch higher than the left."

"You're not serious."

"Wait. You're right. I'm not. That's an embarrassing mistake on my part. It's more like three-sixteenths of an inch."

Lars sat in a stupor. "Dude. Wow."

Johnson repressed the urge to get up. "What now? Can I fix it?"

"You might find this hard to believe, but that's unimportant. I do applaud your honesty, though. And your attention to detail. For now, just put it out of your mind. Let's try to focus elsewhere, okay?"

Johnson repeated the Graeco-Roman phrase and waited for the magic to happen. Soon, the agony of the imperfect window treatment was replaced with another spine-chilling distraction.

"You were making progress," Lars said excitedly. "I could feel it. What happened?"

"Sorry, sir. It's that stupid animal bugging me again."

"Stop with the apologizing. What animal?"

"A squirrel, sir."

"A common tree squirrel?"

"Yes, sir. I know it doesn't make any sense, but squirrels scare the heck out of me."

Lars chuckled. "I've got to ask. Why?"

"Squirrels are just big rats and I've never liked them. They're so unpredictable. If you search online you can find videos of them jumping on people's faces. I have recurring nightmares about one in particular. It always freaks me out."

"That's all right, man. I can assure you we're in a safe environment here. There are no rodents of any kind. Let's move on. I know you can find your Nirvana if you keep trying."

Johnson assumed the position again and chanted. Despite his attempts to repress them, images of the window and the squirrel cycled through his mind like slides in a PowerPoint presentation. First, the window alone appeared, then the squirrel, and finally a third horrifying scenario featuring the evil squirrel perched on the windowsill. There it sat, glaring at him, flaunting the bothersome asymmetry behind it. Eventually, all three visions faded away and were replaced by a memory.

Johnson stood facing the penetrating gaze of his fellow sixth graders. Written book reports were easy, but delivering one orally had nightmarish implications. There was hope, however. As he scanned the opposition for any weakness that might be leveraged, a golden opportunity presented itself. Her desk in the first row was empty. It was a miracle.

Everyone knew Patricia had a thing for him. He never understood exactly why, and the infatuation wasn't mutual. But she was undaunted by his harmless rebukes, mesmerized by every detail of his life. Even his recounting of something as common as a trip to the dentist elicited inexplicable oohs and aahs. He learned to accept her unbridled curiosity and uncanny ability to pinpoint his location at all times. She was one annoying encounter short of albatross status.

Her absence gave him newfound confidence, and he launched into a cogent monologue, fully engaged, with high hopes of showcasing his elementary command of classic English literature. For a time, everything went smoothly. His poise and brilliance resonated with the young audience who appeared fully invested in his lusty tale of buccaneers and buried gold. Then, out of nowhere, the red-haired she-devil appeared, homing in on him with radar-like precision, boldly interrupting the discourse.

"Who dressed you this morning?" she asked, as she slipped into her seat. "Your cardigan is a disaster."

The teacher sternly admonished her for her rude interruption, but for Johnson, everything was already unraveling. A quick downward glance confirmed the awful truth. Each button was indeed in the wrong position, leaving the bottom one homeless. He continued with the report, painfully aware of his sartorial faux pas, but he'd lost focus, maimed a few passages, and mispronounced words that had been firmly in his vocabulary. Still, it wasn't a total disaster until he tried to address the sweater mishap as he spoke, thinking his deft handiwork would go unnoticed. Snickers and howls of laughter soon ensued.

Red-faced, Johnson snapped back to the present.

On the floor, Lars retracted his feet. "Oh, man. I felt that. You were in the worst kind of Stage IV panic. What's the issue?"

"Talking in front of a crowd," said Johnson. "It's always been a problem for me. Lately, it's gotten worse. In fact, my last presentation was a total disaster."

"Don't sweat it. Lots of people have trouble with public speaking."

"That may be true, but not like me. You have no idea."

"All the more reason for you to achieve alpha. You have to make a conscious effort to take slow, deep breaths. Remember, there's no pressure. You are the master."

"Okay, sir."

"That's enough with the sir stuff, man. You're still uptight. Maybe it's time we had the talk about you and your sphincters. It can be a real orifice opener, I promise."

Johnson stared at him, glassy-eyed.

"You've been working hard, and I've got something next door needing my attention. Let's take ten. Now try to chill."

Lars busied himself with something in the attached greenhouse while Johnson lamented his tenuous grasp of human anatomy. He browsed the surrounding canvases, classifying each as either disturbing or deeply disturbing, until one work caught his eye: a series of interlocking grids of increasing density was arranged against a black and white background. At first glance the hatched patterns were static, but as he continued to focus they appeared to expand and contract in a wave-like, hypnotic motion. He stood entranced, his thoughts racing ahead to the upcoming ceremony.

On a gorgeous, bright day, the mood was somber. Among the thousands of mourners gathered for the event were journalists, government officials, and celebrities.

Gramps stood at the podium, preparing to honor the decorated war hero, an exceptional man from a family with a rich tradition of military service. Bill Jennings had been a loving godfather to Johnson, his grandfather's best friend, and a national treasure. Books had been written about his exceptional leadership. Award-winning movies had been inspired by his battlefield valor. To dishonor him in any way on such a special occasion would be tantamount to heresy.

Now all eyes were focused on Johnson, standing at attention in the center of it all, his face flushed with mounting tension, desperately hoping for a reprieve. It was not to be. On cue, the impetuous raven buried deeply within came home to roost once again at the worse possible moment.

When he opened his eyes, Johnson felt clammy and disoriented. He looked around cautiously. Lars was nowhere to be seen.

What the heck. I'm doing it.

Then he was back on the brown sofa, enjoying a rare moment of complacency. And the troublesome blinds hung without a discernible slant.

CHAPTER 24

Lars returned from the greenhouse, bringing the earthy smell with him. He lit another scented candle and led a reluctant Johnson in a hypnotherapy session. Readings from Khalil Gibran followed, along with additional attempts to reach the auspicious pinnacle of alpha. Though his patient never achieved true bliss, Lars was happy with his progress. They retreated to another room with cushioned wicker chairs for an in-depth discussion about Johnson's childhood, the unexpected death of his parents, and life with his grandparents.

"Now I understand why you're so uptight," Lars said. "We could spend a week just on your Gramps. It's time we rap about your pressing issue—besides dealing with your career, your grandfather, and the chick you're currently hanging with."

Johnson stared off into space.

Lars snapped his fingers. "Hello. This is the part where you spill your guts."

"Sorry, bear with me," Johnson said. "I get a little tongue-tied talking about this."

"Why so?"

"Because it's personal. It's weird, and it's sexual."

"I've heard it all, man. Hit me."

"Okay. Here goes. Put bluntly, I'm getting aroused in inappropriate social situations."

"That disgusting!" Lars screamed. "I can't help you with that. Now get the hell out of here and don't ever come back."

Johnson bolted out of his chair.

Lars grinned. "Sit back down. I was only kidding. Man, you've still got a lot of work to do. You know, on the spring-loaded thing. Now tell me more about your arousal issue."

Johnson returned to his seat and Lars coaxed him into opening up about his regrettable experience in the shower and the constant harassment from Brooks.

"Dude, is that all? I don't mean to belittle your anxiety, but I was expecting something slightly more traumatic."

"It wasn't just Brooks. There were a bunch of other guys in the shower at the same time. Now everyone's gotten the wrong impression about me, including Cameron, I think."

"Sometimes our subconscious mind can have a powerful effect on our behavior. Why just the other day I... never mind. Look, you're young and you're horny. I get that you were embarrassed, but one incident in the shower is nothing to freak out about. Shit happens."

"But Mr. Olsen, it keeps happening! And not just in the shower. I was caught on stage during my big presentation in front of all the brass. You can't tell me that's nothing to freak out about. I'm losing it."

"You're doing great. Now, this is getting interesting. Let me take some time to unpack all this before we go on." Lars leaned back and fell into what began as a peaceful trance. As the seconds passed, his languid expression transformed into the slight grin of a deranged sociopath.

Johnson peered into his eyes. "Mr. Olsen, are you okay?"

Lars continued in the same disturbing state, unresponsive to his patient's panicked overtures until Johnson doused him with a cup of cold water.

"What just happened?" Johnson asked.

"Did I zone out? Sorry about that, man. One too many acid trips from last...I mean my younger days. So where were we?"

"I was talking about my continued bouts of unexpected passion."

"That's right. Taking any drugs?"

"Only the legal stuff. I've been on pain medication for my hand. But all this happened before that."

"Okay. You're a weightlifter, right? I've seen some very radical side effects from steroids, even in small doses."

"Never used them."

"That's cool. I think we've eliminated the endogenous causes. That leaves something in your environment that's triggering these episodes."

"I was hoping it wouldn't come to this. The weird part is I know the trigger. It's music."

Lars smiled. "Something seductive, right?"

"If you consider the National Anthem seductive, then yes."

"Are you shitting me?"

"No," Johnson said, hanging his head.

"Man, you really *are* messed up."

"I know, I know. I'm a freak."

"Dude, I'm just screwing with you. There's a rational explanation."

Johnson waited nervously while Lars went into another deep trance. This time he emerged without undue effort, spouting about the id and other Freudian theories which he summed up with examples of similar behaviors described by his other patients.

"What does all this mean?" Johnson asked.

"We're all animalistic at the most basic level," Lars explained. "This kind of reaction occurs in response to a very intense, very sensual experience. The technical term is psychogenic. It's a stimulus followed by a response. Pavlov's dogs heard the bell and they associated that with food, so they salivated. You hear this music, and you associate it with an emotion from some distant memory. In your case, a powerful emotion, from some very erotic experience. Nothing comes to mind?"

"Unfortunately, no. But I've heard the National Anthem before and never had this reaction. Why now?"

"That's one of the defining characteristics of repressed memories. You never know when they'll surface and for how long."

"That makes sense, I suppose. Did I mention the flashbacks?"

"No, you didn't. This is awesome. Tell me more!"

Johnson explained how the music brought back fleeting memories of his last football game at State. The details were frustratingly fuzzy. He recalled the soggy conditions on the field, an angry encounter with a Tech player, but none of the coach's pep talk at halftime.

"Anything else?" Lars asked.

"No. That's it. So, you see, nothing even remotely sexy. Ask me about any other game in my career, and I could write a book."

Lars scratched his head. "If that's true, then I'd say we're looking at a concussion sometime during your game. That would account for the memory loss."

"That stinks! Will I ever remember exactly what happened?"

"Johnson, the mind is a tricky thing. Total recall is not out of the realm of possibilities, but I'm afraid it's not likely. Somewhere in the recesses of your limbic system, a fragile circuit was broken. The repair process operates on its own schedule."

Agitated, Johnson fiddled with his watch. "In the meantime, I still have my problem. I hear that music, and I respond. It all goes down in a few days."

"What goes down?"

"The service for the general I mentioned earlier. It's a huge deal on national television. The president will be in attendance as well as all the top brass from the military. I've been asked to be in the color guard. So, I'll be there, for all the world to see, when the band plays the National Anthem."

Lars broke up. "I'm sorry, but this is absolutely hilarious. Can't you get out of it? Think of an excuse."

"No way. This is the military, and the program is set. Gramps is counting on me to do it, and I can't let him down. Anyway, how would I explain to him or anyone else why I can't do this without sounding like some kind of sicko?"

"You have a point. Now don't sweat it, man. We'll figure something out."

CHAPTER 25

Zipping up her jacket, Charlie wound her way through McKenzie's crowded parking lot to the outdoor seating area. She found a table under a green tartan canopy, sat down, and checked her phone for messages. Still nothing from Shelton. It seemed odd that he was ignoring her texts. According to the Silver Tray website, his conference had ended at noon two days before. A phone call went straight to his voice mail. *Oh no. He's been in an accident. Or worse.* As the specter of foul play stirred up terrifying visions in her head, a young woman clutching a lighter stepped out the door to the bar.

Charlie scowled. "Excuse me, but this is not a designated smoking area. Please go around back."

The woman marched over to Charlie's table. "I think—holy crap. Charlie? Is that you?"

Charlie instantly recognized the flawless makeup, hair, and nails of her college roommate. "Amanda? Oh my gosh! What are you doing here?"

"I could ask you the same thing."

"I work here. My shift starts in about ten minutes."

"You work at McKenzie's? No way!"

Charlie chuckled. "Yes, way. Hey, what's with the cigs? I thought you quit."

"Yeah, I did, too. The patch didn't work for me. Guess I need some behavior modification."

"Doesn't everybody? So, how's school going?"

"It's not. I dropped out after my second semester. My grades were trash. Right now I'm working in custom van and RV sales with my dad."

"That sounds cool."

"It's not bad. Things have been slow lately but I'm sure it will pick up soon. So, what's up with you? I've heard all kinds of wild rumors."

"About me? That's so funny. What's the word?"

"I'd rather not say. What happened to you, anyway?"

"Well, after my mom's accident, I had to drop out of State to take care of her. Money's been tight, so we sold the house and now we're living in an apartment over in Walmsley. I got a job here on the weekends to help out, and I'm taking classes in the evenings."

"Oh my god! I had no idea. I'm so sorry. Is your mom all right?"

"She's much better now, thanks. She's learning to walk again."

"Oh, man. I feel like such a bitch. The way I treated you the entire semester. I hope you can forgive me."

"About that. How come you were so mean to me?"

"To be perfectly honest, Charlie, I was jealous of you. Not only are you smart, but behind those nerdy glasses and frumpy clothing is an extremely attractive woman. You intimidated me."

Charlie laughed. "Wait just one second here. You were jealous of me? Amanda, you're gorgeous. You could have had any guy on campus."

"That's nice of you to say. But that doesn't mean I didn't feel threatened."

"Wow. You think you know somebody. But let's be honest. I

wasn't the best roommate in the world, either. I could have handled things a lot better."

"True. You could be a little OCD at times."

"Only a little?"

"Okay, more than a little."

"So, we both screwed up. We can't change history. Let's just forget about it."

"Agreed."

"I can't believe we finally *do* agree on something," Charlie said.

Amanda smiled. "Good. That makes me feel better."

"Me, too."

"How are your classes going?"

"Not bad. I'm keeping up much better now that I've given up binge drinking."

"Oh, yes. I remember that. Are you seeing anybody?"

"As a matter of fact, I am. Did you ever take any classes from Bruce Shelton?"

"Are you kidding me? Dr. Shelton? That man is so hot. You two are together?"

"We are. Not only that, but he's also asked me to be his TA."

"Damn, Charlie. I haven't had a date in weeks. Now I'm starting to feel intimidated again. It must be that lucky jacket of yours."

"You don't think my radiant beauty and charming personality has anything to do with it?"

"Of course. But that jacket is a bonus."

"This thing? It's not even mine. I found it in a box."

"You were wearing it the last time I saw you."

"You mean in the dorm?"

"Absolutely. Don't you remember? We were partying hard that night after we beat Tech. You came in the room after having been who knows where, drunk off your ass, wearing not much of anything under that big green jacket. We all wanted that thing. Funny, but it seems like it happened yesterday."

"This is so weird. It's all coming back to me now. The game. That stupid sorority prank. The jacket." Charlie let out a high-pitched squeal as another memory surfaced. "Holy moly. I am such a ditz. I've got to call—"

"Yeah, like I said, you were pretty wasted that night. We all were."

"I'd pretty much blanked everything that happened that day out of my mind until the call about Mom."

"Funny how our minds work sometimes."

"It sure is."

"Look, Charlie, I'm glad we got to talk. I'd better get back inside before my friends send a search party. Here's my card. Let's stay connected and let me know if there's anything I can do for you."

Charlie gave Amanda a hug. "Thanks. You've already been a tremendous help. I'll call you."

CHAPTER 26

"Nice work, ladies. Let's finish up. Now that you've challenged yourself physically, it's time to focus on the spiritual you."

Julia paced around her spacious living room, eager to lead her most popular session. The pattern on her long purple dress matched the jewelry around her ankles, and a strong aroma of lemon and ginger root preceded her presence. Tonight's group was new. The two twenty-somethings seemed like perfectly good candidates for therapy, but the older woman's focus was questionable.

Sam rolled up her mat, released her long, dark ponytail, and shook out her hair. She grabbed a few strands to check for any degradation in color. "I want you all to know that I've made a big decision tonight. I've been thinking about it a lot, and I've decided I'm no longer letting myself be defined by men and their needs. From now on, I'm an independent woman."

Madison giggled as she adjusted her gray leggings, the elastic waistband springing back with a snap. Bleached blonde hair framed her cute, freckled face that reflected a constant state of surprise. "You do know this is the twenty-first century, right? We've been liberated since the seventies. We get to work outside the home, vote, drive cars, you name it. We even get to wear pants."

"Of course," said Sam. "But lately, it's like every guy I know has taken the same course in how to be annoying. It's so infuriating."

"They can't help it," said Madison. "They're born that way. I think there's something in their Y chromosome that makes them think they're better than us. But guess what? We're smarter, we live longer, and we know better than to wear white after Labor Day. That's the ultimate Vogue trifecta."

Beth came up from a Downward Dog pose and held her huge, green-framed eyeglasses to the light to check for smudges. Her lithe, slender frame was rubber-like. "You guys are right. I've had it with men and their fragile egos. Why should we kowtow to them all the time? If somebody would invent a vibrator that could clean gutters, we wouldn't need them at all. Someone's working on that now, aren't they?"

"Now ladies," said Julia. "I don't want you to get all stressed out. Our session tonight is all about serenity. We need to be calm and focused. Only positive thoughts, please."

Sighing, Sam tossed her mat in the corner. "I'm sorry, but it's hard to stay calm when you're not speaking to your current boyfriend and your ex is acting like a jerk. I swear, there are no good men left."

"What did that asshole do now?" Beth asked.

"Which one?"

"Your ex."

"Oh, you'll love this. He came over the other night to pick up the last of his things. We started talking about the settlement and he casually mentioned he's started seeing Belinda. I mean, come on. Belinda? Really?"

Madison made a face. "Oh my god! Isn't she that tramp we see all the time at Fit Plus? The one with the big tits? Isn't she a little young for him?"

Beth finished her last stretch, then plopped down on the sofa.

"She can't be a day over nineteen. Those two can't have anything in common. She's a total airhead. And I'd be willing to bet her main attractions are silicone."

Sam dabbed her face with a towel. "I hate to admit it, but I think they're real. I absolutely hate that little bitch. Who does she think she is? Strutting her young stuff around the gym in front of my husband like that?"

"You mean your ex-husband," Madison said.

"Yeah, whatever."

"I don't know what to tell you," said Beth. "They all think with their dicks. After what I've been through with Alex, I've had it. That's it. I'm officially swearing off men."

Madison nodded in agreement. "Oh, I am so over Dixon. I'm with you."

Shaking her head, Julia positioned herself in the middle of the group. "Ladies, ladies. Such hostility tonight! How are we going to channel our MICs with all of this negative energy in the room? Let's get comfortable on the floor and try to have a minute of silence while we refocus."

Sam pouted. "Sorry. It's not happening. I thought the yoga would help, but I'm too keyed up to channel anything."

Beth hunkered down against a pillow and pretended to light up a smoke. "I think we all need to chill."

Julia disappeared behind a beaded curtain and returned moments later with a small wooden box. "Here, I've got just the thing for you," she said, proffering a hand-rolled cigarette. "This is guaranteed to mellow you out."

"Woohoo, I know what that is," Madison said. "Let me get my lighter. Hey Julia, can we have some alcohol, too? I channel a lot better when I'm flying."

"Great idea. We could all benefit from a double dose of mood enhancement." She headed to the kitchen, returning with a bottle of wine and four crystal glasses. The women arranged themselves on the carpet around Julia's rustic pine coffee table and poured themselves generous portions of Merlot.

Madison took a drag of the joint. "This stuff is even better than the last time." She passed it to Beth.

"Good," Julia said. "Let's all have a few hits before we begin our session. Remember, when you're at peace you attract *positive* energy. And positive energy leads to positive thoughts. This is a definite must for our next exercise."

Within minutes, the mood in the room had lightened. The conversation transitioned away from men and relationships to spiritual self-awareness.

Sam raised her glass. "I'd like to make a toast. To sister Julia, our shining light in the forest, our life coach, our frickin' fantastic spiritual leader."

"Yes, to our frickin' spiritual leader," Madison said, slurring her words.

Beth choked on her wine as she laughed. "Couldn't agree more. Here's to Julia, may your mystical inner-tube always float freely down the terminally polluted rivers of our sorry-ass beings."

Madison dropped her glass on the thick carpet, missing the tabletop by several inches. "Whoopsie. Good thing it was empty. I think I'm finally ready to explore my MIC. Now, what is it, exactly?"

Julia stood to address the group. "Excellent timing, Mad. Now for those of you who haven't read my latest book, *Me, Myself, and I: A Self-Guided Tour to Your Inner Self,* your MIC, or your meta-physical inner core, is the energy plant from which your vital life forces are nourished and maintained. Think of it as a beautiful flower within your soul that bears the fruit of awareness. Your MIC is unique to you. Most of us in the spiritual community believe that while there is a genetic, immutable component to it, it is possible, with therapy, to modify it. It is through your MIC that your composite being is projected to the outside reality. The intellectual being, the spiritual being, and the physical being are all derived from your MIC, all inextricably linked. When your three beings are out of sync, that means your MIC has somehow been compromised, and I don't need to tell you what happens then."

Sam gave Julia a frightened look. "You don't mean—"

"Yes, it's unfortunately true. That nightmarish phrase we never want to hear. Cognitive dissonance."

The group let out a collective gasp.

"So our physical actions could be at odds with our metaphysical blueprints," Sam said. "That's scary."

"Exactly, girls. That's why tonight's exercise is so important."

"How do we start?" Beth asked.

Julia scooted closer to Madison. "Great question. It begins by channeling honesty and positivity. You must let go of your apprehension, your negativity, and your doubts. I'm going to go around the table and ask each of you to make a positive, truthful statement about yourself. This is a small but important first step in the journey to self-discovery."

Madison raised a finger. "Okay, I'll be brave and go first, I think. Let's see... It has to be something positive and truthful. Right now, I'm. . . I'm. . . I'm undeniably and positively shitfaced." She screeched in delight, spraying Merlot across the table.

Beth's attempt to maintain a straight face ended with a howl. "And I'm positive she's shitfaced. I just might be, too."

Sam started to speak but broke out laughing with the others. Then a hush fell over the room. Julia stood up, took another sip of wine, and circled the table. Shaking her head, she resumed her seated position before downing another gulp of the aged grape.

"Ladies, failure to maintain decorum signals a serious fault. It appears you are no longer the master of your own physical being. When you are no longer the master of your own physical being, channeling your MIC can be extremely challenging, if not impossible. But you know what? I think tonight it's okay."

"Why?" asked Madison.

"Because I'm shitfaced, too!" Julia shrieked.

The women collapsed in a heap of laughter on the carpet.

When they managed to calm down, they raided the refrigerator for cheesecake.

Beth smacked her lips. "This is so good. I can't remember the last time I was this hungry."

Madison's eyes rolled back with pleasure. "Oh my god, this is orgasmic."

Sam wolfed down her slice, then pretended to lick the plate. "I can't believe I'm still hungry. What else you got?"

Julia stepped into the kitchen. "Let me see." While she studied the contents of her refrigerator, the doorbell chimed. "Can someone get that?"

Sam pushed her empty dish aside, then teetered out of the room and opened the door. A man was standing on the stoop. She stared at him for a while without saying anything, expecting a sales pitch. He looked confused.

"Hi. I'm Johnson Telling. I was looking for my aunt. Is she here?"

Sam, now fixated on his broad chest and shoulders, continued to stare, then abruptly came out of her trance. "I'm sorry. Who were you looking for?"

"My Aunt Julia."

"Oh, Julia. Of course. Please come in. Julia, we have a visitor."

Julia yelled from inside. "I'm not expecting anyone now. Get rid of them."

"He says you're his aunt."

Julia bounded into the foyer, screaming. "It's my little Tommy! Come here, sugar." She gave Johnson a hug while Sam shut the door. "I wasn't expecting you tonight."

"I promised you I'd stop by right after my appointment. And here I am."

Julia led him inside. "So you are. Somehow, I didn't think you would come, but I am so pleased that you did. What happened to your hand?"

"That's a long story. Sorry to interrupt your party. I can come back another time."

"Oh no you don't, mister. You're not getting away that easily. I want you to meet the girls. Everybody, this is Tommy, my nephew."

Sam eyed him while toying with her hair. "Hi, I'm Samantha, but you can call me Sam."

Madison grinned as she introduced herself. "I think I've seen you somewhere before. Are you an athlete?"

"Roger that. I played a little football at State."

Beth sidled up to him. "A little football. Are you kidding? You were in the backfield with Tyrell Brown. You guys were so good. I'm Beth."

"Come sit down with us for a while," Julia said. "Would you like some cheesecake?"

"Not right now. But I might take some later."

The women assumed their positions around the table and Johnson squeezed into a space between Beth and Madison. He looked around and nodded. "Your house looks pretty much the same since I was in high school. I always loved this thick carpet. And you're still using that same air freshener. Some things never change, I guess. I like that."

The women stared at each other. "That's not exactly air freshener," Beth said.

Johnson gave her a puzzled look.

Julia grimaced. "Tommy, what she meant to say is it's a new scent I'm trying."

"Sure smells the same to me. Oh, and I go by Johnson, not Tommy."

Julia cleared her throat.

Madison smiled at Johnson. "Tommy, why don't you have a glass of wine? Then you can tell us all about yourself."

"Girls, Tommy is very inhibited and doesn't drink alcohol," Julia said. "He's in the Army."

Sam stared at him. "We'll just have to remedy that, now, won't we?"

Madison caressed a crease in Johnson's pants. "Ooh, I love military guys. They are awesome."

"Oh, me too," Beth said, pretending to swoon. "They're so rugged. Out there in the fray, defending our country. You know, I feel safer already."

Sam interrupted her fixation on Johnson to gawk at Beth. "So now you like military guys? That's interesting. Just an hour ago you said you were swearing off *all* men."

Beth flashed her a dirty look. "What? I'm positive I never said anything like that. Tommy, don't listen to her. Women her age can't handle their liquor. Anyway, tell us what brings you out into the real world today?"

Julia topped off her wine glass. "He had an appointment with Lars to discuss a sexual disorder."

Johnson cringed. "Aunt Julia!"

"Now Tommy, we've discussed this before. You've nothing to be ashamed of. Everyone has these kinds of problems from time to time. It's all part of the human condition. You're among friends here. Don't be afraid to open up."

"Absolutely," Sam said. "I, for one, want to hear all about your problem."

Johnson looked around at the entranced women and tried to respond but was too embarrassed to speak. When Julia left the room to answer a phone call, he excused himself and wandered out.

Shortly after, Julia popped back in, holding her phone. "Sorry, guys," she said in a whisper. "It's Michelle. She's in the middle of a crisis. I've got to take this. Carry on without me for a while. Why don't you try channeling again?"

Beth poured out the last of the wine. "Sure. When Tommy gets back, he can join us."

Sam joined Johnson in the kitchen, peering over his shoulder. "What are you looking for in there, cutie?"

Johnson stared into the refrigerator. "Some orange juice would be great. I think my blood sugar must be low. I'm feeling a little lightheaded. Or it's the pain medication. I'm not sure."

"We can't have that. Why don't you go back to the living room and sit down, and I'll bring in a big old glass of OJ, just for you."

"Okay. If you don't mind."

"Not a problem at all. And just so you know, if you'd like to talk with me about sex, or anything else for that matter, I'm all ears."

Johnson didn't answer. He pretended to receive a call on his phone, signaled to Sam, and rushed out.

Sam found several bottles of liquor in Julia's cabinet. She poured a healthy portion of vodka into a tall glass with orange juice, slunk back into the living room, and handed it to Johnson.

"Thanks." He downed half of the tainted mixture in a few gulps. "This is good. I've never had a citrus drink like this. It's got a strong kick to it."

"Well, have some more," Sam said. "Juice is so good for you."

Sam sat down and snuggled up beside him. "Now where were we? Oh, that's right. Tommy was going to tell us all about himself."

"I go by Johnson, not Tommy. Believe me, I'm not that interesting. And weren't you in the middle of something? I don't want to interfere."

Beth drained her glass, then peered at him, glassy-eyed. "No problem. You can channel with us."

"Channel? What's that?"

"We're channeling to discover the core of our existence. It's who we are, the very nature of our being. Our inner core."

"Your inner what?"

"Core. It's like a flower," said Madison.

"I'm not sure I have an inner flower, or whatever it is."

Madison grabbed Johnson's hand. "Of course, you do. Everyone has one. It's a life force. Unique to you. And Tommy, I have a feeling the core within you is huge and absolutely pulsing with energy. But to set it free, so that it's visible to the outside world, you need to strip away all your inhibitions. It's a dangerous exercise but oh so exhilarating. Just be brave and you'll be rewarded. I promise."

"Come on," said Beth. "Don't be afraid to bare it."

Sam gazed into Johnson's eyes. "She's right. It's all about letting us see the real you. The one the world doesn't know, your true inner self. Just let yourself go. Let us be touched by your magnificent, throbbing core, Tommy!"

Deeply troubled with the concept of baring his soul or anything else to strangers, Johnson looked at the women in terror. He felt queasy and out of his element, still emotionally drained from the session with Lars.

"Let me see if I can help," Sam said. She got up on her knees and positioned herself behind him, gently manipulating his back muscles. "Oh Tommy, you are way too tense. Let's try to remedy that. Take off your shirt."

"Excuse me?"

"Don't be so nervous. I wouldn't think of hurting you. We're just going to try a little massage therapy. You need to relax."

Johnson was awash in a peculiar surge of warmth as he pondered her request. "I guess that's okay."

His shirt off, the women gaped at his bare torso in stunned silence.

Sam mouthed *Oh my god* to Beth and Madison as she continued to gently knead his upper back, then moved on to his shoulders. "How's that, Johnson? Are you starting to feel more relaxed?"

"I sure am. That feels great. And you can call me Tommy."

Madison leaned over and squeezed his bicep. "Wow, Johnson, you are in great shape. Do you work out?"

"I mostly lift weights."

Sam continued the massage. "It sure shows. You could be on the cover of a fitness magazine."

"I don't know about that."

"Yeah," said Madison. "Look at those arms. I bet you could pick up little ol' me with one hand."

Sam glared at her. "Oh, Johnson, that's true. But believe me, it's not a big deal. Lots and lots of men have picked her up."

"Really?"

"Oh, sure. It's not that hard to do. In fact, I'd say she's incredibly easy to pick up. I know she gets picked up at McKenzie's bar every weekend her boyfriend is out of town."

Madison glared back. "Well, at least I *do* get picked up. Johnson, you might be interested to know that on the other hand, Sam is incredibly difficult to pick up. She hasn't been picked up in weeks."

"I guess some of us have standards," Sam said. "And speaking of standards, when you're in my line of work it's important to keep up your appearance. So, I'm at the gym every day. I do some weights and a lot of aerobics."

Beth gave Sam a snide look. "Absolutely, I agree. It *is* important to have standards. But it must be incredibly difficult for someone your age. I didn't know they offered geriatric classes at Fit Plus. Must be a bitch with all those walkers in the way."

Sam frowned. "They do. Although I've never participated. It's the class right after yours. You know, the special one for twice-divorced ladies who are losing their hair?"

Johnson guzzled the rest of his juice and steadied himself. "Wow. That is an extremely specific requirement. How many are in your class?"

The women looked at each other.

"Johnson, can you excuse us for a minute?" Beth said. She motioned to the kitchen, and the women followed her.

Beth put her glass on the kitchen table, then folded her arms across her chest, eying Sam. "Well?"

Sam looked back indignantly. "Well, what?"

"What exactly are you doing?"

"What does it look like I'm doing? I'm flirting with him. And if I play my cards right, maybe I'll get lucky tonight."

Madison shrieked with laughter. "Oh, please. Honey, you're embarrassing yourself. That ain't no flirting. You're throwing yourself at him. What makes you think he'd be interested in you, anyway? He's much closer to our age. What are you, fifty-five? Sixty?"

"I'm forty-one and why do you care, anyway? I thought you were swearing off men. If so, why are *you* flirting with him, Madison?"

"Because he's hot."

Beth pointed a finger at Sam. "Don't get all high and mighty with us, missy! You said you were swearing off men, too."

"Not true. I never said that. What's different is now *I'm* calling the shots. Don't get me wrong. I'm not counting on anything long-term with him. But why shouldn't I have a boy toy for a while? I just want one evening of no holds barred passion. It's been a long time. Too long. So, you two need to disappear. And I mean right now."

Beth stood on her toes, inches from Sam's face. "You don't get to tell us what to do. How about you disappear instead?"

"Yeah," Madison said. "Why don't you go home? I'm sure you must need your support hose by now."

Sam threw her head back as if to laugh. "Oh, that is uproarious. Not! Ladies, we have reached an impasse. Any ideas?"

The women looked around, avoiding eye contact.

After a while, Madison put an elbow on the table. "Enough of this crap. How about arm wrestling? I could so take you both right now."

Beth scowled. "I don't know about that. Isn't that kind of primitive? Anyway, I might get a hangnail or something. Let's not fool ourselves. We all know who should get the first shot at Johnson. That would be me."

"Are you kidding me?" Sam asked. "Why you?"

"Come on. It's obvious. Because I'm the hottest."

The conversation devolved into an extended diatribe. Each woman unleashed an onslaught of witty barbs and insults carefully crafted to leave her rivals in tears. Whether or not Johnson was truly out of earshot was a matter of a heated and noisy debate. When the rants finally reached a natural plateau, each participant declared herself the winner, unperturbed by the vicious verbal slings and arrows launched against her. The decision came down to a game of rock, paper, scissors from which Sam emerged the victor. Madison and Beth begrudgingly headed home, but not before calling Sam, among other things, a desperate bitch in heat.

* * *

After the other two left, Sam freshened up and returned to the living room to find Johnson sitting upright on the floor, a faraway look in his eyes. "What happened to Meth and Badison?" he said.

"Unfortunately, Beth and Madison had to leave. I think it may be past their bedtime."

Johnson swayed back and forth, then steadied himself with his hands. "Aw, man. Will I get to see them again?"

"I don't think so. But this way it'll be easier for us to get to know each other tonight. Does that sound okay?"

"Sure. You've got nice hair."

"Thanks. So, any questions? What would you like to know?"

"How do you know my aunt?"

"I went to one of her book signings a few months ago. When I found out she lives right here in Parish, I asked if I could join one of her encounter groups. She's famous, you know."

"So I've heard."

"Any other questions?"

"Just one. Can you make the room stop spinning?"

"I can try. Why don't we make you more comfortable?" Sam grabbed a bean bag chair and positioned it behind Johnson. "There. Now lean back and try to focus on one object in the distance."

After a few awkward attempts, Johnson was sprawled out in

the red vinyl sack. He pointed to a framed poster on the wall. "Who's that?"

"That's Janis Joplin. She was a blues singer in the sixties."

"And who's that?" he asked, pointing to another poster.

"That's Jimi Hendrix. He was a famous guitarist, also in the sixties."

"Cool. I've never heard of them. Are they still around?"

Sam unbuttoned the top of her blouse, then curled up next to Johnson. Her silky hair fell in a wave below her shoulders. "No, sweetie, I'm afraid they're both dead."

"Both dead? That's so sad. How did they die?"

"Drug overdoses, I think."

"Well, Gramps taught me to just say no to drugs. And I did. I always do what Gramps tells me to do. You'd like Gramps. And Annie. I would never do anything to disappoint them. That's why I'm staying in the Army. So they're never disappointed."

"You don't like to disappoint people, do you?"

"I sure don't."

"And you wouldn't want to disappoint me, would you?"

"No."

"Good. Tell me, Johnson, do you like older women?"

"Sure."

"And have you ever been with an older woman?"

"Sure, lots of times."

"And the experiences were good for you?"

"They sure were."

"I'm so glad to hear you say that."

"Why?"

"Well, quite frankly, I need some help. You see, I came here tonight in a crisis of sorts. An internal crisis. With guidance from your aunt, I was hoping to channel my true inner core, the essence of my spirit. For various reasons, it didn't happen. But I need to resolve my inner turmoil tonight. I think I'm on the verge of a revelation that will finally answer the question of who I am. But I need *your* help to get there, the kind of help only a man like you can provide. Help from a strong, powerful man."

"When I saw you standing on that doorstep tonight, I heard a voice—a majestic inner voice. It told me something that shook me to the very core of my being. I can't ignore it. Believe me, I've tried all evening to ignore it. It won't go away. The voice told me that only you have the key that unlocks the secrets of my soul. It said that if you and I could be one, all would be made clear."

Johnson stared blankly off into space for a second, then faced Sam. "So, you want me to help you find a core? And it's around here somewhere?"

"Yes, in a way," Sam said, loosening another button. "Think of the core as a seed that turns into the true, beautiful flower of my being. But it's something deep within me."

"So, what kind of flower are we looking for? I've never been much into gardening. My grandmother has a flower garden, though. Gladiolas, pansies, roses, tulips, you name it. She spends hours out there, watering, weeding, fertilizing. They're pretty, but that's a lot of effort."

"It's not a real flower, silly. It's a symbol." She loosened the last button on her blouse and moved in closer.

"But it's inside you? Oh, man. That is some kind of weird, isn't it? This conversation is way too deep for me. I wouldn't have the slightest idea how to discover that."

"It's not that hard," she said, staring deeply into his blue eyes. "Just do what comes naturally, if you know what I mean."

Johnson maintained his blank expression, then stared at his hand as if it were a foreign object. Sam's breathing became rapid and more pronounced. After a slow, sensual caress of his arm, she leaned in, closed her eyes, and waited for a kiss. Clueless, he turned away, suddenly interested in the cast on his other hand. Screaming, Sam threw herself across his lap. "Look, you big lug. Just make love to me!"

He stiffened in horror. She began softly kissing his chest while he squirmed. "What's a girl to do? Don't you like me?"

"Gosh, I didn't know you meant that. I mean I *have* been with older women. And it's true I do like them. But not in *that* way. I thought we were talking about. . . never mind. Man, what is wrong with me? I'm dizzy, I can't focus, and I sound like an idiot. Please don't misunderstand. You're attractive, but I have a girlfriend."

"And I have a lousy boyfriend," Sam said. "So what?"

Julia reappeared. "Sorry that took so long. Michelle was in a bad way. What's going on? Where is everybody?"

Johnson scrambled to get up.

Julia squealed with delight. "Oh, Tommy! I'm so happy to see you you're finally going with the flow. Letting your primitive urges take control can be so liberating. Oh, my, looks like you two need some privacy."

With one hand, Johnson swept Sam off the floor and onto the sofa. "Nothing's happening here, Aunt Julia. We were just talking."

"Holy crap," Sam said breathlessly. "You *are* strong."

"Good luck finding your flower. Or whatever the heck it is. Sorry I couldn't help." Johnson made a haphazard attempt to button his shirt then staggered towards the foyer.

Sam grimaced. "Seriously? You're leaving?"

"Roger that. It was nice meeting you. I had a good time tonight. But I've got some unfinished business to attend to while I still. . . still have a few more hours. . . left on my pass. Aunt Julia, I'll talk to you later."

Julia took Johnson's hand. "Tommy, please don't go. You're not looking well at all. Are you sure you can't stay a bit longer?"

"I wish I could, but no. Don't worry about me. I'll be fine."

Johnson fumbled with his keys, then waved goodbye to a crestfallen Julia who watched him wander down the dark path to the street. Taking a few steps, he fell, picked himself up, then broke into raucous laughter that drowned out his buzzing phone.

He wasn't ready to give up on Cameron. She was gorgeous, fun-loving, and incredibly sweet when she wasn't so domineering. Still, given their emotionally-charged encounter at McKenzie's, he wasn't sure how she would react to his desperate attempt at reconciliation.

He opted to make the short trip to her condo on foot, hoping the exercise and fresh air might help him regain his faculties. As he walked along, rehearsing his speech of contrition, the soothing palette of an early evening sky gave no indication life could be anything but harmonious. Across a clearing, the distant outskirts of the city looked serene, bathed in dusky twilight. For a brief time, he felt calm. Then, reality set in.

Cameron deserved to know the truth, even if it meant risking ultimate rejection. Somehow, he had to explain himself without coming across like a freak. The thought of facing her was scary. How could anyone that petite be so intimidating?

CHAPTER 27

Cameron showered and slipped into her robe. She had an hour to choose the perfect outfit from her extensive collection. Tonight's restaurant was new and chic, so her wardrobe choice had to be smart and stylish but not overly sophisticated. There was no telling whom she might see. She considered several conservative options, then zeroed in on one of her newest and trendiest purchases.

In the bedroom, she got out her curling iron and styled her hair in soft waves, touched up her face, and dressed. As she was admiring her look in a full-length mirror, the buzzer sounded. She grabbed her shoes and headed for the door. "Who is it?"

A voice serenaded her in an off-key falsetto. "Oh, baby. . . I'm losing my mind just a little. Why don't you just meet me in the fiftieth percentile?"

Cameron groaned. "That's not how it goes, you nerd. It's the middle. Why don't you just meet me in the middle?"

"The middle is imprecise. The middle what? The middle of the road? The middle quartile? Who knows what it is?"

"Everyone knows what it is, Johnson. It's the middle! It rhymes with little. Your version sucks."

"I still think mine is clearer."

Cameron sighed. "I can't believe I'm standing here arguing with you about this."

"Well then let your main squeeze in. We need to talk."

"Since when do you call me your main squeeze? I'm sorry mister, but I am no longer your main squeeze."

"Come on, Cameroon," he wailed in another off-key pitch. "Don't say it's over so soon. Open up, baby. Pretty please?"

Cameron covered her mouth, suppressing a laugh. "You promise to tell the truth this time?"

"I promise, babe. Now let me in. You know I can't survive without being in your awesome presence."

"Whatever."

She stared at Johnson as he sauntered in. "My god, you look awful. What happened to your shirt?"

"Nice to see you, too." He kissed her hand.

She snatched it back in disgust. "Look, I'm due to meet my parents shortly so I'm giving you fifteen minutes. Come sit down."

"Thanks for squeezing me in, beautiful. Can I sit over there or is the sofa still off-limits?"

"You take the chair and I'll use the sofa."

Johnson took a few wobbly steps, a slight grin on his face.

Cameron gave him an annoyed look. "Well?"

"Well, what?"

"You know the rules. Shoes over there, Mister Ex-Squeeze."

"Oh, I forgot."

After a struggle with the laces, he set his wingtips aside, then laughed as he sunk into the seat, nearly falling out.

She was not amused. "What is wrong with you? I can't believe I'm asking this, but have you been drinking?"

"Come on babe. You know I don't drink."

"Could've fooled me. You are acting so weird. Now tick tock—what've you got to say for yourself?"

Johnson cleared his throat. "First of all, I want to apologize for my egregious behavior. I've been a very bad boy."

"That's a start."

"I wasn't truthful when we last met and I want to set the record straight." He winced at the sound of his phone.

Cameron scowled. "Don't you dare answer that."

"Now stay calm. I'm picking it up and declining the call. I'm sure it's a wrong number, anyway. Watch me, I'm gently placing it on the table." The phone hit the table with a solid clunk. Pleased with himself, he snorted.

"Smooth. Now go on. Why are you laughing?"

"Because I dropped my phonie."

Cameron rolled her eyes. "What is up with you? You are acting so bizarre. It's like you're high. Wait a minute—I thought I smelled something on you. Oh my god! I do smell it. You've been smoking weed."

"Weed? Weally? Where would I get weed?" Johnson snorted again.

"I'm so glad you're amused. You won't be when you get my fumigation bill. Do you have anything to say to me that makes sense?"

Johnson put on a serious face and cleared his throat again. "Sorry. Like I said, I wasn't honest with you. Truth is, my life's been a disaster over the past few days. The presentation was a bust, then I got in a fight with Tyrell. That's how I broke my hand. And Blanton took me off Tangent."

"Why in the world would you get in a fight with Tyrell?"

"Because I thought he was in cahoots with Brooks to sabotage my part of the presentation."

"Oh, please. Tyrell? He's your best friend. Why would he do that to you?"

"I figured he wanted to get back with you, so he had to make me look bad."

"Get back with me?"

"Come on. Now it's your turn to be straight with me. I know you used to date him."

"Okay. You're right. We did used to date. We didn't tell you because I was afraid you'd get all stressed out about it. In any case, our last date was a long time ago, and I haven't spoken to him since that night at McKenzie's when he was with Alicia. I've never had any intention of getting back with him, you moron!"

"Then the disaster at the presentation must have been all on Brooks, I guess. Tyrell could do no wrong, but somehow when I had to speak the mic cut out."

"So?"

"Well, you see, Blanton wanted me to come down off the stage."

"Again, so?"

"I couldn't get out from behind the podium. It would have been a little awkward, and Blanton lost patience. I was having a moment. Now that's hysterical." He laughed again.

"Johnson! Focus. Why would Brooks do that to you?"

"Because he hates me."

"Why does he hate you?"

"He thinks I'm gay. But that's not why he hates me."

"You're not making any sense."

"Let me explain. Brooks has no problem with me being gay. I mean, not that I'm gay. But if I was gay, he would have no problem with that. It's the fact that, according to him, I'm gay but I won't admit I'm gay. Wow. That's a lot of gays. Anyway, that's what he hates."

"And what reason would he have to suspect you're gay?"

"Well, this is where the story gets a little wacky, so bear with me."

"I'm listening."

"Lately I've had some experiences where I get extremely turned on in socially unacceptable situations."

"Turned on?"

"Yeah, you know, like really aroused. It happened a couple of times in the locker room, during my presentation, a few others."

"And you have no control over this?"

"No. What I'm saying is, from time to time, it just happens."

"I see." Hands on her hips, Cameron paced the room, muttering something under her breath. "Look, I'm trying to keep an open mind, but this is ridiculous. You've been getting turned on, without provocation, at random. And you have no control over it. I'm supposed to believe that?"

Johnson raised a finger, then belched. "No, wait, that's not true."

"Johnson, for god's sake!" Cameron screamed. "Tell me something I can believe."

"It's not random. It happens when I hear music."

"Okay, now we're getting somewhere," she said softly. "So, you're not gay. You're just a regular heterosexual male who has been having instances of uncontrollable desire lately, always brought on when you hear music. Sure, that makes perfect sense."

"So, you believe me?"

"Of course, sweetheart. Thanks for being so open with me."

"So, we're good now?"

"Almost. I just have one more question."

"Okay. Shoot."

"Does this happen with any music or is it a particular tune that gets to you?"

"Oh, no. Not just any music. It's a particular song."

"Just one particular song. That's interesting. So?"

"So what?"

"So, what song is it? I want to know."

"Right. It's a song you've heard before. Very patriotic. One of the best. A national treasure."

"I see. And the name?"

Johnson maintained a straight face for a time but soon lost his composure. "It's the National Anthem," he said, falling out of the chair.

"Very funny, mister pothead. Like I would believe that. Do you think I'm that naive?"

"Come on, lighten up. Don't you think it's a little bit funny?"

"No, I don't." She spotted something on the carpet. "Wait,

what's that? Next to you. It looks disgusting. It's a black hair. It can't be mine and I know it's not yours. Where have you been today?"

"Oh, that's probably from Sam. But I can explain."

"You got it from Sam? Who the hell is Sam? Is this what you do now? You get high, then you hook up with one of your new friends? You know what? Don't answer that. Don't say anything else. I don't want to know what you've been up to. Just get out of here. Now."

"Wait. Let me explain." Before he could finish, Johnson sprang to his feet, holding his hand over his mouth.

"What's wrong with you now?"

"I think…I'm going to be sick."

Horrified, Cameron jumped aside, but not far enough to miss his pungent expulsion. "What the hell? Are you kidding me? Do you know how much I paid for this dress?"

Johnson scampered out of the room.

* * *

When Johnson reappeared, Cameron was sitting solemnly on the sofa. "Are you quite finished in there?"

"Yes," he said, slipping into his shoes. "Sorry about that. Guess it was something I ate. Hey, what's with the robe and slippers? I thought you were going out?"

"I canceled with my folks. I'm in no mood to go anywhere tonight."

"And it's all my fault. Look, I know you don't believe me, but everything I told you tonight is true."

"If you say so. I think you should leave."

"So that's it? No second chance?"

"Tonight *was* your second chance. Now go on, and don't forget your phone. You might want to check your messages. While you were defiling my bathroom, you got an interesting text. Apparently from some long-lost friend. I hope you two can connect again. He sounds nice. Let me read it to you."

Hey. Tried to call a couple of times but it rolled over to voicemail. This is long overdue, but I owe you a huge thanks. What you did for me in the locker room during the Tech game so long ago was incredible. I'd like to somehow return the favor. Oh, and I have something you may want. If you're in town, I'll be at McKenzie's. Just ask for Charlie.

"I have no idea who that is," Johnson said. "He obviously has me mixed up with someone else."

"Whatever. Look, I don't have the energy to be angry with you anymore. I don't want to fight about this, and I don't want to talk it out. We had a good run."

"But—"

"Let me finish. I know I'm not perfect. I can be challenging and demanding at times. I think we were good together. I found your little idiosyncrasies adorable. Straightening all those pictures every time at McKenzie's. Sending your fries back to the kitchen a million times. Showing up thirty minutes early for a date. Now I think we both know it's over."

"But—"

"I'm still not finished. It's too bad. I fell in love with a different person, a person I thought I wanted to marry someday. Bottom line is I don't know who you are anymore. Now please go so I can cry in private."

"Cam, you're sure this is what you want?"

"Yes, Johnson."

"Isn't there anything I can say that will change your mind?"

"I think you've said more than enough tonight."

"I know I've had some issues lately. It wasn't going to be easy, but I thought we could work through them together. To be honest, though, things were moving a little too fast for me."

"I realize that. Unfortunately, I no longer see us happening. And I'm sorry, I can't wait for you while you work through your issues. They're too messy and quite frankly, too perverted. I've got to move on."

"I'm so sorry. I never meant to hurt you like this. I know it doesn't seem like it now, but one day, you'll find a great guy who'll make you happy. And you deserve to be happy."

"Do you really think so?"

"I do."

Though Johnson rarely succumbed to his emotions, he felt a deep sense of remorse. As he stood beside her, silently contemplating the past, he was drawn to her eyes. On the rare occasions when she became quiet and withdrawn they would mirror her most intimate thoughts. Tonight, they seemed different, less engaging, a paler shade of remarkable. The consuming gaze that once held the promise of love was now a forlorn look of despair. Yet somehow reflected in her anguish was a hint of another sentiment: genuine forgiveness. No further words were necessary—he understood and could move on.

Shivering, he stepped outside into a shadowy setting strangely lacking the bustle of a Friday evening. He paused, reminded of an earlier experience with Cameron in the same place. It all came rushing back—the frigid air, the tiny snowflakes melting on his face, and the warmth of her lips during their first embrace. Even then, a nagging uneasiness he never fully understood stained the joy. As the bittersweet memory faded, he peered into the dim light where streetlamps tinged the boulevard in a hazy shade of blue. He continued on his way, steeped in a strange mix of relief and melancholy. Above him, her door closed softly.

CHAPTER 28

Johnson milled around the entrance to McKenzie's, stealing an occasional glance inside. Many of the patrons on their way in or out felt threatened by his curious stares. Like an alligator in a swimming pool, the big man was impossible to ignore.

The text message he'd received earlier bugged him. The only Charlie he knew was a former teammate who had graduated years before. He could have returned to Parish for a visit. Many alumni did. He probably just wanted to reconnect. If not, who was this other Charlie, and what had he done to deserve such gratitude?

He conjured up several scenarios, most of them unlikely. In one, a clandestine meeting had taken place in a foggy locker room. There was Johnson, a monstrous trench coat stretched over his uniform, hat pulled down over his eyes, trading State's game plan to a kid named Charlie for a pirated copy of Windows 10— the Professional Edition. True, he hadn't upgraded his system for some time, and the thought of scoring new software was tempting. But would he have sold out his team for that?

He needed answers. Gathering up all his courage, he marched

through the door and stepped boldly up to the bar. Where was this mysterious guy?

In the corner, an impeccably dressed older man nursed a drink while watching the TV news in closed caption mode. The seat beside him was slightly askew, and a sweater was draped over the back. Nearby, two couples chatted incessantly about politics while sipping cocktails. On the opposite end of the bar, another pair held hands and kissed, their wine glasses untouched. A younger man with short reddish hair occupied a seat near the door, scribbling notes on a small pad. A bottled beer kept him company.

Johnson looked him over and pulled up a chair. "Excuse me, by any chance are you, Charlie?"

The man continued writing. "Yeah, I'm Charlie. Or Rumpelstiltskin for that matter, but I prefer Charles. Who wants to know?"

Johnson cleared his throat. "I'm Johnson. You sent me a text tonight."

"Text? Tonight? I don't think so."

"Okay. Sorry to bother you." Johnson started to get up.

Charles put down his pen. "Wait a minute. I was too hasty. I've seen your face before. It's been a while, right?"

"Yes, a long time. I don't recognize you. How did you get my number?"

"From you, I assume."

"At the Tech game?"

"Sure."

"What were you doing in the locker room? You weren't on the squad."

"I believe the question is what were you doing there?"

"With the State football team, what else?

Charles took a swig from his bottle and smiled. "I know that. I was a part-time trainer back then, but I usually worked with the soccer team. Don't you remember me?"

"No. I can't remember anything about that day because of the concussion. They said it must have happened when I nailed Kupert in the end zone."

Charles patted Johnson on the back. "That's interesting."

"How come?"

"I seem to remember the prospect of you nailing me in the end zone, too."

"Huh? You said you weren't a player."

"No, but I was a *playah.*"

"I'm confused. Did you give me a massage or something? I used to get leg cramps all the time."

"Well, not exactly. There was a massage, all right. But I was on the receiving end."

"So, I gave *you* a massage? Are you yanking my chain?"

"No. It was the other way around."

"I was yanking my chain? Man, I will never get the hang of that phrase."

"Good lord! Do I have to spell it out for you?" Charles broke into song with a screeching, altered rendition of Aretha Franklin's "(You Make Me Feel Like) A Natural Woman," or "man," as he sang it. Before long, everyone at the bar joined in.

Johnson gasped. "Right there in the locker room?"

Charles stared into Johnson's eyes. "I have to say it was pure magic, though I usually like to take it a bit slower. But don't get me wrong. I have no complaints. Say, what are you doing tonight?"

* * *

On her way home after an uneventful shift at McKenzie's, Charlie took a detour. Another round of texts to Shelton had gone unanswered, and her anguish had reached a tipping point. Worried and out of ideas, she needed to find him.

Speeding down the interstate, she took the exit for the university and drove past the campus until she reached the familiar lights of The Brentwood. After an exasperating search past scores of embarrassingly large, late-model SUVs and expensive sedans, she found a parking space in the rear next to a dumpster. *I guess this is where we belong, Dieter.* She got out and headed for the hotel entrance. On the way, she spotted Shelton's smoke-colored sports car in the front row. A tinge of excitement washed over her.

Walking past the front desk, she ignored an offer of assistance and took the elevator to a luxury suite on the top floor. She paced outside for a while, then tapped on the door. There was no response. She tapped again. The sound of movement inside was followed by a woman's voice.

"Do you know what time it is? What the hell do you want?"

"I'm looking for Bruce."

"Bruce who?"

"Bruce Shelton. I know this is his suite."

"You're wrong. There's no Bruce here."

"I don't believe you. I saw his car in the parking lot."

"Oh, yeah? If the President's car were in the parking lot, would you expect him to be in here, too?

"At the moment, I don't care about the President. I'm worried about Bruce."

"Look, I've never heard of Bruce Shelton, and I've told you he's not here. Now get your ass out of here before I call security."

"Okay. My mistake. So sorry!"

Charlie crept down the hallway to the elevator. The doors opened, exuding the overpowering odor of alcohol. A well-dressed couple spilled out, enmeshed in foreplay. They continued to grope each other, teetering and stumbling towards the other end of the floor.

The woman glanced back just as Charlie stepped around them. "Look, this young lady's been watching us," she shrieked. "I guess we'd better find our room."

Charlie dashed into a dimly lit stairwell and heard the man call out. "Hey, whoever you are, don't run off. Why don't you come back and join us?"

The woman giggled. "Oh, Bob. You're such a pervert. Leave her alone."

"Girl, you are *so* not fun. Okay, killjoy. Let's go."

Charlie took the stairs to the lobby where she alternately sat, stood, and paced. After an hour, she became more anxious. *Where is he?* She checked her phone again for messages. In a panic, she approached the desk.

"Excuse me, but can you tell me if Dr. Bruce Shelton is registered here?"

A well-groomed older man in a dark gray suit stepped up and stared down at her through glossy designer glasses. "Is this a matter of law enforcement?" he said in a refined accent. "If so, I'll need to see your credentials."

"No, this has nothing to do with the police. I just need to know if he's here."

"If so, then I'm sorry. I am not at liberty to divulge that information, young lady."

"Thanks, anyway."

Charlie stepped aside, glancing at the crowd gathered in the hotel lounge. In the corner sat a man conversing with a server. *Is that him?* Flushed and excited, she fussed with her hair and clothes, then moved closer to get a better look. A woman from the lobby interrupted her laser-like focus.

"Charlie?"

"Yes. Who are you?"

"I'm Lindsey. I'm a grad student at State. I've been sitting in on some of the evening classes and thought you looked familiar."

"Oh, Lindsey. That's right. Sorry I didn't recognize you. I'm a little preoccupied at the moment."

"That's okay. Do you work here?"

"No. I was hoping to meet a friend here tonight, but it looks like he's a no-show."

"That sucks. Bruce and I were about to have a drink. Why don't you join us?"

"Bruce?"

"Oh, sorry. You know him as Dr. Shelton."

"Of course. My English Lit professor."

"Exactly. Don't you just love this place? Bruce picked it out. It's simply perfect."

"It sure is. Just like Bruce. I mean Dr. Shelton."

"So, you must know him fairly well."

"A little. He and I have been working on a paper together, among other things. Did he happen to mention that?"

"No, I'm afraid not. But he's always so busy. Lots of irons in the fire, if you know what I mean."

"Has his iron been in your fire?" Charlie muttered under her breath.

"What was that?"

"I mean he works so hard."

"I know. Yet, somehow he's making time this weekend to take me to the Caribbean."

"Imagine that. The Bahamas?"

"You're right! How did you know?"

"Just a guess. So how long have you been together?"

"Not long. He invited me to a conference in Atlanta, and we just clicked. He's so fascinating. Every day with him is amazing."

"Yeah, freakin' amazing. I'm so happy for you."

"I don't want to brag, but starting next week, I'll be his new TA. Can you believe it?"

"I'm impressed. Congratulations. A word of advice, though. Don't ever say no to him."

"What does that mean?"

"Oh, nothing. It's just my thinly-veiled jealousy rearing its ugly head."

"Come on, don't be like that. Now, how about that drink?"

"Lindsey, sounds like you and Dr. Shelton need some alone time. I don't want to be a third wheel. I'm calling it a night."

"You sure?"

"Yes. But please give him a message from me."

"Of course. What is it?"

"Tell him to go to—I mean tell him I'll have my edits ready soon."

* * *

Back in the parking lot, Charlie climbed into her car and started the engine. How could she have been so naive about Shelton? The miserable snake cared only about himself. She was tempted to storm back inside and deliver a potent dose of shaming, but her pain and humiliation would be too high a price to pay for his shock and embarrassment.

She knew exactly how the scenario would play out. He would point out in his didactic, rational manner that implicitly they were never exclusive. He'd remain calm, even disdainful, while she dissolved into tears, blathering accusations peppered with blue-collar obscenities and clumsy epithets. And to what end? To win him back? Their little fling was over as far as she was concerned.

As she drove away staring out into the night, she was struck by a startling vision. In the light of a brilliant full moon, the back-drop of Parish's great divide was painfully evident. Directly ahead stood a members-only racket club, flanked by two large swimming pools. On the adjacent property, an exclusive gated community beckoned, where spacious homes towered over sprawling, immaculate landscapes. Lest the slightest bit of pros-perity find its way out, a monstrous stone wall secured the inhabi-tants' posh lifestyles. Nearby, but barely visible, the living quarters of the needy and less fortunate were crammed together in odd juxtaposition. Here, in a prison of tiny, crumbling proper-ties, common workers of all races and ethnicities led lives of uncertain destiny, left behind to fend amidst the rubble of economic ruin.

She thought of their plight, and how the division between the haves and the have-nots had grown dramatically in just a few years. Her thoughts were interrupted by the sight of another green receptacle only a few feet away. *Hey trash bin, thanks for the not-so-subtle symbolism on the state of my love life.*

She maneuvered her way through the maze of narrow outlets to the street, still mired in disappointment. When the driver of the Lexus ahead slowed to a crawl, she snapped. "Come on, pokey man. Move your ass or get the hell off the road!" She pulled closer. The initials on its license plate looked familiar. Was it the same car they had seen weeks before during the stakeout at the liquor store? Instantly, her scorn for Shelton was forgotten and she was energized by the thrill of a new lead. *Let's see where you're going, Mister RMP.*

Charlie followed the vehicle across town to an industrial park, turned into a vacant lot, and watched as the Lexus continued down a street closed to traffic. Its taillights disappeared into an older complex nestled in the woods at the far end of the drive. She turned off the ignition and jumped out.

As she trudged through the darkness, a strong chemical smell led her to an old plant which had been closed for years. It was heavily barricaded with "Keep Out" signs posted everywhere, but it looked to be in full production. Barbed wire topped the surrounding chain-link fence, giving the building a harsh, prison-like appearance. The gate at the entrance was controlled by an electronic sensor.

She skimmed across the grounds, stepping around fallen trees and edging through thick brush filled with thorns and brittle stems that never seemed to snap at the right moment. As she made her way out of the overgrowth, she stumbled into a deep ditch. *Way to go, dumbass.* She sprang up, nearly losing her balance. After another wobbly step, she fell in again. *Damn. This day just keeps getting better and better.*

She sat up to get her bearings. In the moonlight, she could see an even larger rut inside the property. Rising, she scurried over to the fence, scooping out rocks and dirt below it until she could squirm underneath. On the other side she sprang up, brushed herself off, and charged ahead.

She scraped through another stand of prickly vegetation and found herself on a battered concrete drive leading to a well-lit loading dock. The Lexus was parked nearby, along with a few other vehicles. An armed guard appeared briefly, then disappeared in the opposite direction. Sensing a narrow window of opportunity, she took the stairs up to the platform. There, she managed to squeeze under an enormous roll-up door.

Inside the warehouse, materials were stacked on dozens of wooden pallets, each covered with a bright blue tarp. She peeked underneath the heavy plastic and found layers of foam insulation. Sandwiched near the bottom were plastic bags filled with white crystals. She stuffed one in her jacket, took out her phone, and shot a series of photos.

Then she tiptoed to the other side of the facility and through another door. A large window in the dimly lit hallway caught her attention. On the other side, workers in hazmat suits moved around large stainless-steel vats and tubing. Open barrels of the familiar crystals sat nearby. Fascinated, she captured a video of the operation as the containers were sealed with lids, labeled as 'Rock Salt,' then hauled away with impressive precision. The entire activity unfolded like a well-orchestrated production, each participant moving with drone-like efficiency.

Still itching to explore, she was startled by the sound of footsteps and chatter from a radio.

"Mitch, report."

"We're all clear here on two."

"Good. Finish your rounds and get your ass back here."

"Yes, sir."

A man with an automatic rifle appeared from around the corner and stood inches away from her. "Who the hell are you and what are you doing here?"

Charlie continued to watch the activity below. "I could ask you the same thing."

"How did you get in here?" He shoved the barrel of the rifle in her face.

"Good question. How *did* I get in here?"

"Listen, smartass, start giving me answers before I get irritated."

Charlie tapped the barrel aside. "Well, pardon me. So, you're irritated? Now you listen to me, jackass. I'm way beyond irritated. I've been snooping around here undetected for the past twenty minutes and I don't like what I've seen. Your security, if you can call it that, is lax. No, let's make that non-existent. What if I turned out to be a Fed? My boss is not a patient man, and he's none too happy right now."

"Are you a Fed?"

"No, you idiot. Why would you even ask that? I'm on your side. This is an inspection. And guess what? You've failed miserably."

"That's bullshit. Nobody said anything to me about an inspection."

"That's because it's a surprise, you moron."

"Well, I'll need to report this." He grabbed his radio.

"Sure, go ahead. Should be fantastic timing. Enrico will go ballistic. He's tearing your boss a new one right about now. Or worse. And guess who's next?"

"Did you say Enrico?"

"Yes, why?"

"Enrico Scolina?"

"Yes."

"Enrico Scolina is your boss, and he's here right now?"

"Congratulations. You finally caught on."

"Holy shit!" He turned pale.

"Holy shit is right. If I were you, I'd lay low for a while."

"Yeah. Excuse me. Make yourself at home. I suddenly need to take care of some business." He disappeared into a stairwell.

She hurried back through the warehouse and out to the loading dock, then stopped short. A guard was combing the area with a flashlight. In the opposite direction, someone was getting into the Lexus. "Hey, excuse me, could I bum a ride?" she yelled.

The man gawked at Charlie standing outside his door. "Who the hell are you?"

She instantly recognized his voice as the man from the hotel elevator. "I'm Kim. Just started working here tonight."

"Oh, yeah? I didn't hear anything about that. Who recommended you?"

"Mitch."

"Who's Mitch?"

"He's in security. About six-two, dark hair, trigger happy. I can go back inside and get him if you want. He'll vouch for me."

"Oh, *that* Mitch. That's okay. I'm in a hurry. Hop in."

"Thanks." She took a seat and shut the door.

He started the car and they proceeded through the entrance.

In the side mirror, Charlie saw a guard mulling around behind them as the gates closed. She slumped down in her seat, checked something on her phone, then put it back in her jacket. "My brother. Texts me a lot. He's a worrier."

"I see. Rough night, huh? You look like you've been through it."

"I sure have. Hazing the new kid, you know. But I passed every test with flying colors."

"I swear, I've got to get out here more often. Seems like every time I show up there's somebody new."

"I know. I was lucky to get this job. Not a lot of opportunities here in Parish."

"Are you sure you're right for security? You don't look big enough or badass enough to handle it."

"Oh, I'm a badass alright. Like a ninja. And you should see me with a rifle. You don't want to mess with me."

"I'd love to see you in action. But not tonight. I've got to get home to the wife."

Charlie giggled. "That's so sweet. So, tell me, how's the business doing these days?"

"It's doing great. We can't manufacture the shit fast enough. And the money keeps pouring in. Shutting down the plant was the best decision I ever made. It's turned into a goldmine, an absolutely perfect setup. Who would have ever believed all this going on in little ol' Parish?"

"Aren't you worried about someone finding out?"

"Oh, hell no. I've got this town in my back pocket. Plus, most of the officials are clueless. I've paid off everyone else. Anyway, too many people around here are getting fat off this. They'd have to be idiots to jeopardize that. It's a great example of trickle-down economics."

"Trickle-down?"

"Sorry. Reagan was before your time."

"A little. Where are the buyers?"

"All over the country. A few here in town, but most are down south on the coast. And like I said, demand is growing."

"That's good for me. Job stability is important."

"Sure. So where are we going?"

"Just up to the next intersection. My brother is picking me up. He thinks I work in that all-night garage on the corner."

"That's a good cover. But do you know anything about cars?"

"Absolutely. I specialize in antique German imports."

"That's cool. I used to drive an old BMW years ago. It was a great car until I totaled it."

"Was it an E30? My personal favorite line."

"It was a 1989 325i. You tell me."

"Oh, yeah. I love the E30. They stopped making it in '94. The US version had an inline-six with the Motronic fuel management system. It had 168 horsepower at 5800 rpm and 163 pound-feet of torque at 4300 rpm. With the manual, about eight seconds from zero to sixty."

"Damn! You do know your cars." He pulled over to the corner and stopped.

"Thanks for the ride. I appreciate it." She slid out and shut the door.

Lowering the passenger window, he leaned over. "Hey, what is your name again?"

"It's Kim."

"Okay, Kim. Good to have you on board. Let's get together some time. I'll buy you a drink."

"Sure. I'd like that."

He eyed her briefly, then sped off.

* * *

Charlie trudged into the living room where Aunt Viv was in her usual position on the sofa. Remote in hand, she was engrossed in television. She glanced up at her niece. "You're late and my god, you look like shit. What the hell have you been doing?"

"Nice to see you, too. What's the attraction tonight?"

"*The Thin Man.* William Powell and Myrna Loy. It starts right after the late news. Care to join me?"

"No thanks, you enjoy. I'm going to bed."

Vivian hit the mute button and sat up. "Come on kiddo, your clothes are dirty and it looks like you're bleeding. You want to tell me what's going on?"

Charlie sank next to her and sighed. "Oh, man. So much stuff. You wouldn't believe what I've been up to."

"Tell me. Maybe I can help."

"For one thing, I'm not in love anymore. Go ahead and say I told you so."

"He turned out to be married, didn't he?"

"No, I don't think so. He just turned out to be a jerk."

"Oh, you poor baby. I'm so sorry. Are you okay?"

"I was upset at first. Tried to cry but I just couldn't. I guess it wasn't love after all. Now I'm more angry than anything else."

"That's perfectly normal. Give yourself some time. You'll be fine."

"I hope you're right. But you know, what sucks is knowing how naive I was about the whole thing."

"Don't beat yourself up about that. We all succumb from time

215

to time. Even me. But don't give up. There are still a few good ones out there. FYI, this guy on TV is not one of them."

"Holy moly. I saw him tonight. Who is that?"

"Robert Mansfield Perry. Now talk about your jerks. This guy is the king."

Charlie stared at the image in front of her. There sat the mayor of Parish, a drug kingpin, and the man at the center of a huge ring of corruption in city government. The same man who, unbeknownst to him, bragged about it all while she recorded it on her phone. This was huge, all unfolding before her like a dream. The prospect of collaborating with Alex on a tell-all story intrigued her. Suddenly, there was much to do.

"Aunt Viv, what I'm about to tell you will be hard to believe, but I swear it's all true. I'm in way over my head, but I have a plan. I need a favor—a very big favor. Let's talk."

CHAPTER 29

Vivian sat alone in McKenzie's lounge, nervously tapping a heel on the floor as she finished her Mai Tai. She gestured to the bartender. "Another one, please."

Pete nodded at her from behind the counter as he filled a tall glass with beer. "In a sec. I need to get some more lime juice."

"No rush. I'm not going anywhere."

She studied the host of imbibers around her, most of whom were dim-witted men. One by one, they'd tried to chat her up, but she had no time for nonsense. With Charlie in the throes of final exams, Vivian was in charge of the operation. It was simple—keep the jackass out of his office long enough for Lydia and Reggie to do their work. So far, McFadden wouldn't budge, appearing only once to make a cursory pass around the establishment. Now, yet another pretentious patron of swill seemed fascinated by her presence. How could she get rid of these losers? The latest peacock checked himself out in the mirror, adjusted his plume, then strutted over in her direction. *Oh, crap. Don't come over here, don't come over here!*

"Well, that is just music to my ears," he said.

Vivian scowled. "Excuse me. What is?"

"What you just said. That you're not going anywhere."

"What if I told you I'm changing my mind?"

The man laughed, then downed the contents of his shot glass. "Let me guess. You've got to go feed your cat or something? I get that a lot."

"I can't imagine why."

"You must be new. Don't think I've seen you in here before. Hi. Mac McDonough. And you are?"

"Not interested."

"Oh, snap! You're funny. How are you doing tonight?"

"Fine, except for all these gnats buzzing around me. They're so annoying."

"Maybe it's your perfume."

"I'm not wearing any."

"Have you tried bug spray?"

"No, but I do have some Mace on me if I need it."

"That's cold. Why the attitude?"

"Since you asked, a few things. First, you came over without an invitation. Second, it looks like your belt is out of place because you missed a loop in your pants. Oh, and third, your fly is open. In my book, that makes you both sad *and* annoying."

Startled, he looked down to check his zipper. "Oh, snap again. You got me. You're good."

"You're not. Now, why don't you run along and bother someone else?"

"Not yet. I'm just going to be honest. You're alone and smoking hot. You see, that in itself is an invitation in my book. You're obviously on the prowl. I'm not half bad once you get to know me. Come on, give me a chance."

"Look, I'm not your type."

"I beg to differ. Sexy is definitely my type."

"Okay. I'll put this another way. You're not *my* type."

"I don't believe it. I'm tall, good-looking, successful, modest. What could possibly be wrong with me?"

Vivian paused as she thought of a crushing response. She didn't want to be cruel, but this guy and any future annoyances needed to be out of the picture. After a thorough analysis of his unruly eyebrows and damp hair laden with gel, she decided on her fallback approach. "Something you can't change," she said. "At least not easily."

"I doubt it. I'm always up for a challenge. I can change. Believe me, I've done it before. So, what do I have to do to win your love?"

"Just one little thing for starters."

"And that is?"

"Become a woman."

"Ha. Good one. No really, what do I have to do?"

Vivian maintained her stone-faced expression.

"Wow. You're serious. I didn't see that coming. That explains all of the earlier rejections. I just assumed you had high standards."

"I do. Obviously."

Mac tossed a business card on the table. "In case you happen to change your mind." He started to walk away, then stopped. "Hey, I didn't get your name."

"Let's keep it that way." *What a buffoon.*

He smiled, then meandered back to the bar.

Pete arrived with her drink. "There you go. One more delicious Mai Tai for the mystery lady in red. I'll put it on your tab. And don't worry about Mac. He's harmless."

"I disagree. Those are the ones you have to watch."

"You think?"

"Oh, yeah."

"You raise a good point. I once went out with this chick who was very soft-spoken and reserved, basically a mouse. Or so I thought. She was always wearing the same jeans and an 'Ask Me About My Cat' T-shirt. I couldn't tell much about her eyes behind these impossibly thick glasses, and her hair was wound up in a bun so tight those peepers could have been spring-loaded. This one night, she invited me back to her place for a couple of drinks. We started making out on her couch, and it wasn't too long before things got hot and heavy. We were in her bed when I started to feel strange. I have no idea what was in that liquor, and I don't remember what happened after that. All I know is the next morning I'm wearing a maid's costume, making crepes in her kitchen, and speaking French to three strangers. That ever happen to you?"

She stifled a chuckle. "You're not weird at all, are you? If you'll excuse me, I'm going out for a smoke. I'd like to speak to your manager when I return."

* * *

Vivian walked toward a van parked in the rear of the lot. The driver waved to her, then stuck his head out. "*Qué pasa*? You're looking fine this evening. Girl, if that dress were any tighter, your eyes would be bulging out of your head. Are those Jimmy Choo's on your dogs?"

"No, they are not. I can't help but be flattered, though. I didn't know you were so knowledgeable about women's fashion."

"Yeah, baby. I keep up with all that shit."

"You sound a little too animated. Like you're compensating for something. Is everything okay?"

"Yes, ma'am."

"What are you doing?"

"Watching *The Notebook*," he said with a quiver.

Vivian took a step closer. "Reggie, are you crying?"

"No."

"Oh, god. You *are* crying. What is wrong with you?" She took a whiff of the air. "So that explains it. You're stoned. You want to tell me what's going on?"

"I met the most incredible person today. She rocked my world with the most amazing insights into the spiritual being. Did you know that we all have a metaphysical inner core? She's helping me learn to channel it. You should try it. It will set you free."

"I'll think about it. I'm assuming your road to self-discovery led you to make some dramatic wardrobe changes?"

"A bit, yes. I'm showing the world how confident I am in my masculinity."

"I see. That explains the feather boa. It's quite a bold fashion choice for a guy, especially when you consider the dark glasses. But far be it from me to question your personal taste. Anyway, I have another question if it's not too much trouble."

"No problem," he said, lifting his sunglasses and dabbing his eyes with a tissue.

"Are you sure you don't mind? It's personal."

"Of course not. Shoot."

"Where are your pants?"

"That's funny. The guy in the toll both asked the same thing! I have no idea what happened to them. It doesn't matter, anyway. I won't be needing them tonight."

"Whatever. Let's try and stay focused on the task at hand. You do remember what you're supposed to do, don't you?"

"Yes, ma'am," he said, voice cracking.

"You've got to be kidding me. Are you crying again?"

"I can't help it. This movie destroys me every time. Especially the scene where Allie remembers who Noah is. They talk about their lives until she forgets. She starts screaming, and then Noah cries. I can't take it. It's just so sad."

"Turn that thing off and wait for further instructions. And under no circumstances are you to get out of this vehicle until it's time."

"I got you, chief."

Vivian rolled her eyes. *What did I get myself into?* She marched back to the bar, again drawing leers from the male contingent.

She apprised Lydia of Reggie's hysterical, half-naked state, and they agreed that some combination of black coffee and Midol might be necessary to keep him under control and functional. Regardless, they wouldn't waver from the plan.

When she returned to her table, McFadden greeted her.

"Hey there. The bartender said you wanted to speak to me. Is there a problem?"

"Not exactly. You probably don't remember me. We met a few weeks ago while I was having lunch. I'm Vivian."

"Vivian. That's right. You were three years behind me in high school. You said you had a crush on me."

"Guilty as charged."

"Well, what can I do for you?"

"I'm a little embarrassed to talk about this. Especially since we don't know each other. It's complicated. Do you have a minute?"

"That depends. What's this about?"

She trembled. "Gosh, it's so warm in here. I'm getting a little flustered. Sorry. It's a personal matter. I was hoping you'd be able to help me."

"Look, I don't have time for this. Do you have a legitimate complaint, or not?"

She put her head in her hands, and her top sank lower across her chest. "I don't know where to start."

The appearance of cleavage and a hint of black lace got McFadden's attention. He took a seat beside her. "Talk to me."

"Okay. I'll try. Let's see. Now I'm getting all tongue-tied. This is not easy to discuss." She toyed with a strand of her hair.

"Well?"

She leaned in so that her lips grazed his ear. "I want you," she whispered.

"Now I'm interested."

Vivian caressed his arm. "I was hoping you would be. To be completely honest, I've been thinking about you ever since we met a few weeks ago. Seeing you again has rekindled all kinds of feelings."

"And?"

"And I wanted to know if you could spare an hour or so."

"Right now?"

"Yes."

"Sure. Come on back to my office."

"That won't do. I was hoping for something a bit cozier. I'm staying at The Brentwood."

"Sorry, I can't be away that long tonight. Maybe we can get together later. After closing." He gave her a lengthy gaze, then disappeared into the dining area.

Vivian sighed, partly relieved. She had no intention of sleeping with the man. The thought of being alone with him made her skin crawl. She knocked back a few more ounces of courage, then answered her phone. "Amanda? Good timing. We may need to implement Plan B. Are you ready?"

"Hold that thought," Amanda replied. "I can't find a place to park this thing. There's some sort of major demonstration going on. A TV station's van is here, and the street is crawling with reporters. Women are picketing everywhere. Looks like some city official just arrived."

Vivian glanced outside. "Oh crap. I see it. What the hell? This is going to be interesting. I guess just keep circling the block until a space opens up."

"Okay, I'll try. But this is turning into a nightmare. Fast."

As Vivian contemplated a new strategy to lure McFadden out of his den of iniquity, a commotion near the entrance disrupted her thoughts. In walked the mayor, immaculately appointed from head to toe, and flanked by two burly primates in ill-fitting suits. Throngs of adoring admirers followed and began taking selfies with him. Her heart sank. *Perry. Oh, no. Not him. Not now.*

When the excitement tapered off, the master politician directed his two associates to take a seat. McFadden rushed up. "Welcome to McKenzie's, sir. It's truly an honor to have you here."

Perry stood beaming, soaking up the attention like a rock star mingling with his groupies. He looked even more devious in person and strangely distracted. His jaw visibly tensed while emoting, as if anger lay fermenting just beneath the surface.

Giddy with excitement, McFadden followed his every move, smiling awkwardly and laughing for no reason. Vivian saw through the masquerade, noticing a hint of anxiety in his fawning facade. His movements were stiff and unnatural, like a schoolboy on his way to a whipping. "What can I do for you tonight?" he asked.

Before he could answer, Perry caught a glimpse of Vivian. "We'll get to that in a minute, McFadden. But first, I must say hello to that incredibly beautiful lady seated over there next to the bar." He walked over to her table.

Vivian faked a smile. "Mr. Mayor, please sit down. I'm Viv. It's very nice to meet you."

"Likewise, Viv," he responded while settling into a chair. "I was going to ask you what you do for a living, but it's obvious. You must be a model."

"Ex-model, yes. I'm more of a consultant these days."

"Interesting. Perhaps you'd like to consult with me on my re-election campaign? I could use a female perspective."

"Re-election? Isn't it a little early for that?"

"I like to think ahead."

"Why would you assume I know anything about politics?"

"You don't need to know anything about politics. Just what women in this town want. You do have a handle on that, don't you?"

"I do, but couldn't you ask your wife for some advice in that area? It might be cheaper."

"Are you saying you're expensive?"

"Very."

He chuckled. "I'm afraid my wife is much too busy spending the family fortune to be bothered with my campaign. She never gets involved in politics. I'm in a bind right now because my last consultant didn't work out."

"That's right, I read about that. You gave her a high-profile job and she turned on you. Something about a lawsuit, I think. What an ungrateful bitch. Women don't know how to be accommodating anymore, do they?"

"At last, someone who gets it. I like you, Viv. I like you a lot. We should get together. Soon."

"Would that be for business or pleasure?"

He winked at her. "Why, all business, of course. I want you to work for me."

"I'll check my calendar."

Looking at his watch, Perry motioned to McFadden. "Would love to talk more with you, but unfortunately I've got some urgent business to discuss here with Mr. McFadden. Would you excuse us, please?"

Vivian ordered another drink, fearing what the men might be plotting as they absconded into the shadows. The noisy disturbance outside continued to grow. Shortly, McFadden returned, but he was staring at something outside.

"Where's the mayor?" Viv asked.

"He's in my office. Needed to make some calls."

All heads turned as a young vixen dressed in a sheer dress, fishnet stockings, and leopard-print heels waltzed through the door.

Vivian shrieked. "Amanda? Is that you? Get over here, girl. I didn't know you were in town."

The newcomer bounced over to Vivian's table and took a seat.

Amanda hiked up her dress, then gave the stunned McFadden a sultry gaze. "Yep. Just got back from a shoot for a camping wear company. Who have we here?"

Vivian smiled. "This is Gavin. He runs McKenzie's. Gavin, this is my friend Amanda."

McFadden plunked down on a chair with a jolt, unable to speak. Amanda put a hand on his knee. "Ooh, you run this place? That is so hot. I love men in power."

McFadden's eyes lit up. "Hi. Yes, I'm the manager and soon to be owner. Do I know you? You look familiar."

"Maybe. I specialize in erotica. This latest was the tamest gig I've had. I'm not a camper, but the money was good. It's a funny thing—my idea of roughing it is staying at a three-star hotel."

McFadden wiped his brow. "Erotica?"

"Yes. You might have run across an ad or two of mine. They

tend to appear on porn sites and such. Think garters, leather, whips, handcuffs, the usual stuff. Does that turn you on, Gavin?"

He nodded.

"Good, because I've got a few items most men would find interesting in the RV."

Vivian snorted. "You with an RV?"

"Yes, believe it or not—parked only a few blocks from here. It's been my home for the past couple of weeks. It's quite comfy and private, a great place to unwind. The perfect place for other activities, too. Would you like to see it?"

McFadden sprang up, a devilish grin on his face. "Hell yeah. I'd love to."

Vivian grabbed her purse. "Me, too. We could make it an evening. The three of us."

"What are we waiting for?" Amanda offered. "Let's go."

At that moment, a man with a trim physique in a form-fitting jacket appeared inside. He inspected every face in sight until finally settling on one. "Thank goodness. I finally found you."

Vivian gasped. *Oh shit.* "Dylan? What the hell are you doing here?"

"Looking for you, obviously. You don't return my texts. You don't return my calls. For days I've worried about you. What's a bloke to do?"

The man was supposed to be back in Australia where she left him. She was too shocked to respond.

Mac streaked over to gush at Amanda. "Wow. Hello, Abercrombie!"

McFadden shook his head. "Mac, what are you talking about? Abercrombie?"

"The way I see it, she's Abercrombie, and the other one is a bitch. So together, they're Abercrombie and Bitch! Get it?" He roared, pointing to Vivian. "Sorry, honey. I couldn't resist. I tried to pick her up earlier tonight, but she turned me down cold. Apparently, she prefers the ladies."

Dylan glared at Mac. "Vivian? Into women? No way, mate. Believe me, I know. Maybe she just doesn't like *you*."

"Now hold on a minute, Skippy," Mac blurted. "Don't get your knickers in a bunch. I'm just telling you what happened."

An older woman wearing a bright tie-dyed T-shirt joined the group. "Excuse me, the server over there said I should speak to the manager. Which one of you is Mr. McFadden?"

Irritated, McFadden waved her off. "Hold on a second, lady. Vivian, if you're into women, why were you hitting on me?"

Dylan squeezed in closer. "That's a fair question, Viv. Why *were* you hitting on him?"

Vivian stammered. "Well, —"

"Tell me this," Dylan said, putting his face close to hers. "Why are you so afraid of me? What did I do to hurt you? Do you have any kind of explanation? Can you please say something?"

Vivian sighed. "Look. Not a good time for this, okay?"

"I get it. So sorry. Let's just wait until the next time I fly all the way across the world to talk to you."

The woman in the T-shirt crouched beside Vivian. "Let's give her some room. Relax, dear. Forget about him and free yourself. It's okay to come out. Let the world see the real you. Keeping yourself bottled up is not good for the soul. I can help you calmly navigate these troubled waters. Just say the word."

Vivian leaned away from the woman. "Excuse me? Are you on crack?"

Before she could answer, a young man with red hair squeezed his way in next to McFadden. "Hey, guys. What's going on? Anybody check out the newspaper today? They were supposed to roll out a new Helvetica ten-point font, but I'm skeptical. Looks more like nine and a half to me. I liked the old Nimrod better. Don't even get me started on those new weather charts. Some of those axes have no labels. Seriously, can you believe it? Man, I am so constipated today."

McFadden rolled his eyes. "Not now, Charles."

Then, a large, distinguished-looking older man made his way

over from the bar, laughing and sneering as he poked his head into the motley assembly of characters. "I thought that was you, Julia," Thomas Telling said. Nice T-shirt. Trying to get more recruits for your bleeding-hearts club? Good luck with that at McKenzie's."

Julia scoffed. "If you must know, Thomas, this poor girl is in crisis. I'm trying to help her. She's dealing with core issues of sexuality. She's in denial."

"I'm totally lost," Dylan cried. "Will somebody please tell me what the hell is happening here? Is this some sort of intervention?"

Vivian shot out of her seat. "There is no intervention. This is just a huge misunderstanding. I'm perfectly fine!"

In a near hypnotic trance, Julia continued. "Are you sure, dear? You seem like such a suitable candidate for my Wednesday evening support group. There are so many souls like you struggling to find their identity. You'll learn to embrace the true essence of your being and love yourself for it. Let me guide you down the river on the inner-tube to self-discovery."

Vivian shook her head. "I don't get it. What inner tube? What river? I'm not following you."

"It's a metaphor for spiritual awareness. You see, discord arises when your brain and metaphysical inner core are at odds. It's a common problem, unfortunately. I can tell you this. You will never be at peace with yourself unless both are in sync. With the right therapy, I can make you whole again. The soul you were meant to be. Achieving holistic bliss is possible. But it's up to you to take the first step."

As Julia went on to explain her belief system, and the power of her particular form of transcendentalism, every patron within earshot became interested. One by one, they inched closer until a flock of listeners encircled the table, encouraging Vivian, asking questions, and sharing their own stories.

Losing his composure, the general growled, "Oh good grief,

lady. Don't listen to this horseshit. The only thing you need to embrace is the man who loves you. He's standing right over there. I don't know him, but he looks like a decent guy."

Applause and cheers arose from the crowd.

Mac continued to stare at Amanda. "Hey, beautiful. If *you're* not in a crisis, let me buy you a drink. Then we can go back to my place. If you play your cards right, I'll let you help me break in my new waterbed."

Amanda broke into laughter. "Wow. A waterbed? Are you kidding me? We can hit some discos, too. That is, if you'll wear your polyester leisure suit. Oh, wait. Never mind. Turns out I *don't* have boogie fever."

Charles gestured to Mac. "Hey, my man. Here's a fact you might find interesting, given your current situation. Did you know as a courting ritual, a male giraffe will rub the female's ass with his head until she pees?"

"Oh my god," Amanda cried. "Don't even think of rubbing *my* ass with anything. In what universe is that relevant?"

Charles took out his phone and tapped on the screen. "It's very relevant. I can even show you the reference right here. It's one step in the process of finding out if the female is ready to mate, you see. Then, the male—"

Amanda cringed. "That is, without a doubt, the grossest thing I have ever heard."

McFadden grabbed a menu from the table and threw it at Charles. "What the hell is the matter with you. Can't you act normal for once?"

Thomas groaned. "I, for one, have had enough of this crap. I need another drink."

"Thomas, I would think you'd be a little more understanding," Julia said. "And a little more patient. Especially given your grandson's situation."

"What are you talking about?"

"His problem."

"What problem?"

"Why don't you ask him, instead of ordering him around all the time like one of your minions? You must know he's deathly afraid of you. He'd rather die than disappoint."

Incensed, the general fired back. "Geez, Julia. Everything's a problem with you. Something to solve. I can assure you there's no problem. He's doing fine. He's on his way to a distinguished career in the military, just like me."

"Don't get me started on the military. That's a different issue. This problem has nothing to do with that."

"Don't you think I'd know if my own grandson had a problem?"

"Would you? Talk to him. And for once, please just listen. He's struggling right now."

Charles took a drink of his beer, then stifled a belch. "Excuse me, but I'm going to have to side with the lady, here. I ran into Johnson here a few nights ago."

The general towered over him, sneering. "So. What about it?"

McFadden exploded. "Damn it, that's it. I've heard enough. I don't care who's straight, who's not, or who can't make up their mind. I care about metaphysics as much as I do about quantum physics because I know nothing about either one. You folks can discuss this all night if you want. I've got more important things to do."

"Me too," cried Dylan as he stormed away.

The others focused their attention outside where an army of women had surrounded the restaurant, screaming in unison for the mayor. Police in riot gear tried to maintain order, but the protesters locked arms and refused to move. The bright lights and cameras from the local television station added a cinematic twist to the event as the crowd became increasingly agitated. Soon, Vivian joined the throngs of the curious wanting a better look.

A reporter stood nearby, conducting a live interview. "I'm standing here with Julia Chatham, political activist and celebrated author of dozens of self-help books who lives right here in Parish. Julia, what prompted you to organize this demonstration?"

"I represent a group of concerned citizens who are opposed to the appalling treatment of women by the existing city administration. In particular, we hold Mayor Robert Perry responsible. These decent, hard-working individuals deserve better."

"What evidence do you have of this?"

"We have sworn statements from several female employees who were dismissed from their positions without cause. As I'm sure you're aware, the most recent victim managed the mayor's election campaign. The people of Parish have a right to know about the atrocities taking place in their own town. This man cannot and will not be tolerated."

"And what are you hoping to accomplish tonight?"

"We want answers. The mayor's office has refused our repeated requests for a meeting. We're not leaving until he addresses our concerns."

Seconds later, with McFadden standing in the background, Perry bounced into the spotlight. Boos and chants of derision erupted. The reporter rushed over and requested a comment.

Perry stepped up to the microphone. "These are serious allegations and I assure you my office will take them up as soon as possible. It is our duty to maintain the highest standards of conduct as we represent the fine citizens of Parish."

"Sir, were you aware that Ms. Chatham's supporters have repeatedly requested a meeting?"

"Perhaps there was a miscommunication. I'm not aware of any such requests."

"What do you know about the pending lawsuit brought by your former campaign manager, Taylor Stanfield?"

"Unfortunately, Ms. Stanfield did not live up to expectations, according to our latest demographic analysis. We won the election, but we should have done much better with several key groups. I think what we have here is just a case of sour grapes.

That's all I have to say about that. Now, if you'll excuse me, I must tend to city business."

Julia grabbed the microphone. "Don't listen to him. That's a lie. All you ever do is lie, Perry. Why don't you be honorable for once and own up to your actions?"

As the mayor and his entourage tried to make their way through the demonstrators, McFadden became entangled in the resulting chaos. A few of the women tried to confront Perry, but his security guards stepped in. Infuriated, Julia flung the microphone in their direction. A melee ensued as the officers and the angry mob were gnarled in a shoving match. McFadden, still stuck in the fray, was too preoccupied with his own predicament to take notice of anything else. A man with no pants shouted "power to the people" as he rushed headlong into the middle of it all.

Horrified, Vivian could only watch as Reggie accosted the befuddled mayor who stood alone, briefly vulnerable in the momentary confusion. Perry pushed him away, but Reggie charged back, flailing his boa wildly. With each swing, it shed more of its feathers. To the delight of the onlookers, much of the plumage stuck to Perry's sweaty face despite his best efforts to remove it. When officers intervened, Reggie dazzled the crowd with lightning-fast moves to evade them, all the while taunting the mayor with a chicken dance, replete with syncopated clucks and squawks.

Additional patrol cars arrived, and Reggie fled the scene. A few of the men in blue gave chase but returned empty-handed. They were no match for the speed and agility of the mysterious agitator who gained brief notoriety as the "pantless wonder." When Julia and several of her supporters were hauled off in a paddy wagon, the crowd finally dispersed.

* * *

At The Brentwood, Vivian and Amanda dined on smoked salmon sushi rolls and white wine as they dissected the disastrous evening.

"I don't see how things could have gone any worse," Amanda said.

Vivian dabbed at a soy sauce stain on her dress with a wet napkin. "I know. We absolutely sucked tonight. And to top it off, I don't think this spot is coming out. Oh, screw me. I've got to break the news to poor Charlie somehow."

"How do you think she'll take it?"

"I'm not sure," Vivian said, "but she'll have to appreciate your efforts. I know I do. You looked amazing tonight, by the way."

"Really?" Amanda gushed. "That means a lot, coming from you."

"I have no doubt you have what it takes to become a model. I could make some calls if you're interested."

"I'm flattered, but no thanks. Working for my dad has opened my eyes. I'm going back to school to get my degree. This time I'll be serious about it."

"Good for you."

As the evening continued, Vivian delved into her relationship with Dylan. Amanda talked about her own misadventures at State as well as Charlie's numerous alcohol-induced episodes. Vivian relived her days in Omega Chi, then launched into salacious stories about her career in modeling. Amanda listened intently. Even her wildest experiences seemed tame by comparison. After a sobering discussion on the state of political affairs in Parish, she headed home.

As Vivian sat alone, collecting her thoughts, a late-breaking story appeared on the television in the bar. The recent demonstration at McKenzie's looked even more frenetic on the screen than it had in person and rekindled her distaste for local government officials. The mayor came across as decent and sincere as he smarmed his way through a second interview. *You don't fool me, you prick.* Absorbed in the critical commentary, she was oblivious to the man approaching.

"Hi, Viv," Dylan said.

She flinched. "My god. How do you keep finding me?"

"You do know I'm a detective, right?"

"Yes. But what do you want?"

"Great to see you, too."

"I'm sorry. That was rude. Let's start over. It *is* great to see you. I've just had a very shitty day."

"Kind of like mine?"

"Sorry. Yes."

"Care to tell me about it?"

"It's a long story. A very long story."

"I've got all night. And no place to go."

"Okay. Sure. We can talk about that. But first, you didn't answer the question. "What do you want?""

"Look, Viv, I—"

"Oh, please. You're not about to get down on one knee, are you?"

Dylan smiled. "You never know. I might just surprise you."

"Don't screw with me. We've been over this before."

"Whoa. Relax. No need to make a scene. You've made your position on the subject clear. This is *not* a marriage proposal."

"Thank goodness for that. Exactly what is it, then?"

"I missed you, and as I said earlier, I was worried about you."

"I see."

"Look, Viv. I like you. I want us to spend more time together. Since I've never been to the States, I'd love it if you could show me around a bit. Who knows? Maybe I'll consider staying for a while."

"Okay."

"You do like me, don't you?"

"Of course."

"Then what's the problem? You don't seem excited."

"I just don't want this to turn serious too fast."

"Neither do I. That's why we're going to take it a day at a time. No pressure."

She looked away. "Well—"

"Damn it, Viv. What are you so afraid of? I'm not asking for a commitment. I just want to know you better. What's wrong with that?"

"I like you, Dylan. More than anyone I've ever known. That's why I don't want to screw things up."

"I take it that's happened before?"

"I'm afraid so."

"What did you do?"

"I got drunk one night and slept with his best friend."

"Okay. An unfortunate mistake. And he never forgave you?"

"No."

"Why not?"

"We were married at the time."

"Oh."

"There you have it. Now you know, I'm not exactly perfect."

"And you think I am?"

"Have you ever cheated on someone?"

"No."

"I didn't think so. You're kind, understanding, smart, and incredibly sexy. Why waste your time with me?"

"I get it now. You made a mistake. And you think you have to keep beating yourself up for that. The string of failed relationships. Putting up barriers. Never getting close. Viv, you don't have to live like that. You'll never be able to move on unless you can forgive yourself."

"Maybe. But I'll completely understand if you walk away."

Dylan took her hand. "What? Do you think I have a few kangaroos loose in my top paddock? What kind of a bloke would I be if I walked away from the best thing that's ever happened to me? When we were together back home, I was on top of the world. I don't want to lose that feeling. Ever."

Vivian smiled. "Okay, bloke. What now?"

"Can you please tell me what that was all about earlier at McKenzie's? Were you on the piss?"

Laughing, Vivian handed him a menu. "Somewhat. I'll tell you all about it. But you might want to order a drink first and settle in. Like I said, it's a long story."

* * *

Charlie trotted into the apartment and tossed her bag on the sofa. Now that her Sociology final was out of the way, she felt a tinge of relief. Only the English Lit exam stood between her and the end of the semester and the dreaded encounter with Shelton. While the test posed little threat to her wellbeing, the idea of facing her professor again weighed on her like an eerie passage from a Stephen King novel. Despite her best efforts to shed it, the terrifying thought kept hanging on.

In the kitchen, she made a grocery list, then heated up leftovers from the fridge. As she savored her homemade lasagna, muffled sounds emanated from the hallway. "Mom, why are you still up? Have you had your dinner?"

"Yes."

"Did you do your exercises tonight?"

"Yes."

"Did you take your meds?"

"Yes."

"Did you take them with food?"

"Yes."

"Do I nag you and ask too many questions?"

"Yessss."

"So, everything's okay?"

"I think so. How was your exam? Did you ace it?"

"Let's just say I passed. Now go to sleep. You need your rest."

"Yes, doctor," said Beverly. "But first, can I see you for a minute?"

Suddenly worried, Charlie shot out of the kitchen and rushed down the hall to her mother's bedroom. "You're scaring me, Mom. What's wrong? Did we get an eviction notice?"

"No, dear. But I'll tell you what *is* wrong. I'm a complete ass."

"What are you talking about?"

"After all you've done for me, after all of the sacrifices you've made to get me though this, I've never thanked you—not once. I've been so bitter about the accident I was totally focused on myself. Please forgive me, honey. From the bottom of my heart, I'm sorry. And thanks for being such a wonderful daughter."

Charlie smiled. "I haven't always lived up to that standard but you're definitely welcome."

They hugged, then continued bonding by reliving some of their happier days as a family—a summer trip to Europe, hiking the Appalachian Trail, and frequent visits to the beach. When Beverly drifted off to sleep, Charlie felt a mix of joy and bitterness. She and her mother had never been closer, but why had it taken a tragedy to bring them together?

Back in the kitchen, her thoughts turned to English Lit and what questions Shelton might ask on the final. She studied her notes until a knock from the front stoop interrupted her mental essay on the poetry of W.B. Yeats. *Who the hell could that be so late?*

Charlie looked through the peephole and gasped. Speechless, she opened the door and stared. There he was in the flesh—the same unruly hair, the same piercing eyes, the same broad shoulders. Her lips quivered as her stoic façade began to melt. Tears held captive for months flowed freely.

"You've got to cut out that crying stuff," he said. "You know what it does to me. Hey, can you give your old man a hug?"

"Holy moly, Dad. I sure can."

They embraced for a moment, melded as one, each clinging to the life force that was so embedded in their existence. The long time apart had been kind to neither. Without her adoration and uplifting presence, his life had had little meaning. Without his daily dose of warmth and paternal guidance, she'd been lost.

Even so, her elation was short-lived. She could no longer ignore the mounting resentment simmering within.

Inside, he took a seat on the sofa while Charlie kept her distance, eyeing him suspiciously.

"You look so amazing. Just like your mother. Where is she, by the way?"

"She's asleep. It's after eleven."

"Okay. So, tell me how you've been."

"Don't bullshit me, Dad."

"What kind of talk is that? So this is my welcome home?"

"Are you kidding me? What did you expect! You waltz in here after disappearing for years with no explanation and act like nothing's happened. Do you have any idea what we've been through?"

"Well.."

"Why did you abandon us? Why couldn't you bother to make one damn phone call to explain?"

"Charlie..."

"Never mind—I can see it in your face. And I'll have you know while you were out chasing the bimbos, Mom's been through hell and back. She was working two jobs after you left to keep us afloat. One night she was so tired she fell asleep at the wheel on the way home. Do you know she almost died in that accident? We couldn't afford insurance, so the medical bills were insane. We lost the house. We're still up to our ears in debt. And it hasn't exactly been a picnic for me, either. I mean, how could you do that to us?"

"I'm sorry for what happened. I had no idea. I've got some money, so I can help."

"That's not good enough, Dad. You were my hero, and you let me down. I deserve some fucking answers, and I want them now!"

He looked away for a moment to hide the humiliation on his face. "Charlie, I never meant to abandon you. I was in over my head. One thing led to another, and things just spiraled out of control. It's inexcusable. The pain and suffering I've put you and your mom through—I can only imagine."

"But why? Were you so unhappy that you needed a series of trollops to fill the void in your life?"

"No, honey. I still love your mother. And you. With all my heart. That will never change."

"Dad, I'm not a stupid little kid anymore. I'm not buying that crap. If that were true then you never would have disappeared in the first place. Why can't you just be honest with me?"

He took a shaky breath. Then, misty-eyed, he answered. "Okay. I'm in trouble and I need help."

Astonished to see her father in such a state, she stepped closer. "What kind of trouble?"

"It's a long, sad story. I've been through my own personal hell. I'm a drug addict, Charlie."

"Oh my god, Dad! You? But how? You were always so together. There was never any indication—"

"I *was* in control. Until the day I hurt my back."

"I remember that."

"That's when it started. Prescription opioids. They took care of the pain at first. I was able to fake it at work and at home most of the time, but then I needed more and more to manage it. My source dried up, so I was forced to venture into other areas, but nothing seemed to work as well. It got out of hand and your mother got suspicious. I would do anything for that high. I got mixed up in some shady business deals. First in Parish, then down south. Some days, I didn't even know who I was."

"I'm so sorry. Are you getting help for this?"

"I just got into a program. So I've got a long way to go. Is it okay if I sleep here tonight?"

"Of course."

"Charlie, I'm embarrassed to admit this. I've done some horrendous things, illegal things. I've hurt people. Hell, I should probably go to prison. I've been a failure as a husband and a father."

"But you're not, Dad," she said, sliding in next to him. "You're turning your life around and Mom and I are going to help. We'll get through this together. What you're doing takes a lot of guts. You've come back to us. You're admitting your mistakes. I'm proud of you for that. You're not a failure. You're a survivor. And I still love you. I promise that will never change."

"I don't deserve you, or your mom," he said, the guilt still written on his face.

"Yes you do. We're here for you. Always."

CHAPTER 30

Charlie drove into McKenzie's vacant parking lot and shut off the sputtering engine, ready to begin her shift. She sat for a while, enjoying a warm breeze as it passed through the cabin. She didn't think it possible, but with her family reunited she felt sane again. Even Aunt Viv seemed like a different person. The wounds from her father's long separation were still fresh but she had confidence they would heal in time. The new normal was weird but good.

It had been a busy and productive week. Wednesday night's carefully planned sting operation at McKenzie's was a success despite the multiple hiccups. In the end, Reggie gained possession of the huge volume of meth scheduled for delivery, and the Cuban buyers received several boxes of lovely paper napkins. Only one had the hidden prize inside. Julia Chatham's wild demonstration against the mayor and Reggie's well-timed antics had made it possible for Lydia to make the switch.

Charlie breezed through Shelton's final exam and submitted the remaining edits on their journal article as promised. Their brief interaction turned out not to be the nightmare she anticipated. She treated him with an air of professional courtesy, and he returned the favor by acting as if nothing had happened between them. Leaving his classroom with a smile, she closed her English Lit text with a thud, marking the end of the course and their brief relationship.

A chemist at the university had confirmed the powder she'd lifted from the plant was more than ninety-five percent pure crystal methamphetamine. Using this, along with the video evidence she'd recorded that night on her cell phone, Alex was well into their tell-all story, soon to be supplemented with information from McFadden's ledger. Without question, the sleepy little hamlet of Parish would be in for a rude awakening when the exposé hit the media. According to Alex, this was career-making stuff, and fodder for all the major news outlets. Not bad for a small town, part-time first-year student who schlepped inferior cuisine and spirits for a living.

McFadden ran out to greet her. "Gosh! You're early, Charlie. Even for you."

"Yes, sir, and I'm ready to roll. Is the list of specials ready?"

"Not quite. Say, you're in a good mood, and you look great. Have you done something different with your hair?"

"No. But thanks anyway. Something tells me we're going to be busy today. Is Chelsea here?"

"Not yet. But Lydia's on her way. And I've got a new girl coming in. So, we should be fine. In fact, I was thinking about taking the day off."

"Really? Why?"

"Why not? It's a beautiful day—too nice to be cooped up in a stuffy restaurant. You should do the same."

"Mr. McFadden, I'd love to, but It wouldn't be fair to the others. And to be honest, I need the money."

"I love your car. Is this the original upholstery? Mind if I check it out?" Before she knew it, he was sitting next to her, admiring the interior, and asking dozens of questions.

"It's cool that you're so interested, but shouldn't we be getting inside?"

"Not now. Tell you what—let's go for a little drive."

Charlie thought it was a joke, but McFadden didn't look amused. He pulled a revolver out of his jacket and stuck it in her side.

"What the hell?" she yelled. "Have you lost your mind?"

"Shut up and drive, bitch!"

"Okay, okay." Charlie started the engine.

"Take a left out of here, then follow my directions. And don't do anything stupid."

Charlie obeyed his orders. Minutes later, as they were approaching the outskirts of Parish, her tension had reached a peak. She knew this escapade was not likely to end well. He might be able to overpower her, but under no circumstances would she give in to him without a fight.

McFadden noticed her white-knuckled grip on the steering wheel. "Don't be nervous, honey. I thought you deserved a little break, so we're going on a retreat. That's all. I've been waiting so long to pay you back for everything."

She fidgeted in her seat. "Where is this place?"

"A little off the beaten path. Most people don't know about it."

"What's it called?"

"You'll love it. It's on the water. Just keep driving. You're doing great. A few more miles and we'll be there."

As the scenery rolled by, Charlie willed herself not to panic. She hadn't been on the west side of town in years. It was a sparsely populated area consisting of open land, mobile homes, and the occasional convenience store. From the looks of it, little had changed. Here, you'd be more likely to encounter a chicken ranch than some classy resort. This was not good.

When they crossed the city limits, McFadden had her turn off the highway and on to an unmarked dirt road. After dozens of twists and turns through a series of muddy lanes, they came to a stop at a secluded hideaway overlooking a small inlet on the water.

Surrounded by tall pines, the rustic A-frame was badly in need of repair, with a sagging roof, rotting cedar siding, and broken windows. An attached deck looked even worse, with missing floorboards and a collapsed railing.

"Nice place," she said. "Do you mind taking the hardware out of my ribs?"

"No problem. It wasn't loaded anyway." He stashed the gun in his jacket. Come on, we're going inside for a few minutes."

Charlie didn't budge. "And then what? A lovely picnic on the lake?"

"Something like that. Just cooperate and everything will be fine."

"I'm not an idiot. I know what's happening. But what did I do to deserve this? I've been a model employee."

"Model employee my ass! He flung open his door, grabbed Charlie, and dragged her out of the car with him. She tried to pull away, but his grip was firm. "Don't pull that innocent shit on me, girl. It's high time you get what you deserve."

"What are you talking about?"

"Do you think *I'm* an idiot? I know what you've been up to. First, you had no business snooping around my office, but that wasn't enough. You had to go sticking your nose in where it doesn't belong at the plant. I don't know what you were doing, but for damn sure you're not doing it again."

Charlie screamed while struggling to free herself as he dragged her over the soft terrain towards the run-down chalet.

McFadden smiled. "That's what I love about this place. You can yell all you want. There's nobody around for miles."

Inside, he took off his jacket and ordered her to strip. "I've waited so long to violate that pert little body. Now get on with it."

Charlie stood firm. "Go to hell."

He pushed her against a wall, then took off his belt. Striking her repeatedly on the legs and torso, he tossed her to the floor. As she scrambled to escape, he struck her again. "That's for leading me on, you whore! And I'm just getting started. By the time I'm through with you, you'll be swimming with the fishes."

When he stopped to catch his breath, Charlie grabbed a cushion from an old couch and assumed a defensive position. He lashed out, narrowly missing her. On the next attempt, his fierce blows shredded the shabby material, scattering grimy remnants everywhere. She darted across the room, slinging any object she could find in his direction. First a lamp, then a folding chair, and finally three framed photographs from a dusty table landed at his feet. Undeterred, he charged after her, but she slipped past him and up the stairs.

The loft was bare except for a recliner and a stack of old newspapers. McFadden stood below, a deranged look on his face, waiting for Charlie to make a move. "If you want to get out, you'll have to get by me. And I'm in no hurry."

"You don't think you can get away with this, do you? My family will report me missing. The police will investigate."

"Are you kidding, me? You *are* naïve, Charlie. The police here don't give a shit about what happens to you. Or anyone else for that matter. They're conspiring with Scolina and Perry, and they'll continue to be for some time. As far as I know, you didn't show up for work today. Who knows? Maybe you decided to leave town. Happens all the time."

"And what about you?"

"Oh, I've been with Perry all day on business. He'll vouch for me."

"So, you've got it all figured out."

"You're damn right I do. It's too bad it had to come to this. You should have slept with me when you had the chance."

"What difference would that have made?"

"Well, for one thing, you probably wouldn't be stuck in my loft right now."

"I doubt that. Why should I even listen to you?"

"Because I still have a thing for you, Charlie. I might even cut you a deal. Why don't you come down and we'll talk about it?"

She gazed out the window where the lake lay like a silver sheet, taut and uncompromising. The lush, green growths of spring surrounding it were brilliantly reflected on its surface. To any other observer, it was a sight to behold. To Charlie, it was a stark reminder of the deadly depths awaiting her. It seemed a cruel fate, to fade into dank murkiness forever. She vowed to take the lunatic down with her. "Okay. You win. I'm coming down," she said, taking slow, deliberate steps. Near the bottom, she paused. "I have one condition. Lose the belt."

He laughed. "Little lady, you are in no position to negotiate. I own your ass. And your father's, for that matter. That's right. I knew your name sounded familiar. I went back through my records. He worked with us some time ago. So, you see, you have no choice."

"Don't you dare do anything against my father, you asshole." She took a quick step and braced herself between the wall and the railing. A lightning-fast kick to his chest sent him flying into the corner. She nearly made it to the door, but he lunged forward, and a swipe of his hand sent her stumbling to the floor. He was on her in a second.

"Okay, we'll do this the easy way," he said, clutching her throat.

She wriggled underneath him, unable to breathe. Slowly, his expression changed. His eyes rolled back, like a wild animal about to feast on its prey.

As she began to lose consciousness, Charlie flashed back to the night in his office when he brazenly stroked her leg. Now again, his cold, lifeless finger was on her skin. Summoning all her strength, she snapped it back with one quick motion. He rolled aside, howling like the beast he was. She unlatched the door and scrambled outside to the deck.

McFadden leaped after her, but his weight was too much for the rickety structure, which swayed, then gave way completely, trapping them both beneath a jumble of rot and decay. Charlie inched forward through the rubble and grabbed a loose board with a rusty nail sprouting from its edge. Slicing through the air, she landed it in his mangled hand.

He flailed about in the dirt, then screamed as he eased the nail out. Blood oozed down his shirt sleeve. "You're dead, you little shit!"

Charlie fought to escape his meaty arms as he encircled her legs, stood up, and hauled her backward through the open field like a farm implement. But she thrashed at him relentlessly until he lost his balance and they both fell to the ground near the edge of the water. As they lay panting on the soggy earth, a car careened onto the property, fishtailed through the loose soil, and skidded to a stop only a few feet away.

A heavyset man with dark hair and a mustache jumped out of the passenger side. He grabbed McFadden by the collar and hauled him to his feet. "*Buenos noches, Senõr*! We've been looking for you. We need to talk."

"Get the hell off my property. Now," McFadden spat defiantly.

"I would love to oblige, but you see, I'm afraid there's the matter of some product we paid a lot of money for that you failed to deliver. Twenty-seven boxes, to be exact. My boss does not take kindly to getting the short end of a business deal. He wants to see you. There needs to be restitution."

"I don't know what you're talking about."

The man took out a gun. "Oh, I think you do. Let's go. Now!"

Charlie watched as McFadden was bound with tape and forced into the back seat of the car. At the same time, a petite female emerged from the driver's seat. The man with the gun took her place at the wheel and drove off, ignoring his captive's screams of protest.

The woman ran over to Charlie and helped her up. "Are you all right?"

"Lydia? It's a miracle you showed up. He was trying to kill me."

"Are you hurt?"

"A few cuts and bruises but I think I'll survive."

"We should get you to the hospital."

"No, it's okay."

"So he didn't—"

"No."

"I was so worried about you. When you didn't show up for work, I knew something bad had happened."

"It almost did. Who *was* that guy?"

"Not a clue. All I know is he came into McKenzie's looking for McFadden. He paid me five hundred dollars upfront to drive him here."

"That was a very brave thing for you to do. But how did you know where to find me? This place is in the middle of nowhere."

Lydia looked away, hiding the anguish on her face. The sight of McFadden's shabby retreat had rekindled her shame at the forced intimacy she'd endured there. Each occurrence had been brief, turbulent, and impossible to forget—moist breath reeking of booze, sweaty hands groping her flesh, the perfunctory act rooted in vengeance more than desire. After his quick departures, she'd stay there terrified and alone, consumed by anger. How many others had paid the price for his deep-seated hatred of women?

"Sorry to be so emotional," she said. "He used to take me to this godawful place when I first started at McKenzie's. I've tried to put it out of my mind. But it's hard."

"Oh, sweetie. That's terrible."

"You know what? I'm getting over it. I'll survive. It's good this happened because I learned a valuable lesson tonight. I trusted my instincts and it worked. You're okay and our bastard of a boss is gone. Something tells me he's not coming back. Now let's get out of here."

"Sounds good to me. There's this thing I need to take care of at the restaurant, then I'm calling it a night."

Charlie took the wheel and they headed for the road.

"Wait," Lydia asked. "How much gas do you have?"

"Nearly a full tank. Why?"

"There's something *I* need to do—for my own sanity."

By the time they rolled into McKenzie's parking lot, flames

had gutted the dilapidated A-frame. In a matter of minutes, it would be reduced to a heap of ashes. Months would pass before it was discovered.

249

CHAPTER 31

Johnson sat in his usual booth, picking at the well-done steak on his plate. It felt strange to be dining alone at McKenzie's on a Friday evening, and the crowd made him uncomfortable. Everyone was focused on him as if the big, blinking "L" in his latest nightmare were visible on his forehead. His life was dreadful.

He was still on the outs with Tyrell, and the memory of his encounter with the man at the bar bewildered him. Now he understood why so many people drank. He stared at the glass of golden brew in front of him and summoned the courage to take a sip. *Yuck. Who drinks this stuff?* He settled his bill and left.

As he strode across the tattered asphalt, he continued to ruminate, likening his shadow to the secret he couldn't escape. *Why am I so bothered by this?* Surely, the act was out of character for him, a one-time fling between two consenting adults, but it didn't have to define him. Or did it?

Ahead, he noticed a woman hunched over the fender of a red convertible, flashlight in hand, muttering to herself. He walked up to her and poked his head under the hood.

"Hi there. Need some help?"

She acknowledged him with a grunt, then continued her inspection of the engine.

Johnson circled the car, then poked his head in again. "You're on your way to a flat rear."

She hiked up her skirt. "Excuse me? Are you talking about my ass?"

"No. I mean your rear tire. On the passenger side. Not flat, but it isn't fully inflated. Almost imperceptible, but I notice these things. You should check the pressure."

"Thanks, but I've got bigger problems right now."

"Also, your front's lopsided. That's to be expected, though. From the looks of your body here, I'd say it's been driven pretty hard."

"Excuse me, but are you trying to be insulting? If so, you're doing a pretty good job."

"Huh? I'm talking about your front suspension. On this side. See how it droops? It may be a strut. Or a shock absorber. I don't know which one you have. In any case, you should have that checked out."

"Got it. Anything else?"

"I'm no expert, but I'd be willing to bet your chassis could use some work. It'll make an enormous difference. Trust me."

"My chassis is just fine, thank you. Let me guess. You think I need a grease job."

"Yes! When's the last time you were properly lubricated?"

"Are you kidding? Now that you mention it—oh, never mind. Look, you'll need to excuse me, I've had a bad day and I'm trying to troubleshoot this starting problem."

"Oh, I see. Have you checked the—"

"Ground connection?" she asked, tugging on a cable. "Doing that right now. It may be a little loose, but that's not it."

"What about the—"

"Fuses? Yes."

"How about the—"

"Fuel pump relay? It's brand new."

"Starter solenoid?"

"I don't think so."

"It might start if you try re-seating the main relay. It's the one—"

"I know which one it is."

"Roger that."

"Hey, since you're standing right there, can you hand me a twelve millimeter?" She pointed to a toolbox on the ground.

Johnson handed her the wrench.

She checked the battery terminals. "These are tight. How did you learn about automotive electrical systems?"

"My grandfather taught me a lot about old cars. He loves them."

"Cool." After disconnecting a small silver box from the engine bay, she held it up to the light. "Look at this. You were right. One of the contacts has some corrosion. I can fix that. There's a file somewhere in that tray. Thanks for the tip."

"No problem," Johnson said. "By the way, nice jacket. The one there in the back seat. Where did you get it? I used to have one just like it."

"I got it during my first semester at State. It belonged to a foot-ball player."

"No way! That's funny. I used to play football at State. I had a jacket just like that one, but I lost it somehow."

"Holy moly! Wait a minute. Did you put your phone number in the lining, by any chance?"

"As a matter of fact, I did. It was special. It belonged to my dad, you see."

"I can't believe this. You're the guy. I tried to call you one night some time ago but got your voicemail, so I sent you a text. I'm Charlie, and that's your jacket."

"Hold on. I'm confused. *You're* Charlie? From McKenzie's?"

"If I didn't know better, I'd think you're a little disappointed."

"I didn't mean it that way. It's just I already met Charlie from McKenzie's. At the bar. He told me all about what happened. I mean he gave me a lot of details I didn't need to hear."

"I don't know what to tell you. *I'm* Charlie. I'm the one from the locker room during the Tech game."

"So, you were there, too?"

"Sure was. Am I that forgettable?"

"Not at all. I don't see how I could have ever forgotten your face. But that's the problem. I'm having trouble remembering anything that happened that day. I just can't figure how this other Charlie knew me."

"Well, I'm fairly sure it was just the two of us. Maybe he knew you from State. Was he a football player?"

"No. He said he was one of the trainers, I think."

"You said you met him at the bar?"

"That's right."

"What did he look like?"

"As far as I could tell, about my height, slim build, with red hair. I didn't recognize him at all."

"Oh my gosh. I'll bet that was Charles Dennison. He comes into McKenzie's every night. Drinks a lot. He'll say anything. He's a little out there."

"So, are you saying he was just messing with me?"

"I'm afraid so. But why in the world would you believe that wackadoodle in the first place?"

"Because I'm a first-class idiot! His name was Charlie, he had my number, he sent me a text. What's not to believe, right? I have little recall of that day. When I told him I couldn't remember, he told me all about our little meeting. Oh man, this changes every-thing! What a dirty trick to play on someone."

"My memory's been a little hazy, too. In my defense, I was very drunk that day. I finally pieced things together when I ran into my old roommate. What's your excuse?"

"Concussion. Got it at the end of the game when I collided with a linebacker. The whole day's been a blur ever since."

"Well, I'm glad you ran into *me* tonight. I've wanted to thank you for what you did. Rescuing an inebriated damsel in distress and all. Most guys would have taken advantage of the situation."

"I have no idea what I did, but I'm glad it worked out."

"Me too. So, what are you up to these days?"

"I'm an Army Specialist at Camp Conrad. I work with an IT unit that develops software applications for national defense."

"That's awesome. I would love to get some technical training at State. I'm thinking about switching my major."

"You're actually interested in that stuff?"

"Absolutely. Computers. Programming. Stats. Data science. I'm a true nerd at heart. Can you recommend some courses?"

Delighted, Johnson launched into a lengthy overview of his studies at State, talking passionately about processors, logic, mathematics, and programming languages. Equally excited, Charlie asked dozens of questions, leading to a discussion about applications and career paths. When the topic of conversation shifted to sports, Johnson elaborated on his football career and theories on offensive formations.

"Holy moly, do you ever know your stuff. Do you miss it?"

"Miss what?"

"Come on. It's so obvious. Now don't get me wrong. I can tell you love your work. But your face lit up like it was Christmas morning when we started talking about football. You're so passionate about it. You have an amazing memory and a keen sense for detail."

"You're right, Charlie. I never realized how much I've missed it until now. This is amazing. I just had, what do they call it—an epiphany?"

"I think so."

"Yes! I finally got a word right!"

"Glad I could help. Would it be okay to call you sometime? I still have lots of questions."

"Roger that. Now I know it's getting late, but I have a burning question for you. It's been on my mind for quite a while."

"Okay. Shoot."

"What were *you* doing hanging around the locker room that day?"

"That's a fair question. The truth is, I was pledging a sorority. I was supposed to prance into the locker room at halftime and get the football team jazzed up for the second half. Under the guise of school spirit, of course. As I told you, I was very drunk at the time and mostly naked."

"Did that happen?"

"Nope. I never made it inside the actual locker room."

"Why not?"

"As I remember, we were having a very interesting discussion, but at some point, I think I passed out."

"So, I saw you?"

"Well, not exactly. I was hiding in a bathroom stall trying to muster up the courage to make my grand entrance when you showed up."

"That's right! It's coming back to me, I think. I slipped out just before Coach began his pep talk. I walk in and I see one of your fancy shoes on the floor. It didn't look like something one of my teammates would wear."

Charlie laughed. "Probably not. Then you called out, and I must have answered in a drunken stupor. There was some banter back and forth. You said something about a similar incident happening when you were a freshman."

"That's right! It didn't end so well for that poor girl."

"I gathered that. Then you said something about me keeping my dignity."

"Yeah, that sounds like me."

Charlie tossed the file and the wrench back into the toolbox. "That's all I remember. When I woke up, I was in the basement of my dorm."

"And you think I did that?"

"I don't think I could have walked that far in my condition. So, you must have scooped me up and taken me all the way across campus."

"You know what, I did. I remember that walk, now. It was getting cold that day and the campus was deserted. Every soul at State was at the game. I think you had mentioned your dorm, so there I am trudging along in the rain with this beautiful, almost naked female in my arms while the band played on at the stadium. I get to Anderson Hall, and I must have wrapped you up in my jacket to keep you warm."

"So, you think I'm beautiful? That's funny. I've been called a lot of things in my life, but no guy has ever said *that* to my face."

"How could they not? Are they blind? I mean, look at you. Your face, your hair, your...everything is perfect."

"Oh, stop making fun of me. Even on a good day, I know I'm a mess. But tonight—"

"Shh." He leaned in closer, gazing into her eyes. They were kind and inviting, a mysterious shade of blue. He couldn't look away.

"Wait. Holy moly. You're not kidding. You really think so, don't you?"

"Yes, I do. I remember now. It's all a lot clearer. I wanted to kiss you that day. I don't suppose I could do that now?"

"Okay by me."

Their lips met, tenderly at first. Then their kisses became deeper, more urgent. Johnson tingled with excitement as the emotions came flooding back. In an instant, everything crystallized. The walk across campus. The National Anthem playing in the background. His uncontrollable passion for her. Just as it had the first time, holding her in his arms felt right. But with this kiss came no uneasiness, no second thoughts, only pure joy. It was true what they said. Some things were meant to be.

CHAPTER 32

As the business-as-usual day began, commuters filled the highway, students attended classes, and shop owners readied their wares, all of them ignorant of the coming changes. The persistent haze of deceit in the Parish skyline would soon be lifted, altering the lives of many, and resulting in a turning point for one. In the ensuing hours, Mayor Robert M. Perry, the Chief of Police, and several other city officials would be charged with corruption. Federal agents would raid the old factory, seizing hundreds of pounds of crystal meth. A major news article would appear and be picked up by media outlets around the country. Interviews would be held. Endless questions would be asked.

Around midday, Charlie sat on her favorite bench in the town square, feeding pigeons with the leftover crumbs from a pastry. A man wearing dark glasses and a light summer suit approached and sat beside her. He placed a shiny briefcase in his lap and opened it, took out an envelope, and handed it to her. "Here you go. Your share. You earned every penny of it."

Charlie opened the envelope, took out some bills, and handed it back to him. "Thanks, Reggie. This will do."

Reggie took off his glasses and thumbed through the money. "You didn't take it all. What's up?"

"I'm splitting my portion with Lydia. I want you to take the remainder and give half to a woman named Emmaline. You can find her at the shelter. Give the rest to Antoine, your former associate. Those two need it much more than me."

"Man. That's generous. Are you sure about this?"

"I am. I've been fortunate. Things could have turned out differently. I got my family back. I'm in school. I've got a future. There's no need to be greedy."

"You're a good person, Charlie J."

"I'm trying to be. So, what's next on your agenda?"

"I'm out of the business for good, enrolling at State in the fall to get my bachelor's. Then I'm going to seminary school. I feel the calling."

"That's wonderful. I predict great things for you, Reverend Reggie."

"That's Reverend Just Reggie to you, princess."

"Of course. My bad."

"So, what about you? When's your story hitting the streets? I can't wait to read it."

"By the end of the day, I hope. Alex is making the final edits."

"Things will never be the same around here, you know."

"You've got that right, and it's a good thing."

Reggie smiled. "Amen to that."

* * *

Later, Charlie meandered the downtown streets in a solitary confinement of angst and guilt. Yet another text message was ignored as she wrestled with her conscience. Hers was not the only future at stake, and any decision she made would have long-term consequences. Over and over, she debated the pros and cons of each course of action, sometimes doubting herself as well as her intentions. At last, she was resolved. Only one course felt rational, but it would change everything. She readied herself for the conversation, then phoned Alex.

"My god, Charlie, finally. I've been trying to reach you all morning. We need to talk."

"Sorry. I got tied up with some other business."

"Whatever. Look, I've got some questions. We're supposed to go to press this afternoon, but there are some serious gaps in the stuff you sent me."

"Can you give me an example?"

"For one thing, the information you photographed from his records isn't complete. There's activity for a period last year that's missing. What happened to it?"

"I'm not sure. I was in such a hurry to get out of McFadden's office that night I must have missed some of the pages. But that's okay. The police should have the source document. You can just fill in the blanks with that."

"Come on. You know better than that. It would take days for us to get access, if at all. It doesn't matter, anyway. The investigators haven't been able to recover the ledger from McFadden's office. Like him, it has vanished."

"That's a bummer."

"You wouldn't know anything about that, would you Charlie?"

"No. I guess McFadden must have stashed it somewhere else."

"But they checked his apartment. Where else could it be?"

"I wouldn't know."

"Charlie, I'm sure you know tampering with evidence is a criminal offense."

"Alex, I want my name off the byline."

"What the hell are you talking about? Why?"

"I've had second thoughts about this story, and investigative journalism in general. It's a lot harder than I thought. It's painstaking, laborious. So much checking, so many details to consider."

"Are you crazy? You said that's the kind of stuff you love.

Getting your hands dirty. Discovering the truth. What happened?"

"I don't know. I'm just not cut out for it. I'm thinking about something not so stressful, like a career in the tech field."

"That's okay, I guess. If you like that sort of thing. But Charlie, most of my colleagues would kill for a chance like this. This is the big time. I think you're making a huge mistake."

"Maybe so, but I wouldn't feel right otherwise. I screwed up gathering the evidence, and I didn't give it my best effort. I don't deserve the recognition."

"Not from where I'm sitting. Come on. You worked your ass off. You even risked your life. What's going on here?"

"It's a personal thing. A change of heart. It's that simple."

"Charlie, don't bullshit me. I've been in this business a long time. I know when something doesn't add up. You sure you don't have something to tell me?"

"No, I don't."

"Okay, if that's what you want. I hate to see you miss out. Call me if you change your mind. Our deadline is four o'clock."

"Thanks, but no thanks. Look, Alex, I appreciate all you've taught me. I'll carry it with me for the rest of my life. I think this should be about you. This is your time. You deserve it. I'm happy I could help. We'll talk later."

She turned off her phone and continued to stroll in the afternoon sun, at peace with her decision and excited for the future. Many possibilities lay ahead. Challenges would always arise, but she would meet them head-on. The next chapter in her life could wait. She sorely needed some alone time and the kind of therapy only a throaty engine coupled with a 5-speed manual transmission could provide. Smiling, she dropped the canvas top of her convertible, jumped in, and hit the open road.

* * *

During the eulogy for Bill Jennings, Gramps had become highly emotional, pausing more than once to regain his composure. His passionate address about the heroics and dedication of the national icon was punctuated with war stories, humorous anecdotes, and tears.

Johnson was relieved. The part of the ceremony he'd feared so terribly had gone off without incident. As it turned out, herbal remedies weren't necessary to treat his condition. He had learned how to tune out the world on command and find his happy place. It was a huge, liberating milestone. Lars would be proud.

For the first time in days, he felt relaxed and in control. He wondered how different things might have been had he not found Charlie. In one amazing evening, she had uncovered the essence of his trouble. Now he could pursue his dreams and desires, but he'd need a healthy dose of courage to follow through on his convictions.

As the crowd slowly dispersed, a raspy voice called out to him. "Hey, Telling, need to see you for a minute." There stood Carson Brooks, flanked by Dutch and Tyrell.

Johnson cringed. "What do you want?" he snarled, anticipating yet another twisted diatribe.

"Calm down a minute. I've got something to say to you, and you're going to listen. Ever since your presentation, I've been trying to understand what went wrong. I couldn't figure out how he did it. But then I found it. A patch installed on the A/V controller. After a set period, it would turn off the mic. I'd say it did a surprisingly excellent job of disrupting the flow of things."

Dutch hung his head like a disgraced schoolboy. "I admit it. That was rotten. Despicable. I thought it would be a funny little prank. I had no idea it would cause you so much trouble. At least I decided against making you sound like a chipmunk. Now that would have been hysterical."

Johnson shook his head. "You know what? You're a lucky man. An incredibly lucky man. The old Johnson would be all up in your face right now. But it's history. Can't change anything and pummeling you now wouldn't solve anything. But I am curious. Why'd you do it?"

"I did it because I want her back."

"What? Who?"

"Cameron. She and I were together for some time. I liked her. Then she dumped me and started dating you. I tried, but I just couldn't get over her. So, I planted that pink uniform in your locker and then mucked up the sound system in the auditorium. All's fair, right?"

"Not sure about that, but it worked."

"What do you mean?"

"Cam and I broke up. She's all yours, buddy."

"Oh, man. I'm sorry."

"Don't be. Just be careful what you wish for. She's a little high maintenance!"

Dutch grinned. "You think?"

"Just do me one favor. Give her some time to get over me, okay?"

Brooks scowled. "Yeah, yeah, yeah. I'm sure she's devastated. A day ought to do it. Now off you go, A/V man."

As Dutch filtered through the attendees, Brooks gestured to Johnson. "Now it's your turn."

"My turn to do what?"

"To apologize, you moron. I didn't ask Brown to come along just for the hell of it."

"Brooks, for once in your life, you're right. Ty, I'm sorry. I was an absolute idiot. It was temporary insanity, I guess. I thought the worst of you, and there was no excuse for it."

Brooks looked on in disgust. "Oh, god, this is getting mushy already. You guys do whatever you have to do to mend things, but I'm out of here. Oh, and Johnson, just so you know, this doesn't change anything between us. I still don't like you."

Johnson sighed, then blew Brooks a kiss. "But we'll always have those moments in the shower, now won't we, Carson?" Brooks dashed off, a look of terror on his face.

Tyrell grinned. "Okay. I think you've suffered enough. We're good. Just try not to be so jealous of my awesomeness next time."

"Oh, man. Your awesomeness? I think I'm already starting to have second thoughts about that apology."

"Come on dude, you know you love me. Too bad about Cameron. I was looking forward to another double date."

"You and Alicia? Still?"

"Yes, sir. She has a lot of potential."

"Good for you. And speaking of women, we've got a lot to talk about." Johnson caught a glimpse of something in the background. "Hey, can you excuse me for a minute? I've got this thing I need to do."

Tyrell snapped a salute. "Sure thing, my man. See you back at the hut."

* * *

The lone figure seated at the podium was a decorated officer and strict authoritarian who, like Bill Jennings, had inspired a generation of patriots. Johnson felt queasy as he approached him. Anyone could be intimidated by the legend and his impressive accomplishments, but he wondered why fear always consumed him in the man's presence. Was it partly due to his own feelings of inadequacy? Compensating with obedience and a strong desire to please could only take him so far. It was time to stand up and face him man-to-man, even if it led to disapproval.

General Thomas Telling stared wistfully off in the distance, his face tired and drawn. His eyes, usually shining with verve and a hint of mischief, were listless. He looked lost. Johnson was careful to disguise his shock at the sight of his grandfather in distress.

"Hey, Gramps. You did a nice job today."

Gramps stood solemnly, facing the flag. "You know, Bill loved his country more than anything else. And when the situation presented itself, he never hesitated to risk his life for me or anyone else. He was a hell of a soldier and a hell of a man. He was also a hell of a friend. I can't believe he's gone."

"I can't either. I'm going to miss hearing all those war stories. He sure loved the Army, didn't he?"

"I should have been a better friend," the general said, again on the verge of tears.

"You were his best friend, Gramps."

"I suppose. But still, I should have listened better. He needed help. The signs were all there, but I just ignored it, like a lot of people do."

"I don't understand."

"Son, you're old enough to know the truth. The man drank himself to death because he hated his job. All that partying and carousing was just his way of dealing with it. He was fine early on, but combat changed him. He never got over the horrors we faced. He hid his anxiety and depression for years. By the time he went through therapy, it was too late. I should have tried harder to help him. It just took hold of him and wouldn't let go. That poor son of a bitch."

"That's a terrible way to live. I had no idea."

"Yes, son, it was. All those years of pain. I agonized over what to say about him today. It's not always easy to know how honest to be. I finally decided the truth would be too harsh. He galvanized such an important movement in this country. I wanted his legacy to be one of duty and honor, not the tortured soul he'd become. Do you think I did the right thing?"

"Absolutely, Gramps. Yes. He was a military hero, regardless of how he dealt with it on a personal level. I'm glad I was here today to honor him."

"I am too. You made me proud. You always make me proud. I'd do anything for you, you know that don't you?"

"Of course. But there's something I've got to know. How much *have* you done for me? I mean, I know you and Grandma took me in after Mom and Dad died, and you raised me and I'm eternally grateful for that. But I've always wondered how much I've accomplished in life on my own. Do you understand what I'm asking?"

"Do you mean did I call in any special favors for you?"

"Yes and be honest with me."

"Well, never, son. I have too much respect for you to do anything like that. Telling men always learn to stand on their own two feet. I wouldn't have it any other way."

"So, the scholarship to State?"

"You."

"Camp Conrad?"

"You."

"Project Tangent?"

"You. It's all you. Each one. And passed them all with flying colors."

"Not exactly, sir. There's a lot I need to tell you, and it's not all good. In fact, I know you'll be disappointed in me, but I've got to get this off my chest."

"What's wrong?"

"Last week was crazy, both personally and professionally. My career took a nosedive. The presentation was a disaster and I got dismissed from Tangent. Not only that, in the fallout from everything, Cameron and I broke up over a giant misunderstanding."

Gramps leaped out of his seat. "Good!"

"What do you mean, good?"

"I never liked that girl. She was a little too pushy for my taste."

"Hold on. I thought you loved Cameron?"

"Only because I thought *you* loved her!"

"Well, she did have some good qualities, but I think I knew all along she wasn't a keeper."

"Better to find out now."

"Don't you want to know why we broke up?"

"No."

"Why not?"

"Because it doesn't matter a bit to me, son. That's your business."

"Okay. But I royally screwed up with Tangent."

"Hell, that's just a bump in the road. That's no big deal. You'll get another chance to prove yourself."

"Probably not, Gramps. You see I'm not re-upping. I'm getting out of the Army."

"What's this?"

"I've got to be straight with you. The real reason I enlisted was so I wouldn't be a disappointment. I felt like I had to carry on the Telling tradition. I'm sure Dad would have wanted it that way. Don't get me wrong. I've got nothing against the Army. I've learned so much. But what I want to do is coach football. At the high school level at first. Then someday I hope to be a head coach for a university. That's my dream. I love football. It's my passion. It makes me happy."

Gramps eased into his seat. "Well, this is quite a shock. You're right. I *am* disappointed in you. Why didn't you come talk to me about all this?"

"Since we're being honest, I'll tell you. I was afraid to."

"Afraid? Why?"

"Gramps, I don't know how to say this. You've been incredibly good to me over the years. But you've always been more like a commander to me than a father figure. I was just trying to follow orders like I always do."

"Oh, god, your aunt was right. She said you were having problems. I just passed it off as more of her psychobabble. I should have been more aware. Just like I should have been more aware years ago with Bill. You've been living your life to make me happy and that's nothing but bullshit. If you want to coach football, coach football. I know you'll be excellent, no matter what you decide to do. I'll support you all the way."

"That's great, Gramps! You have no idea how relieved I am to hear you say that. I feel like a new man. Hey, what's wrong?"

Gramps wiped away a tear. "You remind me so much of your

father. You have that same drive, that same fire, and you're honest to a fault. And listen, I'm so thankful every day that I have you in my life. I'll always love you, son, no matter what happens."

Shocked and overwhelmed with emotion, Johnson stared, as if seeing his grandfather for the first time. Never in his wildest dreams had he expected to hear him speak from the heart.

"Son, I feel bad. I never knew how much you wanted to please me. I should have set you straight a long time ago. I promise I'll do better. Any time you need to talk to me about anything, don't hesitate. I'll listen. So will you give me a second chance?"

"Yes, sir. Absolutely."

They shared a brief, manly hug, then sat in awkward silence, avoiding eye contact, resisting the urge to give in to the moment. Johnson turned away, almost losing his composure. They were both relieved when Brooks appeared out of nowhere, panting and red-faced.

"Guys, guys! They didn't want me to say anything, but I thought you should know."

"Know what?" Johnson snapped. "And why are you whispering?"

"The mic here is still live. The crowd back there has heard everything you said for the last fifteen minutes."

Johnson gulped.

Gramps turned pale. "Oh for the love of—are you kidding me? They heard everything?"

"I'm afraid so," Brooks said. He maintained a straight face for a while, then broke into a grin. "Okay, not really. I was just screwing with you."

Johnson's rage quickly dissipated.

Gramps snickered.

And the men laughed until they cried.

THE END

For years, Bickford "Bick" Penn's shopping lists, snarky letters to the editor, and feeble attempts at prose were written by hand in his signature blue ink. Now, they emanate from a platform on the cutting edge of 20th century technology—a Commodore 64. When not writing or debugging ancient operating systems, he can be found looking for his three pairs of glasses.